Capturing a Knight's Heart

For the Love of a Shaw
Book Four

By:
Debbie Hyde

Debbie Hyde Books

Cover image: Jimmy Thomas, Romance Novel Covers
Background Image: Ralph Klein, fotosforyou_rk, Pixabay

Cover Design: Debbie Hyde
ISBN: 9798596127942

This book is dedicated to Drusilla Alewine. Thank you for loving and caring for me and my little family. Your friendship is a true treasure to me. You are amazing and I am honored to have you in my life! Thank you for giving me my little buddy. Nancie has sure made this series fun and exciting. I love you, dear lady, and I hope to see you soon!

Chapter One

Jackson Shaw used the back of his hand to wipe the trickle of blood from his chin. The tin ale mug, that had slammed into his face, had busted his lower lip. Thankfully, he did not lose any teeth in the incident. Jax's hair and clothes were drenched from the ale that was in the mug when it hit him.

Jax shook off the ale that was now running down his arm and onto his hand. His eyes bore into the object of his fury. He now had Edmond Prescott pinned the front corner of the Blume'N Brew pub. Edmond's eyes radiated with fear as Jax took a step toward him.

"It is time for you to pay for every evil thing that you have done to my family!" Jax shouted as he took another step closer to Edmond.

"It is time for you to die, Shaw!" Edmond dropped the tin ale mug onto the floor and reached for his pistol.

Before Edmond could pull the pistol and take aim, Jax closed the distance between them. Jax slammed Edmond into the wall of the pub. The jolt caused Edmond to drop his weapon. Jax took Edmond by the back of his head and slammed him, face first, into a nearby table.

Several other fights had erupted around the two angry men. Edmond Prescott had not come to the Blume'N Brew pub alone tonight. His friends jumped up and started more fights as distractions. Soon, the entire pub was in a brawl.

Before Jax could take another swing at Edmond, he was hit across the back with a wooden chair. Jax whirled around and snatched the two remaining pieces of the chair out of Brody Williams' hands.

Jax threw the pieces of wood onto the floor. He grabbed Brody by his shirt. With all his strength, Jax lifted the man off the floor and tossed him through the front window of the pub.

Edmond used this distraction to save himself. He rushed outside, and with the help of Randal Gates, Edmond pulled Brody to his feet. The three men quickly hurried into the shadows of London.

Jax shook off the effects of the fight and braced his hands on a table. Before he could stand up straight, the table flipped, causing Jax to fall to the floor, with the table landing on top of him. Jax could not believe this just happened to him.

A single gunshot was fired into the side wall of the pub, demanding everyone's attention. Jerry Griffin, the pub bartender, walked into the middle of the pub, his rifle still in his hands. Every member of Edmond's party, that had been left behind, took one look at the fury on the bartender's face and fled from the Blume'N Brew.

Jax groaned as he pushed the wooden table to the side. He struggled but managed to get to his feet. He turned around to find himself staring into the bright green eyes of Miss Nancie. The little pub owner was furious, and her eyes bore holes into Jax.

"Why did you flip that table on me?" Jax was furious too. He had clearly seen the little pub owner's face just before she flipped the table on him.

"It was either that or shoot you!" Nancie shouted at Jax. "Look at what you have done to my pub!"

"I did not do all of this." Jax was defensive as he pointed around the room.

"You started it!" Nancie poked Jax in the chest with her finger. Jax caught her by her wrist.

"I was after Edmond Prescott." Jax leaned toward Nancie.

"Well, you failed at that." Nancie pulled her hand away from Jax. "Prescott was the first one out the door."

"What happened?" Maxwell Spencer asked as he walked through the broken pub door.

"Need I say more?" Nancie asked as she motioned toward Jax.

"You are going to fix this." Maxx pointed his finger at Jax as he walked further into the pub.

"Did anybody die?" Paul asked. He and Maxx watched all the men getting up from the floor.

The entire front room of the pub had been destroyed. The tables were overturned. Most of the chairs were broken into pieces. The front doors hung loosely, and the huge main front window was shattered.

Nancie walked over and put her hand on the piano. Sadly, even this beautiful instrument had not been spared. The entire scene before her was heartbreaking. There had not been destruction like this at the Blume'N Brew since Captain Sayer and his pirates started a brawl. At least Captain Sayer had reimbursed her for the damages his ruffians had caused. Who was going to pay for this?

"I should have shot them all," Jerry mumbled.

"Why would you do this?" Maxx asked Jax.

"I did not mean for all of this to happen." Jax was finally coming to grips with just how badly the pub had been destroyed.

"It was not all Sir Jackson's fault." Will Carter set his piano stool upright.

"Of course, it was his fault!" Nancie glared at Jax.

"Hold on, lil buddy." Maxx put his arm around Nancie. "Let us hear Jax's reasoning for this before we flog him."

"He threw the first punch!" Nancie angrily pointed at Jax.

Nancie threw her hands up. She was overwhelmed with the destruction of the pub. She went over to the only section of the pub that had been spared. Thankfully, no one had went up on the raised platform section in the back corner. Every pub patron knew that this was Maxwell Spencer's private table.

"Yes, I admit it. I threw the first punch." Jax followed behind Nancie. He tried to get her to listen to him. "I am deeply sorry that your pub has been destroyed like this."

Nancie was not listening to Jax. She sat down at Maxx's favorite table and looked around the room. Jerry set a bottle of brandy on the table for her. Rachel hurried in with a large bowl of cool water and clean cloths, that she gave to the hurt men.

"I am sorry about this, Maxx," Nancie apologized.

3

"Do not fret, my friend." Maxx patted Nancie on her hand. "We will fix it."

Jax watched as Maxx comforted Nancie. In this moment, Jax envied the friendship between these two. He was surprised that Maxx took the time to listen to Nancie. Maxx was able to offer Nancie's mind some peace. Still, he could not figure out how these two, unlikely people, had become such good friends.

"How did the brawl start?" Paul looked over at Jax, after he had helped to set the tables upright again.

"Edmond Prescott was here." Jax sighed deeply.

"Roger Holden is getting extremely brave sending his brother in here like that." Maxx walked over to the bar and grabbed a bottle of rum.

"That was a bad lot that Prescott was with tonight." Will continued picking up the piano keys off the floor.

"Will, what do you know?" Maxx sensed that the piano player had more information about what had taken place here tonight.

"The piano is a lost cause. We are going to have to get another one." Will stood up and shook his head as he stared at his piano.

"Will." Maxx walked over to the man and motioned toward the rest of the pub. "The brawl, what do you know about it?"

"If Sir Jax had not of thrown that first punch, he probably would be dead by now." Will nodded his head at Maxx and sat down on his piano stool.

"I am glad that somebody is on my side," Jax mumbled.

"How exactly did Jax starting this brawl save his life?" Paul was confused. The little piano player made no sense.

"That bad lot was sitting here." Will pointed at the table that was the closest to his piano. "They were planning on killing Sir Jax before he could leave the pub tonight."

Will's words stunned everyone in the pub. All eyes turned to Jax. Jax sighed deeply. He closed his eyes and shook his head. It was not comforting to know that his death was being plotted tonight.

"It looks as if Holden has a new plan." Maxx put his hand on Jax's shoulder. "Sadly, you seem to be his new target. But, since you did start this, help clean it up."

4

"Take this." Paul handed Jax a board and a hammer. "Start boarding up the front window."

"I do not work here, and I do not take orders from you." Jax set the hammer down on a nearby table.

Nancie was angry and heartbroken over the way the pub looked. She jumped up from her chair. She grabbed Jax Shaw by his ear and dragged him over to the front window of the pub.

"Until this pub is restored, you most certainly do work here!" Nancie pointed at the window. "Now, board it up!"

Jax looked down into Nancie's bright green eyes. He knew she was angry, and he understood why. Yet, Jax saw something more. The little woman standing before him had a huge heart. She was fighting to hold onto this pub because it was, somehow, a part of her.

Something strange and unfamiliar grabbed ahold of Jax's heart in that moment. He had never felt this feeling before and he could not name what it was that he felt. Yet, it was a feeling he could not escape. Somehow, the feisty little woman, with green eyes and golden ringlets of hair, standing before him, had bound him to her.

"I will do whatever you ask." Jax took Nancie's hand and brought it to his lips. His deep brown eyes never left her bright green ones as everything around them faded away from existence.

Chapter Two

Nancie gently pulled her hand from Jax's and stepped away from him. She took a deep breath to calm herself. She was highly upset over the pub being destroyed tonight. Now, she had Jackson Shaw pulling on her feminine emotions as well.

"Board up the window." Nancie handed Jax the wooden board that Paul had laid on a nearby table.

There were too many emotions flowing through her for Nancie to remain standing here in front of Jax. The last thing that she needed now was to have to deal with this handsome Shaw. She hurried over to the bar and grabbed another bottle of brandy.

"Why don't you go and sit down?" Rachel handed Nancie a glass. "We can clean this up." Nancie took the glass and went back to Maxx's private table.

"Are you alright?" Maxx leaned on the bar in front of Rachel as they both watched Nancie walk away.

"I am fine," Rachel assured Maxx. "No one came upstairs."

"You go over and stay with Nancie. The rest of us will straighten things up here." Maxx was deeply worried about Nancie.

"I hate seeing her so devasted." Rachel sighed deeply. "Do you think that it will take long to restore the pub?"

"This place means a lot to her." Jerry continued cleaning up the broken glass around the bar. "This pub was her father's."

"The Blume'N Brew will be restored in a few weeks." Maxx looked around the pub. "The restoration is not what concerns me though."

"Do you think that Edmond Prescott will come back and try again?" Rachel asked.

"If he does, we will be ready for him next time." Jerry was not going to let Edmond Prescott back inside the pub after tonight.

"I have no doubts that Holden and Prescott will try again. They may not try again here but as Jerry said, we will be ready if they do."

6

Maxx looked from Rachel over to Jax. "What concerns me the most right now was that little display by the front window."

"Surely you do not believe that Nancie will fall for Jackson Shaw's charms?" Jerry shook his head at the thought.

"He is charming and handsome." Rachel propped her elbows on the bar and smiled as she watched Jax boarding up the front window.

"Do not look in that direction." Maxx stepped in front of Rachel, blocking her view of Jax. "You go over and comfort our friend." Maxx pointed at Nancie.

"Are you jealous?" Rachel teased.

Maxx, Rachel, and Jerry paused and looked at each other for a moment before bursting out laughing at the thought. Jerry patted Maxx on the shoulder. Rachel smiled and shook her head before she hurried over to join Nancie.

"The pub is destroyed and you three are over here laughing." Jax joined Maxx at the bar.

"I have no doubts that you will have this place back in top shape in no time." Maxx patted Jax on the back as he walked away.

"Me?" Jax followed Maxx over to his private table.

"Yes, you." Maxx sat down next to Nancie. "You are in charge of the restoration of the Blume'N Brew."

"Wait a minute!" Nancie snapped. "This is my pub, and I am in charge."

"He broke it. He is going to fix it." Maxx motioned for Jax to sit down.

"You cannot do this." Nancie huffed and leaned back in her chair.

"You will run this pub, like always." Maxx said to Nancie as he poured himself and Jax a glass of rum. "Jax is only in charge of the restoration."

"Do you honestly trust him with a job like this?" Nancie continued to protest.

"Jax did an outstanding job in Nettlesville." Maxx covered Nancie's hand with his. "I trust him."

"I will not let you down." Jax leaned forward and looked Nancie in the eye. "Trust me."

7

"I seem to have no choice in the matter." Nancie's eyes remained locked with Jax's for several minutes before she turned to Maxx. "If you trust him, then so will I."

"Why don't you go with Rachel upstairs and retire for the night?" Maxx suggested. "We all will start fresh in the morning."

Nancie stood up and looked around the pub one last time for the night. This was her father's pub and tonight it lay in pieces. She sighed deeply and nodded her head. Maxx was right. Tomorrow, things would look differently.

"I am going to hold you to your word." Nancie pointed her finger at Jax.

"I fully expect that you will." Jax smiled at Nancie. She did not smile back.

Jax hated that the pub had been destroyed, but he was looking forward to getting to know the little owner much better. He had been hanging around the Blume'N Brew on every occasion he got for the past few months. Ever since his brother's engagement party, almost a year ago, he had been trying to get in the good graces of Miss Nancie.

Nancie followed Rachel upstairs. She was not emotionally ready to handle Jax Shaw. Tonight, she would rest and get herself together. Tomorrow, she would make this Shaw regret destroying her father's pub.

"She is not going to go easy on me, is she?" Jax watched as Nancie walked out of sight.

"Your world is about to come undone." Paul raised his glass of brandy at Jax.

"Tonight, we will make a plan for the restoration of the pub." Maxx tapped his fingers on the table to get Jax's attention. "Tomorrow, I will send word to your family about what happened here tonight."

"Do we really have to involve my family?" Jax did not wish to have his mother upset over this.

"With Prescott plotting to kill you, they need to know." Paul handed Jax the bottle of brandy.

"Paul is right. Roger Holden and Edmond Prescott are plotting again. You are their target, but they would gladly kill any Shaw that lets their guard down." Maxx had no doubts on this.

"One day, this feud between the Shaw's and Holden's will have to end." Jax quickly drank his glass of brandy.

"I will leave ten men here to help with the restoration of the pub and to protect you." Maxx leaned back in his chair.

"A work crew is a fantastic idea, but I do not believe that I need protecting." Jax did not like being under protection.

"You may not, but they do." Paul pointed up to the second floor.

Jax could not argue with that. He would not be able to keep his eye on Nancie and Rachel, plus lead the restoration of the pub. Since Roger Holden and Edmond Prescott were not fair men, the extra guards would be a blessing.

"Paul, and the rest of my men, will leave with me in the morning. I expect you to take care of things here." Maxx stood up and yawned. "We will return in about two days."

"The Duke is running you ragged." Jax did not like seeing Maxx being used as he was by the Duke.

"There is nothing that I can do about that just yet. You should get some rest yourself." Maxx went upstairs for the night.

"You are going to need your strength tomorrow." Paul laughed and patted Jax on the shoulder.

"She cannot be *that* bad." Jax at least hoped Miss Nancie was not too harsh with him.

"If you stay on her bad side, you would probably be better off dueling Holden and Prescott at the same time." Paul laughed again and went upstairs as well.

Jax folded his hands and propped up on his elbows. He had a lot to think about tonight. He was once again in charge of a work crew. This was something he enjoyed doing.

However, it was an uneasy feeling for him to know that his death was being plotted. He never understood why the Earl of Statham hated his family so much. One would think that Roger Holden would have given up on his plots to destroy the Shaw family by now, but Roger always tried again.

Chapter Three

The next morning Nancie found Jax in her private dining room going over several papers. Rachel was already in the kitchen preparing breakfast. Rachel motioned Nancie away, so she joined Jax at the dining room table.

"I did not expect to see you awake until noon." Nancie poured herself a cup of coffee before sitting down across from Jax.

"I never sleep until noon." Jax did not look up from his papers. "Besides, there is way too much work to be done to allow for anyone to be sleeping in."

"Where is Maxx?" Nancie looked toward the doorway. Maxx was not a morning person, but it was unlike him to sleep in, especially when there was a lot of work to be done.

"Maxx left a couple of hours ago." Jax stopped what he was doing and looked up at Nancie. "We briefly went over these before he and Paul went to the docks." Jax waved his hand over the papers on the table.

"I am pleased to see that you are taking your job seriously." Nancie sat up straight and drank her coffee.

"I always take my work seriously." A sly smile crossed Jax's face. "You look lovely this morning."

Jax liked the way Nancie looked without all the makeup she wore in the pub at night. In fact, she looked younger without the makeup. He also liked how her long blonde hair flowed freely over her shoulders and down her back. Her hair still had curls but not the ringlets she curled it into at night.

Nancie glared at Jax. How could he sit here and use his charms on her like this? She sighed deeply and rolled her eyes. This Shaw needed to stop flirting with her and get to work.

"You look as if you need some help." Nancie held her head high as she gestured toward the papers on the table. "Would you like me to look those over for you?"

"Maxx and I already went over the construction plans." Jax smiled at Rachel as she refilled his coffee cup.

"This was my father's pub." Nancie was irritated. "I think I should have a say in how it is restored."

"You are absolutely right." Jax stacked the papers up and set them aside. "After breakfast, why don't you join me downstairs and share with me your ideas for the pub?"

Nancie tilted her head as she thought on Jax's suggestion. Her bright green eyes never left Jax's deep brown eyes. She wondered what this Shaw was up to. She had heard of Jackson Shaw's charms long ago. She had never expected that she would ever be caught up in those charms in any way. Yet here she sat with Jax Shaw smiling across the table at her.

"Lord Shaw, that is a lovely idea." Nancie smiled sweetly as she accepted his offer.

"I am no Lord." Jax got up and refilled Nancie's coffee cup. "If you insist on formalities, I am a knight, so you can call me Sir." Jax leaned down and whispered in Nancie's ear. "I would rather that you just call me Jax."

Nancie brushed Jax away with her hand. She could not let his charms make her weak like they did those silly high society girls. She was stronger than that. Jackson Shaw was not going to have her swooning over him like a lovesick puppy.

Rachel pushed in the serving cart with their morning meal. Jax helped her set the table before he returned to his seat. Rachel sat down next to Jax and smiled sweetly at him. It was obvious that she was taken in by his charms. Nancie noticed that Jax did not seem to notice Rachel's actions.

"You should hurry up and eat so we can get this workday started." Nancie handed the plate of rolls over to Jax.

Jax took a couple of rolls and passed the plate on to Rachel. He bit into a roll and nodded his head.

"These are good, but Miss Margaret makes the best butter rolls I have ever tasted." Jax reached for his coffee cup. Rachel punched Jax on the arm. He mouthed the word '*Ow*' at Rachel.

"Who is Miss Margaret?" Nancie was curious.

"She owns the restaurant in Nettlesville." Jax turned his attention back to Nancie. He wondered why Maxx had not told her about the people of Nettlesville. "She would not give me the recipe."

"You, Jackson Shaw, were planning on baking if she had given it to you?" Nancie could not help but to laugh at the thought of Jax in a kitchen.

"Do you have no faith in me?" Jax playfully put his hand to his chest.

"Should I get you an apron then?" Nancie teased. She fought to hold back her laughter.

"That is not necessary. I would be lost in a kitchen." Jax leaned back in his chair and grinned. He rather enjoyed this playful side of the little pub owner. "I am, however, very interested in your ideas for the restoration."

"We should get to that then, so you can get your workday started." Nancie stood up and walked out into the hall.

"I guess there is no time like the present." Jax smiled at Rachel before following Nancie downstairs to the pub.

"He is so handsome." Rachel propped her elbow on the table as she watched Jax leave the room.

Jerry looked toward the door and back to Rachel. "I do not see it."

Rachel rolled her eyes and shook her head at the bartender. She was going to enjoy seeing Jax Shaw around the Blume'N Brew every day for the next few weeks.

Downstairs, Jax watched as Nancie silently surveyed the room. The hurt on her face as she looked around the pub did not sit well with him. He vowed to himself that he would do everything that he could to see her smile again.

"Most of the tables and chairs were broken. I will be going around to several shops today to order all the replacements the pub needs. Everything should be replaced in about a week." Jax walked over to where Nancie was standing next to the broken piano.

Nancie placed her hand on the piano and closed her eyes. The memories of her father in this room filled her mind. She sighed deeply as she turned to look around the pub once more. She paused when her eyes met with Jax's. She wanted to be at mad Jax. She should be mad at him but the look of compassion that she saw in his eyes held her anger at bay.

"You need to find a temporary solution then." Nancie could not keep the pub closed for a week.

"Why would you want a temporary solution?" Jax was confused. He thought that Nancie would agree with Maxx's plans for the pub.

"So that I can open the pub." Nancie was frustrated. She walked over to the bar. "I cannot afford to keep it closed for a week."

"Maxx…" Jax was shocked when Nancie interrupted him.

"I am sure that Maxx's plans are great." Nancie whirled around to face Jax. "I want my pub opened now. So, *you* find a solution."

"Yes, ma'am. I will gladly find you a solution." Jax watched as Nancie started toward the stairs. "I do have a question though."

"And just what would that be?" Nancie stopped at the bottom of the stairs.

"Why does Maxwell Spencer have such a strong authority on how *your* pub is restored?" Jax had wondered this after Maxx had gone over the plans with him this morning.

"Maxx is my friend." Nancie could no longer look at Jax.

"Still, that does not explain how he has so much control here." Jax could clearly see how nervous Nancie was. He knew she was avoiding his question.

"You do not need to worry about how things are run here at the Blume'N Brew." Nancie looked Jax in the eye. "You just need to fix what you broke."

Jax was becoming frustrated as well. He did not like secrets and Nancie was, without a doubt, hiding something. One day he would figure out what Maxx had to do with this pub. He was sure that the little pub owner kept many secrets for Maxwell Spencer.

"Then I owe you a window." Jax grabbed the restoration plans off the bar. "That is the only thing that I personally broke. The rest of this, is on Prescott and Holden."

Jax stormed out the side entrance door. The first thing he was going to do was get the front doors fixed. He would then spend the rest of his morning figuring out a temporary solution for Miss Nancie.

13

Chapter Four

Nancie stormed up the stairs. She went back to the dining room and poured herself a fresh cup of coffee. The last thing she needed was Jax Shaw asking questions about the pub.

"He irritates me." Nancie flopped down in a chair across from Rachel. "He makes me so angry."

"That is not what he is doing." Rachel grinned at Nancie.

"Of course, that is what he is doing." Nancie narrowed her eyes at Rachel.

"I do not think so." Rachel's grin widened.

"Then pray tell, what exactly is Jackson Shaw doing?" Nancie would love to know the answer to this question.

"He is handsome. He is also charming. You, my friend, like him." Rachel was sure of this.

"You have clearly been drinking." Nancie did not like Rachel's answer.

"You know that I do not drink." Rachel poured herself another cup of coffee. "I do not know why you will not admit it."

"I cannot admit it, because it is not true," Nancie lied.

"If you say so." Rachel did not believe her friend. "There is nothing wrong with caring for him."

"There is everything wrong with caring for Jackson Shaw!" Nancie snapped. "This Shaw needs to do his job and leave."

She would not let Jax Shaw weasel his way into her heart. There was too much at stake here. Frustrated, Nancie got up and went to her private study. She was bound by her duty to this pub and to Maxx. Her feelings for Jax Shaw, whatever those feelings were, could not interfere with her duty.

Her father had made a vow, and several promises, to Maxx's father many years ago. She had made that same vow and promises to Maxx. Jax Shaw asking questions could destroy what they all had built here at the Blume'N Brew. This pub was important, and it could

14

not fail. She now wondered if Jax's presence here was really a good idea. Perhaps someone else should handle the restoration.

She would have to admit that Jax was handsome, as Rachel had said. Any woman could clearly see this to be true. He was also very charming. Nancie had witnessed his charms several times over the past few months. Jax spent many evenings in the Blume'N Brew, ever since she had danced with him at his brother's engagement party. Jax knew how to draw a woman to him. This was something that she was going to have to fight. She could not fall prey to it. Except at night, for that was when her dreams usually betrayed her.

✳✳✳

Jax left the Blume'N Brew in a hurry. He could not understand why he was being blamed for all the destruction that had happened to the pub last night. Sure, he threw the first punch but only because Edmond Prescott was taunting him. That vile little man had been a thorn in his family's side for years.

From the looks of things, the piano player was the only one that was on his side. Thanks to Will Carter, they now knew that Roger Holden was once again plotting against the Shaw family.

Jax sighed deeply as he remembered the piano player's words. Edmond Prescott, and his band of ruffians, had come to the Blume'N Brew last night with the intent of killing him. Jax wondered if everyone else at the pub had even noticed this fact. Knowing that someone was trying to kill him, had Jax on edge.

The frustration that he had this morning was mainly because of the little tiff he just had with Miss Nancie. Their little argument had Jax's mind clouded. He paused when he realized that he had already walked past several of the shops that he had intended on visiting this morning.

The smell of fresh baked bread reminded Jax that he had not finished his morning meal before leaving the pub. He hurried across the street to Huxley Bakery. Their apple tartlets had always been a favorite for his mother and Aunt Caroline. Jax got one for himself and ordered a dozen to take back to the pub. Perhaps an apple tartlet would help to smooth things over with Nancie. Somehow, he doubted this. It would take more than a sweet pastry to settle Nancie's temper, and he knew it.

When Jax entered Glenn Morten's shop next to the mill, he glanced back over his shoulder. His brother Caleb had described a feeling of urgency and knowing that Jax could never understand until now. Like his older brother, Jax sensed that something was out of sorts. Even though he saw nothing that looked out of place, Jax knew that something was wrong.

"Good morning, Jackson." Mr. Morten walked over to where Jax was looking out the front window and greeted him. "How can I help you today?"

"I need to order a new door and front window for the Blume'N Brew." Jax handed Mr. Morten the papers with Maxx's plans.

"The doors I already have but this window will take a few days." Mr. Morten continued to study Maxx's plans.

"Would it be possible to have the doors delivered today?" Jax smiled. An early delivery would offer a temporary solution so that Nancie could reopen the pub.

"For an extra fee, aye, it could be." Mr. Morten grinned at Jax.

"Of course, just add that to the bill for Lord Spencer." Jax grinned at the mill and shop owner. "The Earl of Hartford would be most grateful that his friend received the doors immediately." Jax figured it would help to use Maxx's title in a situation like this.

"I will see to it that the doors are delivered within a couple of hours and the work on the new window will start this afternoon." Mr. Morten was pleased with the transaction.

When Jax stepped outside the shop, the same uneasy feeling came over him again. He instantly regretted leaving the Blume'N Brew alone this morning. If he had not been so upset, he would have asked Harper, one of Maxwell Spencer's men, to accompany him today. Jax kept a watchful eye on the crowds as he hurried to one of the furniture stores that he had passed earlier.

After leaving the second furniture store, Jax started to wonder if he had been mistaken. Maybe he was just on edge because he knew that Holden and Prescott were plotting to kill him. As he looked around the crowded street, he only saw the everyday activity of the city of London. Caleb had to be wrong about having an unexplainable feeling of urgency.

As Jax turned the corner, someone from behind, shoved him between two buildings. He found Randal Gates waiting for him in the alley. A quick look over his shoulder confirmed that it was Dexter Greene who had pushed him into the alley.

"You messed Brody up pretty badly last night, Shaw." Randal sneered at Jax.

"Today you are going to pay for that." Dexter stepped closer to Jax.

"You fellows did not honestly believe that I would just sit there and let you kill me, now did you?" Jax sized up the fight that was before him.

"Perhaps we will finish that deed now." Randal grinned slyly.

"You two should find a better lot to run with." Jax looked between the two men as they started to circle around him. "Prescott and Holden will get you both killed in the end."

"Seems to me that you are the one on the losing end here, Shaw." Dexter grinned as he advanced on Jax.

Randal Gates helped Dexter to pin Jax to the wall of one of the buildings. Randal punched Jax hard in his stomach causing him to double over. Jax swung upwards as he stood up. His fist hit Dexter in the face. Dexter screamed out in pain as blood spewed from his broken nose.

Wanting no more of this fight, Dexter fled through the back entrance of the alley. Randal Gates rushed to follow behind Dexter when two of the King's Guards entered the alley from the street. Jax never thought that he would be glad to see the King's Guard approaching him, but today, they were a blessed sight.

Chapter Five

Everyone at the Blume'N Brew was alarmed when the King's Guard escorted Jax back to the pub. Jax sat at Maxx's table and told Harper, and the rest of Maxx's men, what had happened to him.

"Looks like Holden and Prescott have hired a few low life scoundrels to help them." Harper oversaw the protection detail that Maxx had left behind. "From now on, you do not leave the pub alone."

"I can take care of myself," Jax protested needing a guard. If he were honest with everyone, including himself, having an extra guard with him today would have been nice.

"Of course, you can." Nancie handed Jax a cool cloth to place at the edge of his eyebrow. Randal Gates had managed to get one good punch in.

"Thank you." Jax's hand lingered for a moment as he accepted the cloth from Nancie.

"You should listen to Harper." Nancie gently pulled her hand away and sat down across the table from Jax.

"Doug and James should return tomorrow. The rest of us can handle guarding the pub tonight." Harper assured Jax and Nancie that everyone was safe.

Doug and James had left after breakfast, heading to Kinsley Estate, to let Jax's parents know what had happened last night at the pub. From there, they would travel on to Ellis Manor to let the rest of the Shaw family know that Holden and Prescott were plotting against them again. Still, eight of Maxx's men, plus Jax, Jerry and the two stable hands should be more than enough to handle things at the pub.

"There are a couple of delivery wagons outside." Jerry came through the side door.

"How did you manage to get deliveries so quickly?" Nancie was amazed at how quickly Jax got things ordered. Jax only grinned as he walked away.

18

"I am sure that he charmed the shop owners." Rachel smiled as she watched Jax follow Jerry out the door. Nancie rolled her eyes and shook her head.

"What is this?" Nancie demanded when Maxx's men carried in several tables.

"You will have to take it up with Jax if you are not pleased." Harper told Nancie as he set his end of the table on the floor.

"Oh, I will surely take this up with Jax Shaw, right now." Nancie stormed toward the side door of the pub. She met Jax as he was coming back inside. "What is the meaning of this?"

"It is only the delivery of the tables, chairs, and the front doors. The window will take a few days." Jax did not understand why Nancie was angry.

Nancie grabbed Jax by his arm and led him over to the tables near the broken piano. She was not happy, and she had no problem letting this Shaw know just how badly he had messed up.

"These are the wrong tables." Nancie pointed at the long tables and benches. "They are supposed to look like those." She now pointed at the round tables being set up across the room.

"I know that these long tables are not on Maxx's list." Jax tried to explain.

"I knew that it was a bad idea leaving you in charge of things." Nancie glared at Jax. "You cannot follow simple instructions. Why would you purchase items that are not even on the list?"

"I can follow instructions." Jax was defensive.

"I think not, or these would not be here." Nancie motioned toward the long tables.

"It's hard to follow everything perfectly when I have Maxx requesting one thing and you wanting another." Jax went over and sat down on one of the barstools.

"Did Maxx request long tables and benches, because I sure did not?" Nancie followed Jax over to the bar.

"No, Maxx did not request long tables." Jax closed his eyes and rubbed his forehead. "This is the temporary solution I found, so that you could reopen the pub."

Nancie now felt bad for yelling at Jax. She did insist on him finding a temporary solution so the pub could open again. She just did not understand how these long tables figured into that plan. Hopefully, Maxx would not be too angry when he found out that Jax had spent the extra money these table were sure to cost them just so she could open the pub tonight.

"Perhaps you should hear Jax out," Rachel suggested.

"You are right." Nancie took the drink that Rachel had poured for her. "Why do we now have the long tables?" She waited for Jax to explain.

"There were not enough round tables and chairs available for purchase today. They are ordered though." Jax looked Nancie in the eye. "I saw these long tables and thought that they would work for now."

"Thank you for honoring my request and in such a timely manner." Nancie politely smiled at Jax.

"You and Rachel are fine cooks indeed." Jax looked between the two women. "I thought that you could use these long tables to serve meals to your patrons and the round ones could be used more for the card players."

"I run a pub, not a restaurant." Nancie shook her head. She was not sure she about this.

"Hear me out." Jax took Nancie's hands in his. "Right now, you only serve food to Maxx and his men. If you offered a simple meal to everyone, it could help you to make a greater profit."

"I'm not sure that I like the idea of serving meals." Nancie pulled her hands away from Jax's, very slowly.

"Think on the matter for a few days. I could help you to plan it all out." Jax was pleased with the idea. "You could try it for an hour or two at dinner time for about a week, and then determine if you wish to continue with it."

"It really is not a bad idea." Rachel added her thoughts on the matter. "I would not mind helping to test it out."

"I promise to think on the matter and if I decide to try your idea, we will talk it over with Maxx when he returns." Nancie patted Jax on his arm and walked away. She hoped that Rachel was not always going to side with everything Jax suggested.

"Why does Maxx have so much authority on what happens around here?" Jax took the drink that Rachel was offering him.

"That is something you will have to ask Nancie and Maxx." Rachel smiled before hurrying upstairs.

Jax turned and looked around the pub. He was proud to see all the tables set up in the room. It made the pub look less broken. Tomorrow, he would see about getting the broken piano removed from the pub. When the new piano arrives, it should cheer everyone here at the Blume'N Brew up.

Jax looked up at the ceiling. There were too many secrets here in this pub. Neither Nancie nor Rachel would tell him why Maxx had so much authority here. With any luck, he would find out before the restorations were completed. Right now, he had to help Harper and Jerry to put in the new front doors. The Blume'N Brew had to reopen. Surely, that would put a smile on Nancie's face.

Chapter Six

The Blume'N Brew pub opened around five that afternoon. Harper placed a few of the men outside the pub, since the front window had not been replaced yet. The rest of Maxx's men were stationed around the main room of the pub. Jax and Harper feared that more men could be working for Holden and Prescott, so they kept a watchful eye over every man that entered the pub.

"I wish she would have waited until Maxx returned to reopen the pub." Harper was sitting with Jax at Maxx's favorite table.

"We both know that Nancie is a strong-minded woman." Jax watched as Nancie helped Jerry behind the bar.

"It is good to know that you have learned that already." Harper chuckled. "That should help to save you some heartache and grief later."

"I am not sure that it will." Jax leaned back in his chair and thought for a moment. "Everything I do seems to keep me on her bad side."

"Those apple tartlets that were delivered this afternoon softened her up for a while." Rachel took Jax and Harper's plates.

Huxley Bakery had delivered the pastries that Jax had ordered this morning. When the King's Guard's presence had interrupted the fight with Randal and Dexter, Jax had forgotten about the apple tartlets. He was surprised but was glad to hear that Nancie had enjoyed them.

"If only I could remain on her good side for more than a few minutes. I seem to irritate her more than anything." The thought saddened Jax.

"She just needs some time." Rachel smiled at Jax, offering him some hope.

Jax looked at Rachel questionably. He wondered what she had meant by that. Before he could ask her about it, Rachel gathered the rest of the dishes from the table and hurried away. Jax had a feeling that Rachel had said something that she should not have said.

"How about another drink?" Harper quickly changed the subject. He could tell that Jax wanted to know more about Nancie.

"I will have to decline that drink for now." Jax stood up. "I am going to have a look around outside. I would hate to find Randal and Dexter lurking in the shadows around the pub."

Jax paused at the front doors and looked over at Nancie. She was laughing with Jerry and a couple of the men that were drinking at the bar. Nancie seemed to have sensed his gaze and looked toward the front doors. Jax smiled and nodded his head at her before he turned and went out the door.

Four of Maxx's men had the front entrance of the Blume'N Brew well-guarded. Jax hated that the front window was still boarded up but that should be fixed in a couple of days. He saw nothing out of place here, so he decided to go and check the stables.

When Jax got to the side of the pub, he noticed the two stable hands, Owen and Woody, go around the far side of the stables. Jax decided to follow them. He had never seen anyone go to that side of the stables before. There was only the wooden fence and shrubbery on that side.

From the corner of the stables, Jax could hear Owen and Woody talking and laughing. Jax took a deep breath before he casually stepped around the corner to greet the two stable hands. To his surprise, the two men were not there.

Jax placed his hands on the wooden fence and leaned closer to it. He could hear the stable hands talking on the other side. Jax wondered, how did they get on that side of the fence?

Jax started pressing his hands against the wooden planks. There had to be a hidden door here somewhere. He had reached the shrubbery, but the wooden panels did not reveal a secret door. Jax reached his hand behind the first bush and felt a latch. Looking back toward the stables, he figured that this panel was about ten feet long.

Before Jax could lift the latch, he could hear the stable hand's voices getting louder again. He quickly slipped into the stables. He hurried over and scooped up a pail of oats. If the stable hands saw him, they would find him feeding his horse.

23

Jax rubbed Blue's neck as he hung the pail of oats on a hook inside the stall. He peeped out the stable doors in time to see Owen and Woody as they entered the side entrance of the Blume'N Brew. Now might be his only chance to see what was behind the stables.

Quickly and silently, Jax hurried back to the secret side entrance. He lifted the latch and pushed the gate panel open just enough so that he could slip through. Hopefully, Nancie did not have a guard dog back here to alert the pub of intruders.

Behind this side of the stables was a huge oak tree that was clearly visible from the back side of the pub. Only the people with rooms on the back of the pub would be able to see this tree and the wooden fence. Jax looked up toward the second floor of the pub. It was convenient that those rooms belonged to Nancie, Rachel, Maxx, and Jerry. All the visitor rooms had a view of the street from their windows.

If anyone ever wondered behind the pub, the huge oak tree helped to provide cover for another section to the stables from prying eyes. This private section of the stables was double the size of the front stables. The private section connected to the back of the pub stables, creating an L shape.

Inside this hidden section, Jax found a carriage that had the Hartford Crest on it. Maxx and Paul's horses were here as well, along with several more horses. Jax assumed these horses belonged to other members of the crew of The Em. There were also a couple of supply wagons near the carriage. In the far back corner were what looked to Jax like living quarters, but they showed no signs of being used at this time.

Somehow, he had managed to stumble across a secret of Maxwell Spencer. Jax was sure that no one here at the Blume'N Brew would explain this to him if he were to ask them about it. For now, the best thing that he could do was leave it be.

On his way back to the hidden gate entrance, Jax noticed that the trees and shrubbery along the outer side of the fence provided cover to several small buildings. He tested each door but found them all to be locked. There were no windows in these buildings, so he assumed that they were for storage. He could not understand why Maxx needed so many storage buildings.

Honestly, Jax could not understand any of this. One day, the little Earl of Hartford was going to have some explaining to do. Tonight however, the only thing that he could do was to get back to the pub before anyone missed his presence. He would have to pretend that he had not seen this hidden area.

Maxx's men, and everyone else at the pub, must have had their minds on other things tonight. Jax was sure that there was no way that any of them would have let their guard down enough to have let him discover this secret area otherwise. Thankfully, he was able to slip back inside the pub without anyone knowing where he had been.

"Did you enjoy your stroll?" Nancie asked when Jax walked up to the bar.

"I enjoyed it thoroughly." Jax smiled at her. "It was very enlightening."

"Did you see any sign of Prescott and Holden's men?" Jerry was worried that there might be more trouble tonight.

"I did not see anyone that is known to be associated with them." Jax looked over his shoulder toward the front doors. "We just never know who might be on their payroll though."

"Perhaps, Sir Jax has had time to think and realizes that he should just return to Kinsley Estate." Nancie leaned on the bar and smiled at Jax.

Nancie's words caught Jax's attention and he turned around to face her again. He was sure that the little pub owner would rather that he left before he uncovered the many secrets that were floating around here, but he was not inclined to leave just yet.

"That would probably be the safest action for me." Jax leaned on the bar toward Nancie. He enjoyed being this close to her. "But, my dear lady, I will never walk away from a job that I have committed to." Jax winked at Nancie and walked away.

Tonight, Jax thought that it was best if he kept moving. Pacing was a Shaw family trait but for him, he needed more room that just the same floor to walk over and over. He was not the type to sit down either, that would drive him insane. His mind was too clouded tonight, and he did not trust his words right now. If he were to sit and talk with someone from the pub, Jax was sure that he would end up asking about the hidden stables.

Nancie watched as Jax went back outside. She wondered what had caught his attention out there tonight. Jax was right though, it was probably safer for him if he returned to his family home at Kinsley Estate. At Kinsley Estate, Jax would have the protection of his family if Edmond Prescott and his men tried to kill him again.

Then again, it was probably safer for her if Jax left. If he stayed, she would only end up getting close to him. Could she manage to remain only a friend to Jax Shaw if he remained at the pub? Somehow, she doubted that would be the case. Nancie could not help but to wonder what a relationship with Jax would look like.

Chapter Seven

Midmorning, the next day, The Em docked in London Harbor. It was noon before Maxx, Paul, and the crew made it to the Blume'N Brew. It was visibly clear that the Duke's special errands were weighing on all the sailors.

Jax went over the restoration progress with Maxx in the private dining room upstairs. Nancie was downstairs getting ready to open the pub. The work crew were moving out the broken piano today and she wanted to oversee the job.

"You are doing a fine job here." Maxx set the papers aside. He leaned back in his chair and closed his eyes.

"You should get some rest." Jax got up and poured him and Maxx a cup of coffee. He doubted that this would help Maxx though. "You look terrible."

"There is no time to rest today." Maxx rubbed his aching head.

"I fear that the Duke is going to work you to death." Jax hated how the Duke of Greyham was taking advantage of Maxx.

"If I die of exhaustion, it would be better than being hanged by the King for some misdeed in the end." Maxx did not always understand the missions that the Duke sent him on. However, he had no choice but to carry them out.

"You only agreed to that deal with the Duke to free my cousin from prison." Jax wanted to help Maxx somehow.

"Lord Alexander should have never been in prison to start with." Paul joined them at the table.

"You just continue to oversee things here at the pub. I will get free of the Duke one day." Maxx did not like talking with anyone about the deal he had made with Samuel Dawson.

When the piano was out of the pub, the three men watched as Nancie hurried into her private parlor and closed the door. Rachel hurried in behind her with a tray of tea.

27

"That piano was a rare piece. It will be hard to replace it." Paul looked over at Jax.

"Aye, hard it will be, but it is not impossible." Jax continued to watch the closed door of the parlor.

Jax had learned from Jerry that Nancie's father played the piano often when the pub was closed. Nancie would sit on the piano bench with him and sing along as her father played. The bartender seemed to be the only one here that really talked with Jax. Everyone else was guarding many secrets.

"If you can replace that piano with another one like it, Nancie will love you forever." Rachel came in and sat down beside Maxx.

"I would not go that far." Maxx laid his head down on the table.

"You really should get some rest." Rachel rubbed her hand across Maxx's back.

"I cannot." Maxx quickly sat up. "Paul and I have some packages to deliver to Delane for the Duke. We will be back in about two days."

Jax walked Maxx and Paul out to their horses. Owen and Woody had brought the horses to the side entrance of the pub. Harper and Ollie would be riding along with Maxx and Paul for this special delivery for the Duke.

"While we are gone, you figure out what to do with those extra tables you purchased for me or I will have to bill your father for them." Maxx mounted his horse.

"I think I might start a small soup kitchen if Nancie will agree to it. They had something similar in Nettlesville." Jax was still trying to talk Nancie into serving meals at the pub.

"Nettlesville sure changed you." Paul admired the man Jax had become, well, mostly anyway. Jax still had to give up barroom brawls before Paul would fully believe it.

"Good luck getting our little blonde friend to agree on that idea." Maxx had a feeling that, somehow, Jax would convince Nancie to give the meals a try. "Doug and James should return sometime today. Doug will oversee my men until we return."

Jax watched as Maxx and the others rode away. It was true, he had his work cut out for him with Nancie. Unlike his brother Caleb, he knew how to be patient. He would find a way to get past the wall that Nancie had built around herself. Perhaps, Jerry would give up enough information that would help him to get closer to the little pub owner. Jax smiled and hurried back inside the pub.

Rather than finding the bartender, Jax ran into Nancie. She seemed to have collected her emotions greatly from the piano being removed earlier. Jax was sure that she had felt like she was losing an important part of her father today. He vowed to restore her some peace on the matter. Another piano would not replace what she had lost, but it would still hold the memory of her father whenever she looked at it.

"There you are." Nancie hurried up to Jax.

"I am pleased to know that you are looking for me." Jax teased as he leaned closer to Nancie.

"You are impossible." Nancie put her hands against Jax's chest and gently pushed him away. "I need your help."

"How may I be of assistance, my dear?" Jax grinned as he took a step closer to her. He thoroughly enjoyed being close to her.

"I need you to oversee the clean-up in the pub while I go and get ready." Nancie held her hand out, halting Jax from stepping any closer.

"I will gladly oversee the clean-up for you." Jax had already noticed the mess that the crew had made while moving the piano. "But why do you do it?"

"Why do I do what?" Nancie looked at Jax questionably.

"Why do you have to 'get ready' to open the pub?" Jax caringly looked Nancie over. "All that make up, the dresses, and your hair style you use makes you look so much older. I do not understand why you do it."

After meeting the real Nancie at his brother's engagement party last year, Jax no longer cared for Miss Nancie the pub owner. He could not understand why she made herself look older. He had always thought Nancie to be several years older than himself. He was now sure that they were about the same age.

"I have to," Nancie whispered before she hurried upstairs.

Jax sighed deeply. He now had another mystery to solve. So far, he had not found any answers to the growing list of questions that he had. The secret stables were probably explainable. Nancie purposely making herself appear to be about thirty years of age did not sit right with him. Whatever the interesting story behind it all was, he was determined to uncover it.

Everyone at the pub had some explaining to do. The problem was, how was Jax going to ask the questions that he needed answers to, without the entire lot at the Blume'N Brew killing him? From what he had seen so far, this group was a close knitted lot that would protect each other and at all cost.

He was an outsider here and he knew that every move he made had to be thought out carefully. He was sure that somehow, just about every secret Nancie and the pub had, was linked to Maxwell Spencer.

Chapter Eight

For the next couple of days, everything at the Blume'N Brew ran smoothly. This was surprising to Jax, but he welcomed the change. There had been no more sightings of Roger Holden and Edmond Prescott's men around the pub. The nightly atmosphere at the pub was almost normal again.

Jax enjoyed seeing everyone happy and hearing their laughter. Even Nancie was being nicer to him. That was, up until the front replacement window for the pub was delivered.

"Send it back!" Nancie shouted at Jax.

"What is wrong with the window?" Jax held his hands out as he stepped closer to Nancie.

No one in the pub could believe Jax's bold move here. Their eyes widened in shock and their mouths dropped open. Usually, when Nancie was shouting, everyone else retreated. The only person they had ever seen to stand up to Nancie was Maxx.

"It's not the same!" Nancie pointed toward the new window leaning against the wall.

"This is the window that was in Maxx's plans." Jax threw his hands in the air. "They do not even make the other window anymore."

"I do not care!" Nancie poked Jax in the chest with her finger. "Fix this, Shaw!"

Nancie was angry and hurt. She was so upset that she could not see straight. The pub was being changed right before her eyes and there was nothing that she could do about it. With a huff and a stamp of her foot, she quickly turned and headed for the stairs. This Shaw was an idiot and she had about all she could take of the messes that he made.

"Maxx will be back today." Jax was also upset. "I will let him handle it, since he has so much control around here."

31

Nancie whirled around midway on the stairs. She wanted to lash out and put Jax Shaw in his rightful place right now. What could she say? Unfortunately, Jax was right on this and there was nothing she could say to set him straight on the matter.

"Ugh!" Nancie exclaimed and hurried up to her private parlor. Everyone watched the stairs in silence long after she had left.

"Can I have your horse?" Doug was now standing beside Jax and handed him a glass of brandy.

Jax quickly turned to look at Doug. "Why would I give you my horse?"

"I estimate that she is going to kill you before the day ends." Doug shrugged his shoulders.

"No, you cannot have my horse." Jax quickly downed the glass of brandy and handed Doug the glass.

"If you wish to sell him, I will gladly buy your horse." Paul offered as he and Maxx walked in.

Paul and Harper helped Maxx over to his private table in the back corner. Paul looked tired, but Maxx was on the verge of complete exhaustion. Jerry carried over a bottle of rum and set it on table in front of Maxx. Maxx did not touch the bottle and laid his head down on the table instead.

"I would rather have a meal and some coffee right now." Maxx did not lift his head, as he declined the rum.

"I will get you all something to eat." Rachel hurried to the kitchen. She hated seeing Maxx in this condition.

"How are the construction plans coming along?" Maxx asked Jax. He still did not lift his head.

"We can discuss that after you have rested a bit." Jax joined Maxx at the table.

As much as Jax would like to discuss the plans for the pub, he was not going to burden Maxx in his present condition. The little guy was wearing himself out.

"Why are you selling your horse?" Maxx sat up and wiped his face with his hands. He could not stay down for too long. There was just too much work to be done.

"I am not parting with my horse." Jax cut his eyes at Doug.

"You have a horse. Why would you want Jax's?" Paul asked Doug.

"Nancie is going to kill him today." Doug motioned toward Jax. "I was just trying to give Blue a good home."

"What have you done now?" Maxx was irritated. He was tired and did not need these two fighting.

"I ordered the wrong window." Jax pointed toward the new window leaning against the wall.

"That is the window that I requested. Are the specifications wrong?" Maxx was unsure how Jax could have gotten this wrong. The order details that he left should have been easy to follow.

"The size of the window is not the problem." Jax leaned back in his chair and folded his arms across his chest.

"She does not handle change extremely well." Maxx looked up toward the top of the stairs.

"No truer statement has ever been said." Just when Jax thought that Nancie was warming up to him, he managed to do something to upset her.

"You go ahead and install the window." Maxx sighed and rubbed the back of his neck. "I will fix things with our little blonde friend."

"If only she saw me as a friend, but sadly, she does not." Jax leaned forward and placed his forearms on the table.

"What exactly are your intentions here, Jackson Shaw?" Maxx was extremely tired, but he was serious on this matter.

"My every intention is true, noble, and honorable." Jax looked Maxx in the eye. "If only they were taken as such."

Rachel pushed in the serving cart and started portioning out bowls of stew. Jax, needing something to do, got up and started pouring cups of coffee for everyone.

"You should just take things slowly with Nancie." Rachel smiled up at Jax. "In time, she will come around."

"I have been taking things slow for months now." Jax had been hanging around the pub on a regular basis for the past ten months, hoping to get closer to Nancie.

"Perhaps that devilish charm of yours is no longer working on the ladies." Paul chuckled.

33

"Would you like some help with that?" Maxx teased.

"I do not need Maxwell Spencer to tell me how to woo a woman." Jax shook his head. He could not believe that things had come to this. "The day that happens, I might as well give up and become a hermit."

"I will be right here, offering my assistance, if you change your mind." Maxx grinned and raised his cup of coffee, in a small salute to Jax.

Rachel placed her hand on Jax's shoulder and looked over at Maxx. "His charm is not the issue here."

"Thank you." Jax smiled at Rachel. He was glad to have someone on his side here.

"You need to go home." Paul changed the subject, but he was serious on the matter. Paul had to place his hand against Maxx's shoulder to steady him as he wobbled a bit.

"Paul is right." Jax hated seeing Maxx so tired. "After you eat, you should head home to Hartford before the Duke shows up with another of his 'special missions' for you."

"You finish up the restoration plans here. I will handle the Duke." Maxx had grown weary of Samuel Dawson's requests months ago. However, he was bound by a deal with the Duke that left no room for defiance on his part in the matter.

Jax wanted to help Maxx somehow. The only way he could think of that would free Maxx of that dreadful deal he had made with the Duke, was to kill the Duke. That just was not an option. On most occasions, Samuel Dawson was usually a decent gentleman. In business, however, the Duke was ruthless.

Maxx was so tired that he nodded off for a moment before finishing his stew. Jax and Paul caught him on both sides and steadied him. Jax and Paul looked at each other, both knew that something had to be done about the Duke.

"You may be right. I should go home." Maxx's voice was low. Even the tiredness of his body hung on his words. Still, he hated giving up like this and having to let others handle his duties.

"You need some sleep now." Paul knew that Maxx could not make the ride to Hartford in his present condition.

"Rachel, get Maxx upstairs." Jax helped Maxx to his feet. "Do not worry my little friend, we all will handle things here in the pub."

Rachel hurried over and slipped under Maxx's arm. She put her arm around his waist and started leading him toward the stairs. After some rest, Paul could carry Maxx on to Hartford Manor.

"I need to help you with the window." Maxx protested being taken care of. It was his job to take care of everyone else.

"Do not fret, my friend. I will take care of the window. The restoration plans should be completed in about a week." Jax assured Maxx that things were handled here.

"When this is finished here, you should head home to Kinsley Estate. Your mother is greatly worried about you." Doug thought highly of Jax's mother. Lady Clara was in great distress when he and James had left Kinsley Estate.

"When this job is finished, I will more than likely retire in Nettlesville." Jax had been considering this lately.

"Why would you move to Nettlesville?" Doug asked. He liked the village well enough, but he would not consider retiring there.

"There are a lot of kind people in Nettlesville." Jax sighed deeply. "At least I know that my presence does not irritate them there."

Jax turned around to find Nancie standing at the bottom of the stairs. Her expression was blank. He did not know if she was upset or glad that he was thinking about leaving. Jax tipped his hat and nodded his head at her, before hurrying over to help install the new window.

Chapter Nine

Nancie battled with her emotions over the next few days. It bothered her greatly that Jax thought he was not wanted here at the Blume'N Brew. Truth was, Jax Shaw was an extraordinary addition to the pub, but she struggled to tell him so.

She knew that she was to blame for Jax feeling unwanted here. Hearing Jax say those words had ripped a hole in her heart. Her heart had enough holes already. She did not need to purposely add more. How could she have ever made someone feel as if they were unwanted, especially Jax Shaw?

When they had danced together last year at that society party, it was the first time that Jax had seen the real Nancie. She had worn makeup that night and fixed her hair, but it was not to the extremes that she did for being Miss Nancie.

Elizabeth Dawson, who was now married to Jax's oldest brother, had insisted on doing her hair and makeup for the party that night. Elizabeth had done a tremendous job of turning her into a society lady that evening. If Maxx had not told Jax who she was, she doubted that he would have ever figured it out.

She had gotten use to Jax stopping by the Blume'N Brew, two to three times a week, for the past few months. She had thoroughly enjoyed dancing with him that night as well. How she wished that it could be that way now. If only there was a way for her to get close to Jax and, at the same time, keep her duty to Maxx.

When she made her promises and vow to Maxx, and the late Earl of Hartford, Nancie was only eighteen years of age. She was in a dark place back then and desperately needed saving. It was a blessing for her to have the help of Maxx's family. She owed the Spencer's everything that she had today. Maxx's family had stood by her through every loss that she had experienced. She could never betray the Spencer's, not even for her own heart's desires.

Nancie pulled the curtains back and looked out the window of her private room at the Blume'N Brew. It was still dark outside, but the sun would be up soon. There was a busy workday ahead for the crew at the pub, so she could not linger here any longer. She sighed deeply and silently prayed for a day of peace between her and Jax.

Nancie met Rachel in the kitchen. With the extra crew members at the pub right now, it meant that a bigger breakfast had to be prepared. She was amazed, and thankful, that Jax had acquired a discount for the pub at the market. She was sure that Jax had used his charms to get a couple of the merchants to throw in extra supplies.

By the time that the two ladies had breakfast ready, Jax, Paul, and Harper were already at the dining room table. The three men were talking about their plans for the work crew for the day. When Jax saw Nancie and Rachel push the serving carts into the room, to help the ladies out, he got up and refilled everyone's coffee cups.

Jax was beginning to enjoy this morning routine that they had fallen into the past few days. Helping Nancie with small daily tasks seemed to make her smile more often. He would do anything to see her genuinely smile every day.

"Are you going to share the details of the construction plans for the pub today?" Nancie asked. She sat down across the table from Jax.

"The restoration is almost complete." Harper was cheery this morning.

"We should have everything thing completed in three to four more days." Doug was happy this morning as well. He passed the plate of rolls to Jax.

"That is good news." Nancie's voice did not sound like she believed that this was good news. She looked between Jax and Paul.

"Tis true." Paul nodded his head at Nancie, confirming the matter.

"Paul will oversee the work crew this morning." Jax passed the plate of rolls to Nancie. "I have to go into the city. A few of the supplies have not been delivered yet."

"You are doing a fine job with the restoration plans." Nancie quickly looked down at her plate. She could not look Jax in the eye any longer. "Maxx was right to have trusted you with this job."

Jax's smile broadened as he leaned back in his chair. He watched Nancie closely for a few moments. She pretended to be concentrating on the food on her plate. He, however, was not fooled. She was a strong and bold woman. Her words of compliments had not been easy for her to say.

"I am glad that you approve, my lady." Jax reached for the pot of coffee and refilled his cup.

Jax was thrilled that Nancie was softening a bit where he was concerned. However, he would not ruin this moment by teasing her. He wanted to get closer to her and perhaps this was the start of something greater between them. If he poked fun at her now, there was no doubt for him that she would stab him with the fork by her plate.

Nancie chanced a quick glance between Paul and Rachel. No one had ever called her a lady before. Jax had done this a few times now. Jax knew nothing of her life. He, like all of London, only knew the rumors that they had purposely set up for Miss Nancie, the pub owner. The expressions on her friend's faces were enough for her to know that they had caught Jax's words, just as she had.

After breakfast, Jax and Harper went to visit the shops in London to check on the delayed deliveries. With Holden and Prescott plotting against the Shaw's again, they all agreed that it was best if Jax did not venture into the city alone anymore.

It was getting close to noon and Nancie was helping Rachel to prepare for lunch. Before they could prepare any of the food, the two women heard shouting coming from downstairs in the pub.

Nancie hurried downstairs with Rachel following behind her. Hopefully, they would not find another brawl taking place. She could not afford to have to restore the pub again so soon. If Jax Shaw was fighting in her pub again, Nancie was going to flog him herself.

From the stairs, Nancie could see that Jax was not the problem today. Today they had a much bigger problem. She found Samuel Dawson, the Duke of Greyham, arguing with Paul near the bar. She silently vowed that if the Duke broke anything in the pub that she would flog him as well.

"Where is he?" The Duke shouted at Paul.

"I have already told you that Maxx is not here." Paul tried to talk calmly with the Duke.

"I do not believe you!" Sam angrily pointed his finger in Paul's face.

"It is true, Your Grace." Nancie stepped forward.

Nancie motioned for Jax's cousins, who had just entered the front doors, to go over to Maxx's private table. She was not sure if having two more Shaw's in the pub was a good idea right now.

"You never leave Maxx's side!" Sam continued to shout at Paul. He could not bring himself to shout at the little pub owner.

"Paul is with me, and like he has already told you, Maxx is not here." The Duke turned to look at the young woman that was standing at the bottom of the stairs, behind Nancie.

Nancie and everyone else in the pub whirled around to look at her as well. Eyes widened and mouths dropped open as they all stared at the woman. Immediately, every crew member of The Em stood and faced the Duke with their hands on their swords.

"What are you doing?" Nancie whispered.

The young woman smiled sweetly and motioned Nancie aside. She held her head high as she walked closer to Samuel Dawson. Paul was immediately by her side.

"And just whom may you be?" Sam was greatly annoyed. "And where is Maxwell Spencer?"

"My brother is at home at Hartford, resting. Maxx is exhausted and Mother insists that he rest." Emily continued to smile sweetly at the Duke.

"Lady Emily, forgive me." Sam slightly bowed before her. "I have not had the pleasure of meeting you until now."

"Likewise." Emily curtsied.

"I need to see your brother. I have a job for him." Sam spoke calmly to Emily.

"After Maxx has rested, and regained his strength, I will pass your request along." Emily nodded her head once at the Duke.

"When do you expect that your brother will be back in London?" Sam hated being put off like this.

"I would say, in about a week or two." Emily's smile widened.

"A week or two?" Sam shouted. "I need Maxx now!"

Emily took a step back. Paul's hand immediately went to the hilt of his sword as he stepped between Emily and the Duke. His eyes angrily bore holes into Samuel Dawson. He was not going to let the Duke shout at Lady Emily like this.

"It is alright, Paul." Emily placed her hand on Paul's arm.

"The Duke will kindly remember his manners," Paul growled. He glared at Sam, but he took a step back as Emily was requesting him to do.

"My brother is extremely tired. If you continue running him ragged, then that horrid deal between you two will be no good to you. Maxx cannot help you if he dies from exhaustion." Emily did not mind letting the Duke know that she thought his little deal was wrong.

"So, you know about the deal?" Sam was surprised. Usually, women of noble birth did not care for the business matters between men.

"Maxx does not hide things from Mother and I." Emily folded her hands in front of her. "I do ask that you kindly grant my brother the time he needs to rest. If the matter in which you need help is an urgent situation, then I will handle it for you, in my brother's place."

Everyone in the pub was shaking their heads at Emily. There was no way that Paul would allow this to happen. Even the Duke shook his head.

"Lady Emily, I greatly admire your devotion to your brother. However, I would never allow you to do the work that is part of the deal between Maxx and I." Sam reached and took Emily's hand in his. "Because of your kindness toward me today, I will grant your request. Tell your brother that I will see him in two weeks." With that, Samuel Dawson left the Blume'N Brew.

Chapter Ten

Paul escorted the Duke to the front doors of the pub. Once Samuel Dawson was gone, Paul locked the doors and told Doug to guard it. Hopefully, the Duke would not return today.

"Ugh!" Emily exclaimed loudly as she threw her hands in the air. She quickly turned to face Nancie, who was standing behind the bar. "Can you believe that pompous windbag?"

"The Duke is quite a handful." Nancie had to agree.

"A handful? He is a nuisance!" Emily reached and grabbed a bottle of rum off the bar. "There are days that I would love nothing more than to run a sword through him."

"That would not be very lady like," Paul scolded Emily.

"No, it is not, but I do not care. Samuel Dawson pushes me to my limit." Emily huffed loudly.

"You do not need that." Nancie reached across the bar and grabbed the bottle of rum away from Emily. "I will have Rachel to make you some tea."

"Have you gone mad?" Emily leaned over the bar toward Nancie. "Why would I want tea? You do know that I can get an entire crate of rum off the ship, do you not?"

"You could do that but again, that would not be lady like." Paul put his fist to his mouth and pretended to clear his throat.

"Are you really going to keep insisting on that?" Emily narrowed her eyes at Paul.

"Why don't you calm down and let me get you some tea?" Nancie suggested as she held the bottle of rum away from Emily. "Or perhaps, you would rather have some coffee?"

"What is wrong with everybody today?" Emily threw her hands in the air. "And why do you keep insisting on tea?"

"Because I am sure that you would not wish for Lord Gavin and Lord Alexander to see you being anything but the lady that you are." Nancie formed a tight smile as she looked past Emily.

41

'*No.*' Emily silently mouthed the word at Nancie.

Nancie nodded her head and motioned toward the private table in the corner. This was totally unexpected, but Nancie thought that it should prove rather interesting. Emily quickly gathered herself and turned to face Gavin and Alexander Shaw.

"Lord Gavin, it is just grand to see you again." Emily smiled sweetly and walked over to the two brothers. "Lord Alexander, it is a pleasure to meet you."

"No. No. No." Alex stepped forward and took Emily's extended hand before his brother could. With his other hand, he pointed his finger at Emily and twirled it around as he spoke. "You pack this prim and proper society lady right back up. I greatly prefer the real you that was here a few minutes ago."

"Please forgive my brother." Gavin removed Alex's hand from Emily's and pushed him aside. "He seems to have forgotten his manners."

"You cannot tell me that miss goody two shoes here is Maxwell Spencer's sister." Alex looked between Emily and Gavin. "Now, the woman that wanted to kill the Duke and drink that bottle of rum, now *that* woman is, without a doubt, Maxx's sister."

"Sit down!" Gavin ordered his brother, as he pointed toward the table.

Alex held his hands up in surrender. He went over to Maxx's private table and sat down. He leaned back in his chair and folded his arms across his chest. His eyes never left Emily's.

"Tell me that I am wrong." Alex looked over at his brother. "You both know that I am not."

"Lady Emily is just that, a lady." Rachel set a tray with tea and coffee on the table in front of Alex.

"Do you really take me for a fool?" Alex asked Rachel.

"Do you really want me to answer that?" Rachel snapped. She still did not like that Maxx had made a deal with the Duke so that Alex would be freed from prison.

"It is alright, Rachel." Emily smiled and sat down across from Alex. "I am sure that Lord Alexander will find his manners again after a nice cup of tea."

"No, he will not." Alex leaned forward and shook his head at Emily.

"Yes, you will." Nancie sat down next to Alex.

"You should apologize to Lady Emily." Gavin sat down on the other side of his brother.

"Forgive me, Lady Emily." Alex put his hand on his chest and bowed his head slightly. "If I have offended you in anyway, please forgive me."

"You did not mean that." Nancie shook her head and laughed.

"I meant it as much as she means this high society lady act." Alex motioned toward Emily.

"I am not offended in any way." Emily smiled.

"See." Alex playfully pushed Gavin. "I'm good."

"What brings you two to the Blume'N Brew?" Nancie thought that it was best to change the subject. Nothing good could come from letting Alex Shaw to continue teasing Lady Emily.

"After Doug and James left Ellis Manor, our families discussed the matter greatly." Gavin propped his elbows on the table and folded his hands together. "We are highly upset that Holden and Prescott are plotting to kill Jax."

"Their attempt last week destroyed my pub." Nancie looked around the room.

Nancie was glad to see that everything was almost back to the way that it was. Still, a part of her was sad. Once the pub's restorations were complete, Jax Shaw would leave and she did not like how that made her feel. Jax was annoying at times, but she was becoming use to him being here. Perhaps it was something greater than that, but she could not dwell on that thought just yet.

"We do not understand why Holden would make Jax his target." This had Gavin's entire family confused.

"Jax is tied to nothing." Alex shrugged his shoulders.

"Jax has done a fine job here this week." Nancie was a tad bit defensive.

"He did a fine job in Nettlesville," Paul added.

"You do realize that you do not have to stand behind her." Alex looked up at Paul. "Lady Emily is perfectly safe here with us. So, grab a chair and relax mate."

"I have my eye on you." Paul told Alex as he got a chair and sat down next to Emily. Emily tried to hide her smile behind her hand.

"Jax's work ethics is not an issue here." Emily poured herself a cup of tea. She narrowed her eyes at Nancie for making her drink this. "Jax not being tied to the Shaw title, or estate holdings, may be the very reason that Holden is targeting him."

Nancie and Gavin quickly looked at each other. Emily's words caused them both to see the situation around Jax in a different light. This new thought caused their hearts to sink. Holden had always plotted against the Shaw's with a hidden angle involved. This one, alarmed Nancie and Gavin greatly.

"Jax is an easier target." Gavin said, out loud, the words that he and Nancie were thinking.

"Holden knows that hurting one member of your family would hurt the rest of you. Killing one of you, no matter which one, would destroy the entire Shaw family." Nancie was now sure that Prescott and his men would try an attack Jax again.

"Where is Jax now?" If this was part of Holden's plan, Gavin was glad that his family sent him and Alex here to watch over their cousin.

"He has gone to check on a few delayed deliveries." Nancie jumped to her feet. Her chair slid back and hit the wall. "I fear that Jax is in great danger."

"Did he go into the city alone?" Alex was deeply concerned for his cousin.

"Harper is with him." Paul stood, with his hand on the back of Emily's chair. He turned to look at the front doors, but he knew that he could not leave Emily's side. This was one time that he would be of no help to the Shaw family.

"Prescott had about four or five men with him here last week." Will Carter was sitting at the bar. He remembered those scoundrels well. "Two of 'em have already attacked Sir Jax in an alley a few days ago."

"We should go and look for them." Gavin spoke to Alex.

"With that many men working for Holden, Jax and Harper will need some help." Alex agreed with his brother. They needed to find Jax and soon.

"Why do we need help?" Jax walked through the side entrance of the pub. He and Harper set a couple of cases of new glasses on the bar.

"Oh cousin, am I glad to see you." Gavin hurried over and hugged Jax. His relief could be heard in his voice. "Come, join us and we will share with you what we believe that Holden and Prescott are up to."

"I do not believe that we will ever figure out Holden and Prescott." Jax was growing weary of the two men. He grabbed a chair and sat down between Gavin and Emily.

"I have to agree on that." Emily sighed deeply.

"Hello." Jax had not noticed Emily until now. "I do not believe that we have met."

"Jax, this is Lady Emily." Nancie introduced them. "Lady Emily, this is Jackson Shaw."

Nancie watched Jax closely as he spoke with Emily. She hated to admit that a part of her was a tad bit jealous. She could not help but to wonder if Emily's beauty would turn Jax Shaw's eye.

"You are Maxx's sister?" Jax was clearly stunned. He looked around at the others. "I thought that Maxx had made her up."

Jax had always been slightly blunt when things shocked him. Manners just did not seem to register in his mind at these moments. The others around the table could not help but to chuckle and snicker. Gavin rolled his eyes and shook his head. Alex leaned back in his chair and winked at Emily.

"You thought that *I* was not real?" Emily's eyes widened as she stared at Jax.

"Forgive me, but I am afraid so." Jax shrugged his shoulders. "Maxx never brings you to London, so I thought the little guy just invented you."

Emily rolled her eyes and shook her head. She could tell that it would be pointless to try and reason with Jax on this matter.

"We all are just glad that you are safe." Gavin quickly changed the subject. He did not wish for his cousin to begin debating with Maxx's sister. "We should discuss a plan on protecting you from Holden and Prescott."

"Why don't we discuss that over lunch?" Jax suggested. "I reserved a table for us at Alston's." He looked across the table and smiled at Nancie.

"That is a lovely idea." Nancie was pleased with Jax's idea.

Nancie was relieved that Jax had returned safely back to the pub. She wanted to rush over and hug him when he first walked in. She could not believe that she was genuinely falling for the charms of Jackson Shaw.

Chapter Eleven

Alston's Restaurant was about four streets over from the Blume'N Brew. Since it was such a lovely summer's day, and they had extra men with Gavin and Alex here, everyone decided to walk to the restaurant. Jax was extremely pleased with the decision. He thoroughly enjoyed escorting Nancie down the streets of London to the restaurant.

"I did not know that Maxx's sister was here." Jax nodded to the people they passed on the street as he talked with Nancie.

"Emily surprised us all." Nancie had her hand around Jax's elbow.

"I think that my cousin just might be smitten with Lady Emily." Jax lightly chuckled.

"I think you may be right about that." Nancie looked back over her shoulder at Alex and Emily. "We should not encourage that."

"Why?" Jax wondered. He looked back at his cousin and Emily. "They look good together."

"I do not think that Maxx would approve." Nancie casually stepped closer to Jax's side.

"Are you still sore that Maxx made that deal with the Duke to have Alex freed from prison?" Jax looked down at Nancie.

He understood why Nancie had been so upset when Maxx first made the deal with the Duke of Greyham. Even he did not like the fact that Maxx had to make that deal. Still, Jax was extremely grateful that Maxwell Spencer had found a way to help his cousin Alex. It had broken his heart to see his Aunt Caroline distraught over Alex being in prison. Jax was sure that his own mother was the same emotional mess over his current situation.

"I do not think that I am upset anymore." Nancie sighed deeply. "I will admit though, it did take me quite a while to accept that it was Maxx's decision. I have no choice but to honor that."

"I know that was not easy for you to do." Jax had listened as Nancie loudly voice her opinion about that deal for months.

47

"No, it was not." Nancie smiled. She had to agree on this.

"I am, however, glad to hear that Maxx is getting two weeks to rest. The little guy sure needed a break. I cannot believe how hard Samuel Dawson is working Maxx." Jax was still trying to figure out how he could help Maxx.

"I am glad that your cousins are here to help look out for you. I do not trust Holden at all, and Prescott deals even dirtier than Roger does." Nancie shuddered at the thought of the two men.

"Afraid to lose me?" Jax teased. "This is a pleasant thought." His smile widened.

"I do not know if I would call it that." Nancie smiled and looked straight ahead. If she looked up at Jax right now, he would know that was exactly what she was thinking.

"Say what you will, but I am taking this moment." Jax enjoyed his little triumph here.

"You are impossible sometimes." Nancie turned to look at the shops windows as they walked past. She did not want Jax to see the grin on her face.

"I am pleased that you agreed to have lunch with me today." Jax was enjoying their pleasant conversation today. It was much better than having her shouting at him. "I thought that you and Rachel would enjoy a break from all the cooking you have been doing for the work crew."

"Rachel and I enjoy cooking." Nancie chanced a look up at Jax from the corner of her eye. "That is something in which I wanted to talk with you about."

"How so?" Jax wondered what the matter could be. His expression was serious as he looked down at Nancie.

"I have been seriously thinking about your idea of serving a few meals at the pub." Nancie was not too sure of this idea just yet. However, it could be a way for Jax to stay a while longer at the Blume'N Brew. "That is, if you will truly help me with it?"

"My lady, I will help you with anything." Jax was beyond thrilled that she was going to try his suggestion for the pub. He was not ready to leave just yet.

"Later, this evening, perhaps you could join me in the parlor, and we can discuss the matter further?" Nancie boldly suggested.

"I am all yours, my lady." Jax's smile broadened even more.

When they reached the restaurant, Gavin held the door open for everyone to enter. He scanned the street before he entered. Thankfully, there had been no sign of Roger Holden or Edmond Prescott this morning.

Alston's host, Walter Kent, met the Shaw family as they entered the restaurant. The little man was thrilled to see Jax and his cousins. Nancie had not realized that the Shaw's frequented this restaurant. Of course, she and Rachel had never been here before. All the sudden, Nancie felt a little uncomfortable here. Would the people of this establishment, the employees and guests, accept her?

"Sir, Jackson, your table is ready." Mr. Kent motioned toward the dining room.

"Mr. Kent, if it is not too much trouble, we need a bigger table so that my cousins and Lady Emily Spencer can join us." Jax was his usual charming self to the host.

"It is no trouble at all, Sir Jackson. We have a table for occasions such as this." Mr. Kent was more than happy to accommodate the Shaw family. "If you follow Jeffery, he will show you to your table." Mr. Kent motioned toward the young waiter.

The waiter led them to a large round table on the left side of the restaurant. Nancie was sure that this was a table that was set up for private parties because the other tables were not too close to this one.

Alston's was not one of the fancy formal restaurants that were further inside the city. Still, it was a lovely place. The guests were not wearing formal gowns and suits, but they were dressed nicely. Nancie was glad that she had not come here dressed as Miss Nancie today. Once everyone was seated, Nancie's nervousness was almost gone. No one here seemed to recognize her and Rachel.

"How much longer do you expect to be in London?" Gavin asked Jax.

"That will depend on a few things." Jax was not sure just yet when he would be leaving London.

"We promised your mother that we would stay with you." Gavin accepted the basket of fresh baked bread from their waiter. He took one and passed the basket to Alex.

"I do not like seeing Aunt Clara so upset." Alex had a close relationship with Jax's mother.

"I would estimate that everything should be finished at the pub by the time Maxx gets back." Jax knew that it would not take two weeks to finish the restoration of the pub, but he was buying time.

"I know the Duke gave Maxx two weeks to rest, but I do not see Maxx taking that long." Gavin hated that he had missed seeing Maxx.

Gavin had only gotten to see Maxx for a few minutes, on three or four occasions, over the past ten months. The special missions for the Duke had kept his friend away most of the time. He deeply missed having his best friend around.

"I highly doubt that he will either." Emily agreed with Gavin. She looked over at Nancie and smiled. It was obvious that Nancie was warming up to Jax Shaw.

"Ms. Rhodes' End of the Summer Party is on Friday." Rachel reminded everyone. "Will you all be joining your family there?"

"I had not thought about the party." Jax looked at his cousins.

"Our families will be attending the party." Gavin told Jax. "They will be expecting to see us there."

"That is one party that I am not particularly fond of." Alex looked Jax in the eye. "But your mother needs to see you. You should attend just to give her some peace."

"Will you allow me to escort you to the party?" Jax turned and asked Nancie.

Everyone, including Nancie, was shocked by Jax's question. Nancie was even speechless. She did not expect to ever be asked to attend one of Ms. Rhodes' parties. Everyone around the table sat in silence as they all awaited Nancie's reply.

"I do not really fit in at those type of parties." Nancie had no idea how to really answer Jax. Her position at the pub did not get her invites to society parties.

"You attended my brother's engagement party at the Duke's house," Jax reminded her.

"Rachel and I got to attend that party only because Elizabeth had insisted on it." Nancie was thrilled to have gotten to attend that party last year.

"You would be attending this party by my side, as my guest." Jax pleaded with her.

"You should go." Emily nodded her head when Nancie looked over at her.

"You should go too." Rachel suggested to Emily. "You can make sure that none of those high society women do anything to insult Nancie."

"I am not fond of those type of parties." Emily declined the suggestion.

"Maxx is not here. So, you should go to represent your family." Gavin encouraged Emily. "I know that the rest of my family would love to meet you."

"As much as I hate this particular party, I will happily escort you." Alex grinned as he leaned toward Emily.

"Of course, you will." Emily gently pushed Alex away.

"Then that settles it." Jax raised his glass in triumphant. The others joined and did the same, except for Emily.

"Oh, I was not agreeing." Emily shook her head.

"Too late, you are going." Nancie smiled sweetly at Emily. There was no way that she was going to let Emily out of this now.

Emily sighed and leaned back in her chair. How did this just backfire on her? It was clear that Nancie was starting to have feelings for Jax Shaw. She wanted to give her friend a wonderful evening by Jax's side. Now, she was trapped into going to that party as well.

"Emily, are you alright?" Nancie leaned forward when Emily's eyes widened.

"Emily, what is wrong?" Alex gave Emily a little shake. She had become like a statue at his side.

"Look over at the windows," Emily whispered.

Everyone at their table turned to look in the direction that Emily was staring. At a table by the windows, on the far side of the restaurant, sat Roger Holden. The Earl of Statham was having lunch with Evelyn Cramer.

Chapter Twelve

Roger Holden had noticed the Shaw family when they first sat down at their table. Two of the women with the Shaw's looked familiar to him. They reminded him of the women at the Blume'N Brew. From this distance, and with their backs now to him, Roger was not totally sure though. However, the woman that was sitting facing him, he had never seen her before. She had long brown wavy hair and she greatly intrigued him.

When it was time for him to leave, Roger sent word for his carriage to pick him and Evelyn up at the side entrance doors of the restaurant. Doing this would allow him to escort Evelyn Cramer by the Shaw's table. He was fine with risking a little public scandal to irritate the Shaw's.

When Evelyn noticed the Shaw family, she came to a sudden halt. She placed one hand to her chest as she gasped loudly. With her other hand, she clutched Roger Holden's arm tighter.

"Alexander Shaw, you should still be in prison for what you did to me." Evelyn was always dramatic, especially when she did not get her way.

"Evelyn Cramer, you should have drowned in that fountain a year ago." Nancie locked eyes with Evelyn.

Nancie had been hoping to run into Evelyn since Ms. Rhodes' End of the Summer Party last year. She had promised Maxx that she would not hunt Evelyn down and give the evil woman a piece of her mind but running into her on the streets of London was another thing entirely. If Evelyn had not have led Maxx into that fight in Ms. Rhodes' garden that night, Alex would not have ended up in prison and Maxx would not be stuck in his deal with the Duke of Greyham.

"How dare you?" Evelyn sighed and pretended to be shocked.

"Oh, I dare." Nancie wanted to reach up and slap Evelyn.

"Do something." Evelyn batted her eyes as she whined to Roger.

"I do not believe that you and I have met." Roger kept his eyes on Emily. He completely ignored Evelyn's theatrics.

Paul was quickly to his feet. With one hand on the hilt of his sword and the other on the back of Emily's chair, he glared at Roger Holden.

"You need to keep moving, Holden." Paul was so angry that his face was turning red.

"My, are you not the protective one." Roger grinned at Paul. "Where is your little captain friend? I have not seen him around much lately."

"Don't you worry about Maxx." Nancie stood up and narrowed her eyes at Roger.

Roger Holden was the one person that Nancie truly hated. The evil snake had already tried to kill Maxx by poisoning a bottle of wine. If it had not have been for Nate Shaw's wife, Olivia, Roger Holden's half-sister, Maxx would have surely died. Thankfully, Nate and Alex had helped Olivia to save Maxx in Nettlesville that day.

"I do not believe that I was talking to you." Roger snapped at Nancie. He hated it when a woman challenged him.

"You will talk to me." Jax stood up and stepped in between Nancie and Roger.

"I think that you should take your lady friend and leave." Emily's voice brought Roger's attention back to her.

"Sitting with this lot, I can understand why you think poorly of me." Roger smiled at Emily. "Perhaps you would join me for a cup of tea, and I will tell you the truth about me." Roger motioned toward one of the other smaller tables. Evelyn was truly shocked this time.

"The tea she has at this table is just fine." Alex stood up with his hand on his sword as well.

"I do not wish to have tea with you." Emily placed her hand on Alex's arm to steady him, as she looked directly at Roger Holden. "However, I would love to see a dagger in your heart."

"I love her." Alex leaned over and whispered to Gavin, who was also now standing. "You should have introduced her to our family a long time ago."

Gavin grabbed Maxx by the arm. "My friend, do not let this woman bait you."

"Ms. Branton, I think you have said enough." Lady Caroline walked over to Mary. "You will not push whatever hatred you have for Maxwell's father onto him."

"I do not hate the former Earl of Hartford." Mary Branton held her head high. "In fact, I loved Daniel Spencer dearly. I was his mistress for many years, and he is Felicia's father."

The entire room fell silent. Everyone turned to look at Maxx. Surprisingly, Maxx did not display shock or anger on his face. Nancie rushed forward and put her arm around Maxx.

"Maxx, could this be true?" Nancie did not understand how Maxx could stand here with a grin on his face after hearing Mary Branton's declaration.

"Not at all," Maxx replied.

"I think our family has heard enough for one night." Gavin proudly stood by Maxx's side.

"Ms. Branton, I do believe that you and your daughter should retire for the evening." Lady Caroline had heard enough from the hateful woman. "Rosa, will you please escort these ladies to their room?"

Rosa hurried over and motioned for Mary Branton and her daughter to leave the room. Lord Mason nodded his head at Mary. She let go of his arm and started following Rosa out of the room.

"I will be visiting your mother soon." Mary said to Maxx as she walked by him.

"The gates at Hartford Manor will never open to you, nor will your foot find rest anywhere on Hartford soil," Maxx informed Ms. Branton.

After the door closed behind Mary Branton and her daughter, relief came over everyone in the room. This was turning into quite an eventful night for the Shaw family.

"Ben, I am going to have to ask that you never bring that woman back to my home." Lord Matthew would not stand for the disrespect of Mary Branton.

"What you Shaw's do with your family name is not a concern to me." Mary Branton stepped closer to Lord Mason's side. "But she does not belong here."

"You are the one that does not belong here." Maxx spoke sternly to Mary Branton. "Your husband was only a lawyer. There is no title for you to cling to."

"She is my guest." Lord Mason defended Mary.

"My daughter and I are linked to an Earl and we should be granted those privileges." Mary Branton informed Maxx.

"It does not matter who you and your daughter know." Jax angrily pointed his finger at Mary Branton. "You have no right to come into one of our homes and disgrace our family in any manner."

"I did not disgrace your family." Mary Branton saw nothing wrong with her actions.

"My son is right." Lady Clara squeezed Nancie's hand. "Nancie is part of our family."

"Just because your son is entertaining the little pub owner, does not make her part of your family." Mary Branton boldly looked Lady Clara in the eye. "You family's reputation would fare much better if your son sent his little plaything away and married my daughter."

Every woman in the room gasped in shock and covered their mouths with their hands. Nancie stood still as a statue from the shock of Mary Branton's words. Lady Clara and Elizabeth tightened their grip on Nancie's hands and stepped closer to her side. Jax could no longer hold his temper at bay.

"That will never happen!" Jax shouted. Caleb and Nick struggled to hold onto their brother.

"Nancie is family." Maxx step in front of Mary Branton. He glanced over at Lord Mason. His anger with the woman clinging to the Earl's arm was clearly displayed on Maxx's face.

"And you, young man, you shame your father greatly." Mary Branton became bolder as she turned on Maxx. "You disgrace your title, *little Earl* of Hartford."

"You, madam, will not turn any of this and your hatred onto my father." Maxx held his temper at bay, but it could clearly be heard in his voice.

"Lady Emily, is there a problem?" Walter Kent hurried over to their table. He was deeply concerned. It was not often that the Earl of Hartford's family visited Alston's Restaurant. The host would hate for the Earl's sister to be offended.

"No, Mr. Kent. Everything here is fine." Emily assured the host.

"Yes, everything is fine. The Earl of Statham was just leaving." Jax stepped closer to Roger.

"You are Emily Spencer?" Roger's head snapped toward Emily.

"That's *Lady* Emily Spencer to you." Nancie sternly informed Roger.

"You need to leave." Jax had enough of Roger. "Now."

"Lord Holden?" Walter Kent was becoming deeply worried about the situation.

"Jax." Gavin reached over and touched Jax on the arm and shook his head. "Not here."

Jax took a step back and folded his arms across his chest. Gavin was right. This was not the place to have an altercation with Roger Holden. His mother, and Gavin's, loved this restaurant. He did not wish to do anything that would cause either of their mothers an issue when they dined here again. However, Jax did step in front of Roger. His broad shoulders blocked Roger's view of the others at their table.

"Yes, Mr. Kent. I am leaving." Roger politely nodded at the restaurant host.

"I will escort you out," Paul offered. He then spoke to Alex, without taking his eyes off Roger. "Alex, you watch Lady Emily."

"Oh, do not fret, mate." Alex smiled at Emily. "I have Lady Emily."

Paul, with his hand on his sword, followed Roger and Evelyn to the side doors of the restaurant. He remained standing in the doorway until Roger's carriage was out of sight. Before going back inside, he looked up and down the street to see if Edmond Prescott was lurking in the shadows.

Mr. Kent apologized a couple of times for the Earl of Statham's behavior. Jax assured the host that his family was fine. Jax hated that Roger Holden had interrupted their lunch. He wanted Nancie to

enjoy this trip to the restaurant so he could bring her here again on another day, just the two of them.

Roger Holden left Alston's Restaurant in a cheery mood. He did not hear one word that Evelyn said to him on the ride to her family's house in London. Evelyn's father had a brother and a sister. Their family shared this house whenever they were in London.

Roger was greatly pleased with how today had turned out. He had now met the mysterious Lady Emily Spencer. She was the very woman that he had been looking for. His mother had told him to force either Lady Emily or Lady Danielle Shaw into marrying him. Lady Danielle was lovely, but she was still a child at only eighteen years of age. Lady Emily was a woman and one that would be a great challenge for him. Roger loved challenges.

Roger smiled slyly as he thought about all the ways that he could destroy Maxwell Spencer through his twin sister. From the look of things, his mother was right. Destroying Lady Emily Spencer would also destroy the Shaw family. Roger had noticed how the Shaw's protected Lady Emily today, especially Alex Shaw.

The only other person that seemed to be very protective of Lady Emily Spencer was Paul. It looked as though he was now going to have to kill Maxwell Spencer's first mate. Roger's smile grew even broader. Paul's death would be another stab to the Earl of Hartford's heart. That was a thrilling notion indeed. Today was just getting better and better for him by the minute. Ms. Rhodes' End of the Summer Party would be just as thrilling as last year's party if Lady Emily Spencer attended.

Chapter Thirteen

Later that evening, Nancie left Paul and Harper to lock up the Blume'N Brew for the night. She went up to prepare a food tray and tea for her meeting with Jax. Well, she was calling this a meeting so that she would not have to analyze her feelings for Jax just yet. One day, she knew that she would have to face her feelings and act on them. After she prepared everything, she went to the parlor to wait for Jax.

No one had to tell her that she was playing a dangerous game with Jax Shaw. Nancie knew it already. She had learned enough, through Maxx's friendship with the Shaw's, to know that they took matters of the heart seriously. She had watched the Shaw men do some idiotic things, over the past couple of years, when they had fallen in love.

Love? Did she seriously just have that thought? Nancie quickly shook her head to try and shake the thought away. Sooner or later, she was going to have to figure this all out. She already knew that Jax was a bit smitten with her. What would she do if he truly fell in love with her?

She could not have a life with Jax Shaw, or any other man for that matter. Her promise to Maxx's family would not allow for her to have a personal relationship. Perhaps that was her thinking and it had nothing to do with her promise to the Spencer's. Whatever this thought of hers truly was, it was something that kept her safe. If she did fall in love with someone, he would have to be from Hartford. Only someone from Hartford would be able to understand her.

Jax was looking forward to spending some time alone with Nancie tonight. He had thought about hardly anything else all day. He was hoping that Nancie would not dress up as Miss Nancie and make her appearance in the pub tonight. He knew that she would though. At least she had not stayed in the pub until closing tonight. With a huge smile on his face, Jax left his cousins downstairs, at Maxx's private table, and hurried up to the parlor.

When Jax entered the parlor, he found Nancie staring out the window. This room was on the backside of the pub. He knew the view from this room would be of the stables behind the pub. He doubted that the secret stables would be visible from here. Maxx had taken the extra precautions to make sure of that.

Nancie was lost in her thoughts and did not hear him enter the room. Jax quietly closed the door and walked across the room. He wondered what she must be thinking about to cause her to not hear him.

Before Jax reached her, Nancie sighed deeply and turned around. She gasped as she placed her hand on her chest. Seeing Jax standing there had startled her.

"Forgive me," Jax apologized. "I did not wish to disturb your thoughts."

"It is fine." Nancie gave a little shake of her head. There were not many men in the pub tonight and there was no piano playing. Normally, she would have heard the noise when Jax had opened the door.

"Would you like to share those thoughts with me?" Jax slowly took a step closer to her. His voice was low and calm. "You were greatly captivated by them for a moment there."

"The only thoughts that you and I need to talk about right now, are the ones that you have for the Blume'N Brew serving meals." Nancie blushed a little as she smiled at Jax. She could not tell him that she was thinking about him.

"I see that you have prepared for us to have a lengthy chat." Jax noticed the tea with cookies and tarts on the table.

"Are your plans for my pub so great that they require a lengthy chat?" Nancie smiled as Jax held the chair out for her. "My, are you not just the gentleman tonight."

"I am always a gentleman." Jax winked at her as he sat down beside her. "If I am ever anything less than a gentleman, my mother will have the final word with me on that matter."

Nancie laughed and relaxed a bit. Their little meeting was starting out simply fine. She now wondered why she was so nervous about this before. Jax Shaw could be reasonable and responsible. He was

also handsome and charming. His dark brown eyes were alluring to her. Nancie gave a quick shake of her head to snap out of that thought.

"What?" Jax had noticed her movement. "You do not believe me?"

"Oh, it's not that. I am sure that your mother would give you a piece of her mind if you were unruly in any way." Nancie poured them both a cup of tea. She had to busy herself to keep her thoughts from straying. "Lady Clara is a strong woman that can surely speak her mind."

"I cannot believe that you actually housed my mother here for a night." Jax had been a little upset when he found out that his parents had spent a night here at the Blume'N Brew a year ago.

"I am sure that night is a matter in which your mother never speaks of." Nancie had enjoyed meeting Lady Clara. Jax's mother had an inner strength that she had greatly admired.

"On the contrary, my mother calls that night her *'interesting adventure'*. She was thrilled to have been able to help Alex and Maxx that night at Ms. Rhodes' party." His mother had surprised Jax when she told him her story from that night.

"I am glad to hear that." Nancie put a tart and some cookies on a plate for Jax. She had already noticed just how much of a sweet tooth he had. "Now, would you mind telling me how you believe serving meals would work out for the pub?"

Jax and Nancie spent the next hour going over the possible plans for the pub to serve a few meals. Jax was thrilled that Nancie was considering this idea of his. Between the two of them, they worked out a plan that seemed pleasing for Nancie and Rachel to test serving meals for a couple of hours around dinnertime.

"Do you believe that Maxx will approve of this?" Jax asked as he got up to leave.

"Since the work would fall upon Rachel and myself, I do not see where Maxx would have too much to say in the matter." Nancie stood up and started gathering their dishes onto the tray.

"Maxx just has a lot of authority here." Jax reached for his teacup at the same time Nancie did.

"He does." Nancie's voice was low. Her eyes lingered for a moment on Jax's hand that was covering hers.

"Why do you do this to yourself?" Jax touched one of Nancie's blonde ringlets.

"This is a wig." Nancie looked up into Jax's eyes. "Did you really believe that I could get my hair to curl like this in such a short time?"

"A wig?" It feels real." Jax was amazed.

"It is real hair." Nancie reached up and removed the blonde ringlet wig from her head. "Maxx gets them from a special shop in France."

Nancie's long blonde wavy hair fell past her shoulders and down to the middle of her back. Jax took several strands of her hair in his hand. He let the long wavy strands run through his fingers to their tips. His eyes locked with Nancie's as the last strands of hair fell away from his hand.

"You are beautiful without these wigs and all the makeup." Jax leaned toward her.

"I have to wear them to be Miss Nancie." Nancie placed her hands against Jax's chest to keep him from leaning any closer to her. It was a mistake, for now she would only imagine more between them.

"You do not have to be Miss Nancie." Jax's eyes never left hers. "I greatly prefer the real you."

"If you truly knew the 'real' me, you would not prefer anything about me." Nancie looked away.

"I seriously doubt that." Jax's voice was just above a whisper. He slowly leaned his head closer to hers.

"I cannot." Nancie took a step back. She knew that if she had not done so, Jax would have kissed her.

Jax strongly felt the coldness of her rejection. He had not come here tonight with the plans of kissing her. Of course, he wanted to kiss her, but this was not a romantic setting. He never imagined trying to seriously court a woman in a pub before. He wanted more for Nancie. He wanted her to know that the world did not revolve around this pub.

"You are right." Jax stood up straight. He continued to look directly in Nancie's eyes. "When I do kiss you, and trust me, that will be soon, you will not be dressed as Miss Nancie. I will have the real you, my dear, and not some dressed up lie." With that said, Jax turned and left the parlor.

Chapter Fourteen

Everything at the Blume'N Brew became strictly business after that night. The pub's restoration would be complete in less than a week's time now. Nancie was beginning to feel uneasy. Ever since their evening in the parlor, Jax had been spending more time with his cousins and less time around her.

It was now Friday, the day of Ms. Rhodes' End of the Summer Party. Emotions at the Blume'N Brew were heightened today. Nancie did not understand why this society party was so important to everyone in London.

It was almost noon and Nancie had not left her room all morning. She sat at her vanity and stared at her reflection. She turned toward the door when she heard the knock. She intended on ignoring the summons, but the knock came again. As she slowly walked toward the door, a third knock came. Whoever was on the other side of the door was not going to go away.

"Nancie, are you alright?" Emily's voice was heavy with concern.

Nancie slowly opened the door. Without saying a word, she motioned for Emily to enter her room. When Nancie turned to walk back to the vanity, Emily gave a little wave to Jax and Rachel, who were watching from the dining room door.

Emily stepped into Nancie's room and closed the door behind her. The room was dark and stuffy. The only light in the room was the lantern by the vanity. Emily pulled back the curtains and opened the window to let some light and air into the dark room.

"Are you planning on becoming a hermit?" Emily pulled a chair up beside Nancie at her vanity.

"It was not my intent." Nancie looked at Emily in the mirror. "It is just working out that way today."

"You are going to have to tell me what's wrong." Emily reached over and covered Nancie's hand with hers. "You cannot stay like this."

"Jax hates me." Nancie looked away and released a deep breath. She could no longer look at Emily.

"Are you blind?" Emily touched Nancie's arm and leaned forward over the vanity. "I actually believe that Jax Shaw just may be in love with you."

"He hates me." Nancie continued to look at Emily in the mirror. "And if what you believe is true, that would be a huge problem."

"Have you been drinking today?" Emily tried to make light of the situation. She sat up and looked at Nancie questionably. "You are talking in circles. Now, I know that you are not off the head, so what is going on with you?"

"Jax does not like Miss Nancie." Nancie closed her eyes for a moment. "He has avoided me since our meeting in the parlor two nights ago."

"Oh no. It has finally happened." Emily leaned back in her chair and laughed. "You, my friend, have been badly bitten."

"Now, you are the one that is off the head." Nancie refused to admit her feelings. "Bitten or not, it is still a problem."

"How so?" Emily did not understand Nancie's reasoning here.

"For starters, Jax hates Miss Nancie," Nancie replied.

"Stop saying that. Jax loves you," Emily insisted.

"Not me." Nancie motioned toward the wigs on the stand next to the vanity. "He hates *Miss Nancie*."

"Oh." Emily now understood what Nancie was saying. "He is a Shaw, after all. I guess, after he met the real you last year at the Duke's house, Jax must see Miss Nancie as a trick of some kind."

"She is one." Nancie hated saying this to Emily. "And she is a lie that I cannot escape."

"You do not have to dress up as Miss Nancie anymore." Emily did not like seeing her friend so sad.

"I have to be Miss Nancie. I have to protect Maxx." Nancie was highly emotional. Emily had to grab Nancie by her shoulders to calm her down.

"You do not have to dress up as *Miss Nancie* anymore just to protect Maxx." Emily gave Nancie a little shake. "And in case you missed it, Maxx has a lot of people protecting him now."

"But…" Nancie was not sure of what to say.

"You have done a lot for my family, and we thank you dearly. When I was nineteen years of age, you became more than my friend. After my father's death, you became my family." Emily spoke seriously. "If your heart has truly fallen for Jackson Shaw, then let me help you. You gave your life for my family. It is time for us to give you back your life."

"You mean, Maxx does not need me anymore?" Nancie's voice cracked.

"Maxx will always need you." Emily assured her. "You are older now. What our fathers started here is secure. You just do not have to play the part of *Miss Nancie* anymore."

"I do not know if I know how to be anyone other than Miss Nancie." Nancie looked over towards the wigs and fluffy dresses that she wore as Miss Nancie. Was it possible that she could truly be her herself all the time? Did she even know how to be just Nancie Blume?

"Why don't you take a little time to think about it? We do not have to decide everything today." Emily stood up and pulled Nancie to her feet as well. "We can pack all this stuff up. The wigs, dresses, and all the heavy makeup and let you live your life as normally as possible."

"I promise to think about it." Nancie gave Emily a hug.

Nancie felt like everything around her was changing too quickly. She was not sure how all this had happened to her. Before, she knew who she was supposed to be, and she played that part extremely well. Now, because of Jax Shaw, her world was crumbling before her very eyes. Did she want for her life to change?

"Take a few minutes and then come join us for lunch. Afterward, we can get ready for Ms. Rhodes' party tonight." This was something that Emily was not looking forward to. Still, she smiled at Nancie and left the room.

Jax was still waiting for Emily in the hallway. He was deeply concerned about Nancie. It was not like her to remain in her room until noon. Jax had not told anyone how his and Nancie's little meeting in the parlor had ended a couple of nights ago. He was extremely embarrassed to have to admit that he had walked out on Nancie that night. This would be something that his mother would not be proud of, he knew he sure was not proud of it.

"Is she alright?" Jax followed Emily into the dining room.

"She will be." Emily sat down next to Alex.

Jax did not want to sit down and eat. He wanted to know what was wrong with Nancie. Emily appeared to be as secretive as her brother was, so Jax knew not to push the issue with her. Jax did not have to wait too long to find out how Nancie was. As they started eating, Nancie walked into the dining room. With her hair down, no makeup, and wearing a simple everyday dress, Jax thought that she was beautiful.

"I am so glad that you decided to join us." Rachel hurried over and got Nancie a plate and teacup from the serving cart. "After lunch, we can start getting you ready for Ms. Rhodes' party." Rachel was as giddy as a young girl.

"I will not be going to Ms. Rhodes' party tonight." Nancie stated as she took the plate from Rachel.

"What?" Jax was clearly shocked. "Why would you not go?"

"I have to be here to open the pub tonight." Nancie poured herself a cup of tea. She refused to look anyone in the eye.

"If she is not going, then I am not going either." Emily patted Nancie on her arm. "Thank you for getting me out of that party, my friend."

"You have to go." Alex protested Emily's decision.

"No, I do not." Emily smiled sweetly at Alex before turning her attention to the food on her plate.

"If you ladies are not going, then neither am I." Jax proclaimed. Like Emily, he now concentrated on the food on his plate.

"You have to go." Nancie was shocked at Jax's statement. "You have to see your mother."

"My parents can stop by here and see me on their way home in the morning." Jax did not look up from his plate.

"Lady Clara will be furious." Nancie was getting upset.

"Aye," Jax agreed. "She will indeed."

Alex started to speak, but Emily lightly elbowed him in the side. Gavin was sitting across the table, next to Jax. He could already see that Emily was working on a plan here with Nancie, that no one else could see just yet. Jax seemed to be fitting into the plan nicely. Gavin remained quiet and hoped that his brother would also. Gavin had seen Maxx do this on many occasions. Usually, in the end, everything had always worked out as Maxx had planned.

"You cannot do this to your mother." Nancie stared at Jax until he raised his eyes to look at her.

"I will go, if you allow me to escort you." Jax was firm on the matter.

Nancie did not know what to say or do. If Jax did not go to Ms. Rhodes' party his mother would be devasted. If Lady Clara ever found out that she was the reason her son had stayed away from the party, the woman would never forgive her.

"That's blackmail!" Nancie snapped.

"If that is what it takes, then tonight, blackmail it what it is." Jax was not giving in. His mind was set.

"Ugh!" Nancie exclaimed. "Alright! This time, you win! I will go!"

Jax nodded his head and went back to eating his food. Nancie was furious that she had no choice but to give in. She quickly stood up, causing her chair to slide backwards hard. She loudly stomped down the hall to her room. After she had left, Jax walked over to the serving cart, behind Emily and Alex, to fill his plate again.

"Thank you." Jax leaned down and whispered to Emily.

Emily reached up and punched Jax on the arm hard.

"Ow." Jax set his plate down and rubbed his arm.

"Before you ask, that was for messing with my friend's mind. She was not like this until you showed up here." Emily got up and left the dining room.

"She's amazing." Alex smiled as he watched Emily walk down the hall.

"Have you gone mad?" Jax looked at Alex as if he had lost his mind.

"He truly has," Gavin replied as he too stared at his brother.

"When Maxx gets back, he is going to kill you for teasing his sister." Jax continued to look at Alex as he sat down. He was still rubbing his upper arm where Emily had punched him. She hit hard for a girl.

"Maxx loves me. I will be fine," Alex said as he looked down the hall where Emily had just been.

"You keep telling yourself that. I will have father to engrave those words onto your tombstone." Gavin laughed at his little brother.

"That's not a bad idea." Jax too laughed at his cousin.

Chapter Fifteen

Ms. Rhodes' home in London was beautifully decorated for tonight's party. Nancie was in awe as she looked around the grand foyer. Ms. Rhodes' house was not quite as elegant as the Duke of Greyham's home, but it was still one of the most beautiful homes in the city.

Nancie walked into the grand ballroom on Jax's arm. She did not recognize most of the women she saw in the room. However, several of the husbands she had seen often at the Blume'N Brew. She had overheard many of these men say that they had come to the pub to escape their wives for a few hours.

The younger girls in the room turned to stare at her. They immediately began to whisper to each other behind their fancy lace fans. She chanced a look back at Emily. It was obvious that Emily was not comfortable in this surrounding either.

"Would you care to dance, my lady?" Jax motioned toward the dance floor.

"I would be delighted." Nancie stepped out onto the dance floor with Jax.

As Jax twirled her around the dance floor, Nancie noticed that some of the whispering going on was directed at Emily and Alex as well. She was surprised to see that Emily was dancing tonight. During the few parties Nancie had been to at Hartford, she had never seen Emily dance before.

"Do you not like dancing?" Alex whispered next to Emily's ear.

"Oh, I like it well enough I guess." Emily had also noticed the women in the room whispering and pointing toward her and Nancie. She rolled her eyes. "It is not one of my favorite things though."

"You might enjoy dancing more if you would relax a bit and let me lead," Alex teased.

Emily sighed. "I will try."

When the music stopped, Jax led Nancie to the side of the room. She was grateful that Emily and Alex had followed them. As much as she had always wanted to be at these society parties, she had not realized just how overwhelming the atmosphere in the room could be. She was not sure if the people here recognized her as the pub owner or not. If they did, she figured that Ms. Rhodes would ask her to leave.

"I need to see my mother." Jax leaned down and spoke next to her ear.

"You go ahead." Nancie smiled up at Jax. "I will wait here with Emily and Alex."

"No, ma'am, you will not." Jax tightened his grip on her arm. "You are coming with me."

Nancie tried to protest but Jax would not listen. All she wanted to do was dance a few dances and then head back to the pub. She was not expecting to have to face Lady Clara tonight. It was different when Jax's parents had stayed at the Blume'N Brew that night last year. That was before she had feelings for Jax. At the thought of those words, the realization of it hit Nancie full force. She truly had feelings for Jax Shaw.

When Lady Clara saw her youngest son approaching, she let go of her husband's arm and rushed across the room. Relief flooded Lady Clara as she threw her arms around Jax. Nancie watched as Jax wiped his mother's tears from her face. Lady Clara was overwhelmed emotionally. Her son was here, and for the moment, he was safe.

Nancie was aware that the Shaw family had a remarkable bond of love. She did not realize just how special that bond was until tonight. Watching that love with her own eyes caused her to be emotional too. It created something else in her as well. A moment of cold and regret blew across Nancie's heart. She missed her parents.

"Mother, you remember Nancie." Jax took Nancie's hand and pulled her close to his side.

"Yes, I do." Lady Clara politely smiled as she looked between her son and Nancie. "Hello, Nancie."

"Lady Clara." Nancie curtsied to Jax's mother. She could not remember the last time she had curtsied to anyone. "It is lovely to see you again."

"Son, why don't you go over and say hello to your father." Lady Clara suggested. "Nancie and I will go over and get a glass of wine and an apple tartlet."

Jax was not comfortable with leaving Nancie. He had promised her that he would stay by her side tonight. He did not trust some of these society ladies here to be nice.

"You go ahead." Nancie encouraged Jax to do as his mother asked. "I will be just fine with Lady Clara." Reluctantly, Jax gave in and hurried over to his father.

"Come." Lady Clara took Nancie's arm and lead her over to where the refreshments were. "Are you enjoying the party?"

"We have not been here long, but it is lovely." Nancie felt nervous.

"How has my son been?" Lady Clara asked.

"Jax has been wonderful. He is almost finished with the restoration plans. He is a great leader," Nancie replied.

"I know that Jackson is an excellent worker and a great leader. He proved that when he helped Nathaniel in Nettlesville." Lady Clara stopped walking, she took Nancie by the arm, and turned her to face her. "Roger Holden is trying to kill my son. I want to know how Jax truly is doing?"

The look on Lady Clara's face broke Nancie's heart. Before her stood a mother that was deeply concerned for her son's life. Nancie instantly loved Jax's mother. She hoped that Lady Clara would one day accept her.

"Jax is strong minded, but we are doing everything that we can to keep him safe." Nancie took Lady Clara's hands in hers. "Maxx has given his men orders to protect Jax."

"Maxwell is such a dear." Lady Clara sighed with relief. It was a bit comforting to know that her son was being watched over.

"Plus, Gavin and Alex are here now for extra protection. You also do not have to worry about your nephews, Maxx has them guarded as well. All three of them will be escorted home when the restoration is

70

complete." Nancie wanted Lady Clara to know that her family was as safe as everyone at the pub could make them.

Nancie was glad to see Lady Clara smile at this news. It was comforting to be able to give the dear woman some peace. Of course, neither Jax nor his cousins knew that Maxx was having them guarded as much as possible right now. Maxx did not think that Roger Holden would stop his attack on the Shaw family until he had killed at least one of them.

"I do not believe that my son will be leaving the Blume'N Brew once the restorations are finished." Lady Clara's tone was serious as she held Nancie's gaze.

This was the moment that Nancie was not ready for. She had not even let it be known to Jax that she truly had feelings for him yet. How could his mother know? Nancie was hoping that Jax would stay a while longer and help with the pub serving meals. Since they had not talked much over the past couple of days, she was not so sure if Jax would stay.

"He has no reason to stay." Nancie quickly looked toward the dance floor. She was not sure what to say to Lady Clara right now.

"If you do not care for my son, then you need to tell him and release him." Lady Clara squeezed Nancie's hands. "I can tell you, as a Shaw, Jax will not willingly walk away."

"I do care for Jax, but I own a pub." Nancie wanted to be completely honest with Jax's mother. "That is something that would not be accepted in your family or with all these society people here."

"It is true, many people may frown upon that. My family and I are not like most of the people in this room." Lady Clara also wanted to be honest with Nancie. "Jax does not hold the family title, and he is not the heir to Kinsley Estate. Even if he was either of those, Jackson will follow his heart, no matter what."

"He does have a huge heart," Nancie replied.

She looked across the room at Jax as he talked with his father and brothers. The sight of him made her smile. Somehow, this Shaw had worked his way into her heart. Could it truly be possible for her to be a part of his family?

71

"I will not pretend or lie to you, your job does concern me greatly, but not for the reasons that you may believe." Lady Clara was deeply concerned for Jax and Nancie's safety. A pub could be a rough and unruly place at times. Edmond Prescott had already attacked Jax once there. How many more times would the evil man attempt this?

"I am not the type of woman that people associate with my job." Nancie was not sure of Lady Clara's meaning.

"You surely are." Evelyn Cramer waved her lace fan as she loudly spoke to Nancie. She lifted her head when she turned to Lady Clara. "I cannot believe that you would welcome a harlot into your family. The Shaw name will dwindle to nothing now."

"Evelyn, you should not speak in such a manner." Felicia Branton, who had been whispering in the corner with Evelyn, spoke in a shocking tone.

"Nancie, why don't you go and get me a glass of wine and that apple tartlet?" Lady Clara suggested. "I will be along shortly."

"I am not leaving you with her." Nancie looked over and glared at Evelyn.

"Trust me, dear, I will be just fine." Lady Clara motioned toward the refreshment tables. "Hurry on now. I promise to join you shortly."

"You better learn how to be nice." Nancie spoke sharply to Evelyn. "And you better learn it fast or I will personally drag you outside by the hair of your head."

Nancie narrowed her eyes as she walked past Evelyn. She did not like leaving Jax's mother, but the refreshment tables were only a few feet away. She could keep an eye on the situation. She would not let Evelyn cause Lady Clara any grief.

"You have a wonderful night, Lady Clara." Evelyn quickly turned to go. She was no longer comfortable being in Lady Clara's presence.

"You, my dear, will refrain from insulting my family in the future." Lady Clara grabbed Evelyn by the arm, halting her exit.

"Are you threatening me?" Evelyn gasped as she pretended to be shocked. "Perhaps I should go and speak to the magistrate."

"We are women. The courts would only laugh at us both." Lady Clara spoke sternly. "I know the company that you keep as of late. If any harm comes to my son, or the woman he loves, I will find you."

"You are off the head!" Evelyn exclaimed. "Perhaps you should be the one that should be in prison rather than that no-good nephew of yours."

"You will also leave my nephew alone." Lady Clara was furious. She tightened her grip on Evelyn's arm.

Evelyn was not pleased that she no longer had the upper hand here. She was expecting Lady Clara to be a much more delicate woman. This was embarrassing her in front of her new friend Felicia. With disgust, she snatched her arm away from Lady Clara. Her small victory was short lived as Emily Spencer grabbed her arm.

"You *will* make it a point to stay away from Lady Clara's nephew, or *snatching your eyes out* will take on a whole new meaning between you and I." Emily's eyes bore into Evelyn's frightened ones.

"You are a lunatic!" Evelyn snatched her arm away from Emily.

"Yes, I am." Emily smiled slyly at Evelyn. "Perhaps you and I should take a stroll through the gardens. I hear the fountain here is quite lovely. We could see just how long you can hold your breath underwater."

"I see why your brother keeps you locked away at Hartford. You are mental." Evelyn was fuming. She grabbed Felicia's arm and hurried away.

"So, you must be Lady Emily Spencer." Lady Clara was smiling when Emily turned to face her. "I see that my nephew is quite taken with you. You are very lovely, my dear."

Nancie returned with Lady Clara's glass of wine and apple tartlet. She now understood Jax's love for these tartlets, they were his mother's favorite. She was glad to see Emily step in to help Lady Clara. She knew that Evelyn could not handle Emily Spencer. It was rather amusing to have watched the situation.

"And where is mine?" Emily playfully asked Nancie.

"You do not like wine," Nancie reminded Emily.

"They do not exactly serve rum at these parties." Emily whispered in Nancie's ear as she hugged her.

"But you do have a sweet tooth and I am sure that you know how to get your own." Nancie laughed at Emily.

"Why yes I do." Emily was enjoying how the evening was going. "Excuse me ladies while I lay claim to one of those tartlets."

"She is rather interesting." Lady Clara said as Emily walked away. Nancie could only nod her head in agreement.

Chapter Sixteen

After speaking with his father and brothers, Jax escorted Nancie out onto the garden terrace. It was the end of July and the night air was warm. It was the perfect evening for a stroll through the gardens. Extra lanterns were lit on the terrace and throughout the garden paths tonight. Ms. Rhodes' garden was beautifully designed for parties such as this.

Nancie stepped closer to Jax's side as they walked through the garden. She did not care much for the atmosphere in the ballroom. She now wondered why these events had ever thrilled her imagination. Out here with Jax was simply wonderful and it was more special than being in the ballroom.

Ms. Rhodes was a true romantic at heart. Her garden was specially designed for romantic moments for couples. No wonder why so much of the London gossip happened here in this very flower garden. It was breathtakingly beautiful out here.

"So, this is the famous garden fountain?" Nancie asked as she and Jax walked around the fountain in the center of the flower garden.

"Yes, this it is. This is where my wonderful cousin tried to drown a woman, or so rumor has it anyway." Jax was sarcastic.

Nancie looked at the water in the fountain. She could clearly see the bottom without touching it. Still, she reached down and placed her palm to the bottom of the fountain. The water did not come up to her elbow.

"I guess Evelyn does not know how to sit up." Nancie raised her eyebrows.

"We know that Evelyn and her father lied." Jax gently pulled Nancie to her feet. "They were able to twist the story in the magistrate's ear, for their benefit."

"Your *wonderful* cousin was only trying to help Maxx and Evelyn got in the way." Nancie looked up into Jax's dark brown eyes.

"You care deeply for Maxx," Jax said.

He took Nancie's shawl from her shoulders and used it to dry off her arm. Nancie wondered how such a simple act could spark such strong emotions within her. A simple touch had now ignited something that she thought was long forgotten for her.

"I do care for Maxx." Nancie could not look away. She was captivated by the tenderness she saw in Jax's eyes.

"Maxx is a lucky man." Jax placed his forehead against hers. He hated to admit it, but he did envy the relationship between Nancie and Maxx.

Nancie looked up into Jax's dark brown eyes. He was tall, he and Alex were almost the same height. Jax had broader shoulders and longer hair. She loved his long dark hair. On so many occasions she wanted to reach up and touch it. To her, Jax Shaw was extremely handsome. Images of him had filled her dreams for months now.

"I care for you in a much different way." Nancie whispered as she placed her hands against Jax's chest. She was amazed at her own boldness here.

This was a place she had vowed to herself to never go again. She had fought her feelings for Jax Shaw for almost a year now. Tonight, was different somehow. She felt different, and surprisingly it did not frighten her as it had before. If she were to let go of the past, could she truly find happiness in Jax Shaw's arms?

"Took you long enough," Jax whispered.

Jax's arms went around Nancie's waist as his lips claimed hers. Nancie did not have time to protest, nor did she wish to do so. She slid her hands up his chest and around his neck. Her lips, having a will of their own, passionately kissed him back.

This was what Jax had been wanting to do for months. If Nancie would admit it, she had dreamed of this moment herself. Jax cupped her face in his hands as he continued to kiss her. Nancie could feel her heart beating faster as their lips moved perfectly together.

Jax slowly, very slowly, pulled his lips away from hers. He wrapped his arms around Nancie and pulled her close to his chest. He could hear her ragged breathing, which was the same as his own. He could feel each breath that she took. He smiled knowing that she was as lost in this moment as much as he was.

The tiny woman is his arms had a passion hidden within her. He looked forward to unlocking her passion even more in the future. Nancie was quiet as she waited for her breathing to return to normal. She snuggled closer to Jax as she continued to rest her head against his chest. Jax's smile broadened for he knew that she wanted to be right here in his arms.

"You are mine," Jax whispered and he held her even tighter.

✳✳✳

Emily smiled when she saw Jax usher Nancie out to the garden terrace. She was happy that her friend had found love. Of course, Nancie was not aware yet that she was truly in love with Jax Shaw. Something told her that Nancie would come to terms with her own feelings very soon.

After everything that Nancie had been through, she truly deserved to find love. The look shared between the couple, as they were leaving the ballroom, told Emily that Jax Shaw would not be leaving the pub anytime soon. This relationship was bound to change things at the Blume'N Brew. Hopefully, Nancie would be able to accept those changes.

She gave the loving couple a few minutes to leave the terrace and move to the gardens. When she thought it was safe, Emily stepped into the doorway. It was nice and quiet outside, but she knew not everything that happened in Ms. Rhodes' flower garden was happy and romantic. Last year's party proved that to be true.

Before Emily could turn around and rejoin the party, she was grabbed around the waist from behind and quickly ushered outside. Something here was wrong. She could feel it. These hands were not Alex's. She was being led to an area off the side of the house.

Emily dug her heels into the ground and quickly spun around. Her blue eyes widened in disbelief as she looked into the green eyes of Roger Holden. Now was the time she wished that she had a dagger hidden in her skirts.

"Forgive me, Lady Emily." Roger slightly bowed before her. "I wished to speak with you alone."

"Most people usually just ask for an audience," Emily snapped.

"I am afraid that you are surrounded by too many Shaw's for that to happen." Roger looked back over his shoulder to ensure that they were not followed. "Plus, that first mate is a handful."

"Well, Lord Holden, you have succeeded. We are out here alone." Emily wanted to get to the matter. "What would you like to talk about?"

"I want you to know that I am not the horrible person the Shaw's portray me to be." Roger took a step closer to her. "Plus, I wanted to offer you more than what you have here."

Emily took a step back. She could not believe what she was hearing. Was Roger Holden really this dense? Could she be hearing him correctly? Surely the man was not suggesting that they be friends.

"What could you possibly offer me?" Emily would love to hear the answer to this question.

"You, my dear lady, are being escorted by a knight with no title. Alexander Shaw is a man that does not matter in this world of ours. He just takes up space." Roger smiled slyly and tried to step closer to Emily again. "I can offer you so much more. Together, we can combine two wonderful family empires."

Emily sighed deeply and shook her head. It was worse than she first thought. Roger Holden truly had no brain in his head.

"Just so that I am clear here," Emily motioned her finger between herself and Roger. "You want a relationship between us?"

"I do, Lady Emily." Roger quickly got down on his knee before her. "Lady Emily Spencer, I am asking you to be my wife. We can combine everything between Statham and Hartford. We would be the most powerful family in London."

Emily put her hand to her forehead. This matter was giving her a headache. She could not believe that she was in this situation. She was being proposed to by Roger Holden. She was unsure if she wanted to laugh or lose her stomach.

"First of all, I do believe that the king has the most powerful family in London. Secondly, I will never marry you." Emily shook her head. "I do not need the Shaw's to tell me how horrible of a person that you are. I already know it for myself. You can forget this notion for it will *never* happen."

Emily wanted out of here before things could get worse. She started to walk past Roger and go back to the party. Roger stood up and grabbed her by the arm. His fingers dug into her skin.

"You are an ungrateful twit! You will marry me, or I will kill that weasel of a brother of yours. After that, I will destroy every Shaw that lives, even the women and children. You should have been taught your place long ago." Roger growled into Emily's ear.

"Trust me, you do not want to try this." Emily challenged Roger.

"You will marry me or the first person that I will kill after your brother, will be your mother." Roger tightened his grip on Emily's arm as he jerked her to him. He did not like women challenging him.

"I do not like your nose." Emily was furious.

Emily leaned her head back and then headbutted Roger in the face. Blood spewed from Roger Holden's long nose. He screamed out in pain before covering his nose with his hand. Emily took her foot and planted it hard into Roger's shin, causing him to drop to the ground.

Roger struggled to stand to his feet. He turned to run when he noticed Jax Shaw running toward them from the garden. Behind Emily, he could also see Paul and Alex rushing toward them as well. Tonight, he would have to give up his prize. Roger hurried around the side of the house. He hobbled to his carriage and quickly got inside. With a shout to his driver, the carriage dashed away from Ms. Rhodes' house.

"Are you alright?" Jax grabbed Emily.

"I am fine." Emily assured Jax.

Nancie hurried over and put her arm around Emily. She and Jax had heard the scream and came running. They did not realize that the scream was from Roger Holden when Emily had broken his nose.

Chapter Seventeen

After Emily's encounter with Roger Holden, and Evelyn Cramer's rudeness, Jax thought it was best for them to leave the party. Jax, Alex, and Paul, along with Maxwell Spencer's men, surrounded the carriage and escorted Nancie and Emily back to Blume'N Brew. Gavin had decided to stay with his wife, Abby, and the rest of their family for the night. He would join them at the pub the next morning.

"I cannot believe that Roger Holden actually proposed to you." Rachel squeezed Emily's hand. She was astonished when they told her what had happened at Ms. Rhodes' party.

"Just another reason to kill him," Alex mumbled. He poured himself a glass of brandy and quickly drank it.

"I will not even try to understand Holden's thinking on this." Jax sat down beside Nancie at Maxx's private table.

"He tried to kill Maxx and now he wants to marry Emily. This makes no sense." Nancie pushed a cup of tea across the table to Emily.

Nancie politely smiled as Emily glared at her. Alex knew that tea was not strong enough for anyone tonight. He set a bottle of rum and two glasses on the table in front of Emily, instantly bringing a smile to her face. Nancie shook her head. She was only trying to look out for Emily. The last time she let a Lady have too much to drink, it did not end well for her.

"We share this." Alex motioned his finger between him and Emily. "Unlike your brother, you do not get a bottle of your own."

"Agreed." Emily was happy to not have to drink tea tonight. She had just had a snake to propose to her and she needed something much stronger.

"You can be the one to answer to Maxx for this." Nancie pointed her finger at Alex. "I am not taking responsibility for this."

Jax reached over and lightly squeezed Nancie's hand. He would not let Maxx blame her for his cousin's mishap if anything went

wrong tonight. He smiled and winked at her, causing Nancie to slightly blush. She was his and he would protect her, even from their friend Maxwell Spencer.

"I am responsible for myself." Emily informed everyone. She then looked at Nancie. "No one will speak harshly to you because I had a glass of rum."

"She was treated rudely for letting Lady Abigail have too much to drink." The entire matter had upset Rachel greatly. She was not going to let her friend go through that again.

"Why did you get Abby drunk anyway?" Jax had wondered this ever since he heard the story, nearly two years ago.

"I did not intend to let Abby get drunk." Nancie sighed as she remembered that day. "She said that she was given time to clear her mind and to decide what she genuinely wanted. I was just helping her clear her mind."

Nancie did regret giving Abby too much to drink that day. She liked Abby well enough when she first met her. Nancie, however, was a little upset when she found out that Abby had left the Duke's home with her father over a lie that Roger Holden had told to her. Abby should have spoken to Gavin rather than taking off like that.

It was Abby's lack of trust in Gavin that had caused him to give her three weeks, the time until their wedding day, to decide if she wanted to marry him or not. Gavin Shaw, Jax's older cousin, was Maxx's best friend, and Nancie hated seeing him so broken hearted those three weeks. Still, she should not have let Abby get drunk that day. It probably made matters worse when she took a drunken Abby to Miss Claudia's to get fitted for her wedding gown.

"It all worked out for Gavin and Abby, so do not trouble yourself thinking about the matter anymore." Jax put his arm around Nancie.

"I am glad that things worked out for them, but I think a few people are still upset over it." Nancie's lips formed a tight smile. She was trying to look at the bright side of the situation, but it was hard.

Before anyone could say more, the new front window of the Blume'N Brew shattered as a rock was thrown through it. The rock landed in the middle of the front room floor with a thud. Paul picked the rock up and removed the parchment that was tied around it.

"We just fixed that window!" Nancie jumped to her feet, as everyone else had.

"Stay here." Jax told Nancie and he hurried toward the front door.

"Wait!" Paul shouted. He handed the piece of parchment to Jax.

"This will not end well." Jax looked over at Emily after reading the note.

"What is it?" Alex demanded.

Jax walked over and handed the piece of parchment to Alex. After reading the note, Alex looked Jax in the eye. The two cousins had a silent moment of knowing between them. Both men knew they had a serious matter on their hands.

"Do you gentlemen want to share with the rest of us what is going on?" Nancie did not like being left out of the matter at hand.

Alex handed the crumbled-up note to Emily. She read it with Nancie and Rachel looking over her shoulders. The note read:

You should have said yes.

"Why does Roger Holden want a wife so badly?" Nancie asked.

Nancie's question went unanswered. Several more rocks were thrown through the front window, sending pieces of shattered glass flying across the floor. Behind them came several lit torches, which quickly ignited the spots of spilled alcohol on the floor from the night's pub patrons.

Doug and Harper took men with them and rushed out the front and side entrances of the Blume'N Brew. Jerry and Will Carter, the piano player, helped Jax, Alex, and Paul to put out the flames from the torches.

Nancie and Rachel grabbed Emily and hurried to the private office on the lower floor of the pub. Nancie shoved Rachel and Emily inside the office and bolted the door. She grabbed a pistol from the cabinet and stood with it aimed at the door. All three women jumped when they heard several gun shots ring out.

Nancie closed her eyes and sighed deeply. She prayed that no one from the pub had been shot. She feared that Jax, being as head strong as he was, would rush into the fight without thinking and get hurt.

She could not lose him. She grabbed the bolt and unlocked the door. When her hand grabbed the door handle, Rachel stopped her.

"I know that you are worried, but you know, Maxx always said, if this happened for us to wait here until they came for us." Rachel wanted to know what was happening also, but this was the best course of action for the three of them.

"This is crazy!" Emily shouted. "I will not sit caged up in here! We can help them fight!"

"Maxx said no." Nancie was stern.

She had to agree, Rachel was right about this. They had to sit here and wait it out. She quickly slid the bolt shut again.

"Maxx is not here!" Emily shouted.

"I am sorry, Lady Emily, this is just how it is for us women." Nancie leaned against the door. She was not going to let Emily out of this office.

"We have no choice in the matter." Rachel went over and stood next to Emily, trying to offer her some comfort.

"I know this is hard, but we have to remember who you are." Nancie pointed at Emily. "You are the Earl of Hartford's sister, and everyone here will fight to protect you."

"I should be out there helping them!" Emily protested, but Nancie shook her head.

Frustrated, Emily threw her hands in the air. She flopped down in the chair behind the desk. She did not like this one bit. She also had not expected Nancie to be so stern with her. On any other occasion Emily would have admired Nancie's strength and courage. Tonight, however, she hated feeling trapped and useless. Some changes needed to happen around here.

Jax put out the last of the flames on the floor. He rushed over and jerked the front door opened. Harper rushed through the door carrying Doug.

"He's been shot!" Harper shouted.

Jax and Alex took Doug and helped him over to Maxx's private table. Jax pushed opened Doug's shirt to reveal the gunshot wound in his left shoulder. Jerry hurried over with a cloth and held it do Doug's wound to slow the bleeding.

"Paul has already sent James and Ollie to get Doctor Ramsey." Harper pulled a chair next to Doug and sat down. Jax was relieved to hear this.

"Where is Nancie, Emily, and Rachel?" Jax was worried for their safety. He had not seen them since the second set of rocks were thrown through the window.

"The women are locked in the office." Will came in with a bowl of cool water and more clean cloths. They had to tend to Doug's wound the best they could until the doctor arrived.

"Any idea who shot him?" Jerry pressed another cloth to Doug's shoulder.

"Paul is after the guy now," Harper replied. He put his hand on Doug's right shoulder. "You hang in there. The doctor is on the way." Jax admired the care that Harper took over Doug.

"Paul could use your help." Jax put his hand on Alex's shoulder.

Alex was just as good of a tracker as his brother Caleb was. Alex nodded his head and hurried out the front door. He hated leaving Emily like this, but he had no doubts that she, Nancie, and Rachel were well protected in the pub by Maxx's men. Alex rushed to find Paul so they could track down Doug's shooter.

Brady and Eli, another of Maxx's sailors, carried in Ned Wilson, one of the men attacking them tonight. Ned had been shot as well. Ned's wound was in his abdomen and it was bleeding badly. Ned was too weak to sit up, so they laid him on the floor. Brady held the cloth that Will handed him to Ned's wound. Brady shook his head at Jax. He did not think that Ned would survive this.

"Ned, are you working for Roger Holden?" Jax leaned down and asked. He did not like pressuring a wounded man, but they needed answers.

"They said that we were after traitors to the crown." Ned's voice was weak. "Did not know that I was attacking the Shaw's."

"It is alright, Ned." Jax pleaded with the man. "Just tell me who hired you."

"Forgive...me." Ned was growing weaker. Jax doubted that he would live until the doctor arrived.

"You are forgiven, Ned. Just tell me who is responsible for this." Jax pleaded again.

James and Ollie arrived with Doctor Ramsey. The doctor went straight to work. He quickly knelt by Ned's side and examined the gunshot wound. He worked quickly to try and stop the bleeding. Ned grabbed Jax by the arm and tried to pull him closer.

"They will not stop until your family is dead, even the women and children," Ned whispered. He had overheard things just before he was shot. "They will kill Lady Emily Spencer first, then you."

Doctor Ramsey pulled Jax away as Ned took his last breath. The blood from his wound was dark. The bullet was lodged in Ned's liver, giving him no chance to survive. Jerry hurried to get a sheet to cover Ned as Doctor Ramsey rushed over to Doug.

Jax, in his frustration, turned and slammed his fist into one of the tables, breaking a chuck off. A good man was tricked into believing he was doing what was right for the king, and he lost his life over a lie. Ned had just died, and Roger Holden was responsible. Jax would not rest until this wrong was justified.

Chapter Eighteen

Nancie rushed over and quickly wrapped Jax's bleeding hand in a cloth. Will had come to the office to let them know that it was alright to come out. She was not expecting the first thing that she would see would be Jax breaking a table with his fist.

Rachel hurried over and helped Jerry with preparing the cloths for him to press against Doug's wound. Emily stood behind Harper, with her hands on his shoulders, for comfort.

Nancie took Jax over to one of the tables in the front of the pub. He was still furious, and she wanted to get him away from Ned's body so that he could calm down. Watching a man die was something that tore through a person's soul, even strong tough men like Jax Shaw.

When enough cloths were prepared, Rachel hurried upstairs to prepare a room for Doug, so that Doctor Ramsey could work better to remove the bullet from his shoulder. Messengers were sent to the Duke's house and to Captain Cromwell of the King's Guard.

Alex and Paul dragged a struggling Dexter Greene into the pub. Alex shoved Dexter into a chair and held a sword to his throat while Paul and Jerry tied the man up. Jerry grabbed his rifle from behind the bar. He put a chair in front of Dexter. The angry bartender sat down and held the gun on their captive.

"This is the man that shot Doug?" Jax was once again furious. Nancie stood in front of Jax, with her hands on his chest, to keep him from ripping Dexter apart.

"I am almost positive of it." Paul took the wet cloth from Will and wiped the sweat from his face. He and Alex had chased Dexter for several blocks before catching him.

"Whether or not he was the one that shot Doug, he was among the men that attacked the pub tonight. That is something I have no doubt of." Alex went with Paul over to the bar for a drink.

Jax trusted his cousin's tracking skills. It was rare to see Alex or his brother Caleb to be wrong. If Alex said that Dexter was one of their attackers tonight, then he believed him. Jax stepped forward. He wanted to hurt Dexter Greene badly.

"You cannot touch him." Nancie pleaded with Jax to see beyond his anger. "The King's men are on the way. If you hurt him, they will take you too." This was something that she could not bear.

The sound of Nancie's voice snapped Jax out of his angered trance. The look in her eyes tore through his heart. She was genuinely concerned for him. A great need to hold her flooded him. Jax wrapped his arms around Nancie. He gave her a quick kiss before holding her to his chest. He closed his eyes for a moment. This was his peace.

It was not long until most of the men in Jax's family arrived at the Blume'N Brew. His Uncle Matthew and cousin, Nate, were the only ones to remain at the Duke's house to watch over the women in their family. The Duke and Gavin's father-in-law, Lord Mason joined the Shaw family at the pub. Everyone was filled with sorrow that Ned Wilson had not survived.

"Did Ned name Holden and Prescott?" Gavin asked as he looked down at Ned's covered body lying on the floor.

"Sadly, no." Jax pointed at Dexter. "We need him for that."

"You lot will get nothing from me." Dexter spat at Jax.

"The King's men have ways to make men like you talk." Samuel Dawson assured Dexter.

"Ned did say that they will not stop until our family is dead." Jax looked up at his father, who was standing next to the chair he was sitting in. "Even our women and children are not safe."

Despair filled every Shaw in the pub. Each of them could feel a loss in their hearts. Then a dark type of anger settled within them as they looked at each other. It took an evil man to threaten innocent women and children. Roger Holden had now crossed a line, into an evil place, that men do not come back from.

Nancie sat beside Jax and unwrapped his wounded hand. She had to busy herself by doing something. Jax's hand did need to be cleaned and wrapped with fresh bandages. His wounds were no longer bleeding but the bandage had blood soaked through it.

"We will get our women and children behind the fortress walls of Kinsley Estate and Ellis Manor tomorrow." Sir Phillip started laying out a protection plan.

"My men will help to escort your family home." Sam put his hand on Jax's father's shoulder. He gave a nod of his head to seal the matter.

Sam's sister Elizabeth was married to Jax's oldest brother Nick. Elizabeth had given birth to his niece, Tori, about two weeks ago. She and Nick had not come to London for Ms. Rhodes' party. He would make sure that the Shaw family returned to their homes safely.

"The Duke's men can help lead the guard detail to Kinsley Estate." Lord Mason stepped forward. "My men and I will help with the guard to Ellis Manor."

Lord Mason's daughter, Abby, was married to Jax's cousin Gavin. He would be staying close to Ellis Manor until this new threat from Roger Holden was diminished. He was not about to let anything happen to his daughter and grandson. Little Alastair was not even a year old yet. Lord Mason and Nancie glared at each other for a moment. It was an action that Jax had not missed.

Nancie went back to tending to Jax's hand. She cleaned the cuts and made sure that there were no splinters from the table in his hand. She then carefully applied the herbal salve that Nate's wife, Olivia, had sent with Gavin tonight.

Nancie figured that Gavin's sister-in-law, Olivia, would be the only one in the Shaw family that would ever understand how she felt. Olivia, like herself, was an outsider. Roger Holden and Edmond Prescott were Olivia's half-brothers. Moments like these were bound to be hard for Olivia.

"We have to protect Lady Emily as well." Jerry said over his shoulder. He would not take his eyes, or gun, off Dexter.

"He's right." Jax looked around at everyone in the pub. "Ned said that they would kill Lady Emily first, then me."

The entire pub exploded in an uproar, especially Alex and Paul. Gavin and Caleb had to hold Alex in his place to keep him from

Just then, a carriage came through the gates of Hartford Place. Jax and Alex quickly looked at each other again. They watched as the carriage turned and took the road heading out into the countryside. Neither of them remembered seeing a carriage in the stables.

"That was a Hartford carriage." Jax had noticed Maxx's family crest on the carriage when it turned. "And it was heavily guarded."

"No!" Alex exclaimed and he rushed ahead to the house.

Jax nudged his horse into a run to catch up with his cousin. A sinking feeling came over him. He was sure that Alex was not going to like what he found, or did not find, at Hartford Place.

Jax dismounted and ran up the front steps behind Alex. They both halted in the front foyer. Alex grabbed the doorframe of the parlor to steady himself. Jax patted his cousin on the back, which was not really any comfort.

"Not happy to see me, I take it." Maxx was sitting in one of the big chairs in the parlor.

"Emily?" Alex asked. "Where is Emily?"

"My sister is on her way to Hartford Manor with our Mother." Maxx said the words that Alex did not want to hear.

"She did not say goodbye." Alex looked Jax in the eye. "She did not even bother to say goodbye."

Alex pushed Jax aside. He angrily stormed out the front door and got their horses. He led both horses to the stables behind the house. He spent the evening hours tending to the horses and sulking around in the stables, where he would remain for the entire night.

"I am glad to see you, but your sister could have been kind enough to tell him goodbye. If she had waited only a few more minutes, she could have told him goodbye." Jax, being disgusted over the matter, went outside to help bring Doug into the house.

"I am sure it will all work out in the end." Nancie was standing beside Maxx's chair.

"It was not a good idea letting Alex Shaw see Emily." Maxx sunk down in his chair.

"It was bound to happen." Nancie put her hand on Maxx's shoulder. "Alex will come around, in time."

Nancie left Maxx in the parlor. She hurried to help Rachel get Doug settled in. Nancie did hate that Alex had not gotten to say goodbye to Emily. Hopefully, one day amends could be made. Still, it was better to have Maxx here rather than Emily.

Chapter Twenty-One

It took Jax, and the work crew, almost two weeks to replace the front window of the pub and to repair the damages from the fire. By the time the repairs were completed, Doug was doing much better. Since there were no signs of Roger Holden's men hanging around, Maxx moved them all back to the Blume'N Brew.

Jax understood that Maxx wanted to keep Hartford Place as a refuge for his mother and sister when they visited London. It would also remain a safe house for Maxx if it were ever needed. With the extra trips from the house to the pub, Maxx feared it would alert Roger Holden to their whereabouts.

The Spencer family had always kept their activities private. Well, the ladies did anyway. Maxx was usually in the middle of things. Eli and James were left behind at Hartford Place for a few days to watch over the four servants that resided there year-round. Maxx felt their presence was needed just in case Holden had found the house.

When the Duke of Greyham heard that Maxx was back in London, he showed up at the pub only once during the past two weeks. Thankfully, Jax was able to convince Sam that their situation was dire, and they needed Maxx to be here at the Blume'N Brew. Sam still sent Maxx on errands, but he did keep them simple and within the city of London.

There were only a few days left before the celebration at Ellis Manor. Nancie was starting to become a little nervous about going. She and Jax were growing closer and if there was a problem with his family accepting her, it was going to be harder for her to send Jax away.

Everyone talked about the Shaw's family celebration while they had their lunch at Maxx's private table in the pub. Well, everyone talked except for Alex. He had been extremely quiet ever since Emily had left for Hartford Manor. Even when word arrived that Emily and

Lady Spencer has arrived home safely, Alex was still quiet. His moping around was starting to get on Jax's nerves.

"Why do you just sit and stare at Maxx?" Jax leaned over and whispered to his cousin.

"He annoys me," Alex whispered back.

"You and Maxx are good friends. You are going to have to let this go." Jax was deeply concerned for his cousin. "Staring at Maxx is not going to bring Emily back. He only sent her home because she is better protected there."

"I know." Alex continued staring at Maxx. "When the time is right, I will talk to Maxx."

"You make peace with this, cousin." Jax was very stern with Alex. He pointed his finger at his cousin. "And you do it by the time we reach Ellis Manor tomorrow."

Jax turned his attention back to Nancie. She was much easier to talk to than Alex. Jax really did want Alex to make peace with Maxx. He did not wish for anything to go wrong while Nancie visited their family with them over the next few days. Before they could finish their lunch, Captain Cromwell and the King's men arrived at the Blume'N Brew.

"I do apologize for disturbing your meal." Captain Cromwell shook Jax's hand.

"Think nothing of it. Would you care to join us?" Jax motioned toward the table.

Nancie and Rachel started toward the kitchen to bring in the serving cart. Captain Cromwell held up his hand to stop Nancie from hurrying to serve him and his men.

"I must decline. We are on our way to the castle." Captain Cromwell politely refused Jax's offer.

"Does that mean that you are here on official business?" Maxx leaned back in his chair and folded his arms across his chest.

"I am afraid that I am." Captain Cromwell had a grim expression on his face.

"Why don't you join us and at least have a cup of tea?" Nancie suggested.

Captain Cromwell sent his men outside before joining them at the table. He was not one to turn down a good cup of tea.

"The investigation into Ned Wilson's death, and the attack on the Blume'N Brew, has not gone well." Captain Cromwell's statement brought great confusion to everyone in the pub.

"What do you mean?" Jax asked. "With all the information we gave you, there should be no problems."

"We cannot put Holden and Prescott in London at the time of the attack on the pub," Captain Cromwell replied.

"The attack on the pub was the same night as Ms. Rhodes' End of the Summer Party." Nancie grabbed Jax's arm. She did not like how this conversation was starting out. "Roger Holden was at the party."

"We questioned several of Ms. Rhodes' guests from that night, hoping to prove that. Sadly, the only person that clearly saw Roger Holden that night was Lady Emily." Captain Cromwell looked over at Maxx before turning to look around at everyone else. "The rest of you only saw him from a distance."

"What was the snake's alibi?" Alex clinched his hands into fists by his side, so the others did not see it. Maxx, sitting by Alex's side, did notice his movement.

"When we got to Statham Hall, Doctor Ramsey was leaving. He had been summoned by the Earl because Lady Holden had taken ill. The doctor went to Statham the day after the attack here at the pub." Captain Cromwell did not like giving the Shaw's this news.

"Let me guess, Roger claims to have been by his ailing mother's side even before Ms. Rhodes' party." Maxx shook his head. He knew how Roger's mind worked. Captain Cromwell nodded his head in reply.

"Was Holden's nose broken?" Alex was furious by this point.

"As a matter of fact, it was." Captain Cromwell set his teacup on the table. "When I acquired of that, he claimed that it had happened when he was sparing with Edmond Prescott."

"Emily broke his nose." This made Alex smile slightly. He was glad that at least somebody had gotten a good punch at Roger.

"What exactly are you teaching your sister out at Hartford?" Captain Cromwell narrowed his eyes at Maxx.

"My mother and sister both know how to defend themselves." Maxx was not ashamed to say that he had taught the women of the family how to protect themselves.

"There is more that you are not telling us." Jax could see it in the Captain's expression.

"We also had to release Dexter Greene." Captain Cromwell braced himself for the explosive response he knew he would get from this.

"Why?" Jax shouted as he jumped to his feet.

"Paul and I caught him!" Alex too was out of his chair, glaring at the Captain.

Maxx stood and placed his hand on Alex's arm. For a moment, the two of them just looked at each other.

"Not here and not now," Maxx whispered.

Alex knew that Maxx was right. He nodded his head and forced his temper to settle. The last thing that he needed right now, was to have Captain Cromwell arrest him again. This time, there would be nothing that Maxx would be able to do to help him out of it. Maxx was already doing too much for him. Maxx's deal with the Duke did not sit right with Alex.

"You caught Dexter ten streets over." Captain Cromwell was impressed with Alex and Paul's determination to capture the man that night. "Dexter has a brother that works in that area."

"Naturally, Dexter's brother was his alibi for the night." Jax threw his hands up.

"What about Ned Wilson's death?" Paul asked. "Are we being held responsible for that?"

"No, you are not." Captain Cromwell was glad to give this news to them. "A few of the shop owners in this area did confirm that the Blume'N Brew was indeed attacked that night. At this time, we cannot prove who was responsible."

"Surely you cannot believe all this?" Jax was beyond frustrated.

"Nancie put her hand in Jax's. She did not wish to see him explode on the King's Captain of the Guard and get himself arrested. She was relieved when Jax turned to look at her. He smiled at her and squeezed her hand. Seeing the worry on her face was enough to calm Jax down a bit.

"No, I do not believe what Holden and his men are claiming, but I have to go by what I can prove." Captain Cromwell walked over and shook Jax's hand again. "One day, the Earl of Statham will work himself into a corner that he cannot get out of."

After the King's men left the pub, no one seemed to have an appetite anymore. Nancie and Rachel cleared the table and left the men to talk among themselves.

Jax did not remain in the pub. He came upstairs and found Nancie. He took her by the hand and led her to the parlor. If he stayed in the pub and discussed this matter with the other men any longer, he would lose his temper. He already wanted to ride out to Statham Hall and drag Roger Holden and Edmond Prescott out.

"I cannot believe that Holden got out of this." Nancie was just as furious as Jax was.

"No, we will not talk about it right now." Jax placed a finger to Nancie's lips to silence her. "I did not bring you here for that."

"Then why are we here?" Nancie motioned with both her hands around the parlor.

"Because I need you to calm me." Jax closed the distance between them and took her in his arms.

Nancie realized immediately that she needed to be calmed as well. She wrapped her arms around Jax's waist and laid her head against his chest. Here, in each other's arms, was where they both found their peace.

Chapter Twenty-Two

On Friday, the day before the family celebration at Ellis Manor, everyone from the Blume'N Brew arrived at the manor in time for dinner with the family. Jax's family had always arrived the day before the party to help with the last-minute details.

The morning of the party, there was a buzz of excitement flowing through everyone at Ellis Manor. Even the servants were overjoyed today. Nancie enjoyed breakfast and lunch with the ladies of the Shaw family. Elizabeth and Lady Clara stayed by her side.

Nancie had enjoyed meeting the three Shaw grandchildren. Abby, Olivia, and Elizabeth were wonderful mothers. Watching these three women with their newborn babies caused Nancie to wonder if that would ever happen for her. There was a time, when she was younger, that she had hoped for such a life as she was witnessing here. Sadly, that had not been her world, so she gave up hoping for it long ago.

The guests for the party started arriving shortly after lunch. The six Shaw gentlemen, along with Maxx, took turns escorting the women guests out to the garden to Lady Caroline. Even though this day was also Gavin and Abby's anniversary, they did not use that to steal the day away from Lady Caroline. Nancie respected Gavin and Abby greatly for this act of kindness they gave to Gavin's mother.

By midafternoon, Nancie was a tad overwhelmed by all the guests and the excitement. She found a table off to the side in the garden and sat down. From here she was able to watch everything going on outside. She knew that this day was special for the Shaw family, but she did not expect so many guests to show up for the celebration.

"Mind if I join you?" Abby asked.

"Please do." Nancie politely motioned for Abby to sit down. She knew that this moment between them would come.

"I am glad that you joined us today." Abby smiled as several children ran by their table.

Nancie was a little nervous. She could tell that Abby was nervous as well. It had been two years since she had let Abby have too much to drink at the Blume'N Brew. In the past two years, Abby had become a wonderful wife and mother. She also helped Lady Caroline and her father, Lord Mason, oversee the running of both their estates.

"I want you to know that I am very sorry for getting you drunk that day." Nancie wanted to end the friction that was between them because of this matter.

"Do not trouble yourself another minute about what happened that day." Abby reached over and covered Nancie's hand with hers. "I am thankful for that day."

"I would have never thought that." Nancie was stunned by Abby's statement.

"You did tell Rosa that I would be a different person after that day, and I truly was." Abby lightly laughed.

"You became cold and bitter, if I remember correctly." Nancie did not see how that was a good thing.

"That is very true, and I had to work through some emotional issues back then." Abby continued to smile. She no longer looked at that day as something bad and she did not wish for Nancie to do so anymore either. "But in the end, I knew the woman I wanted to be and the one that I did not ever want to become."

"I cannot tell you how relieved and happy I am, to know that you are truly happy." Nancie smiled as well. She could now let go of the bad feelings she had been harboring from that day.

"I am just happy that you are here and that this is no longer an issue between us." Abby got up and got them both a cup of tea from the serving cart as the servant pushed the cart by their table.

"I am glad too." Nancie was truly glad that this was all settled. It did relieve a lot in her mind.

"I love your hair like this, but I must ask, how do you get your hair to curl into those perfect ringlets?" Abby handed Nancie the cup of tea.

"Oh, that was actually a wig," Nancie replied.

Abby almost spit her sip of tea out. She quickly covered her mouth with her hand. They both laughed because of it. Nancie told

Abby about the dresses, makeup, and the wigs that she used to be Miss Nancie the pub owner.

Surprisingly to Nancie, the day passed without any issues. Even dinner was wonderful. There were so many guests that everyone was not able to sit in the dining room. Nancie was delighted that she got to have dinner outside with Jax, at the table she and Abby had been sitting at.

"Are you enjoying yourself?" Jax was enjoying the smile he had seen on Nancie's face all day.

"I have been. This is more like the parties at Hartford. I much prefer these types of celebrations rather than those fancy parties in London." Nancie boldly reached over and touched Jax's hand.

"That is something we both can agree on." Jax raised her hand to his lips. He liked that she was becoming more comfortable around him. "But you will have to go to at least one Winter Ball with me. The women in my family love that party."

"Fine, but I will hate it," Nancie teased.

"Then we will hate it together." Jax leaned over and kissed her on her cheek.

After dinner, everyone went to the ballroom for music and dancing. For Nancie, this was a wonderful ending to an incredibly special day. Today allowed her to have hope that she could, one day, be part of a family again.

After dancing a couple of dances, Nancie and Jax left the dance floor. Before Nancie could sit down at one of the small tables that were lined around the wall of the room, Elizabeth rushed over and hugged her.

"You look amazing." Nancie could see that marriage and motherhood were wonderful for Elizabeth.

She and Elizabeth sat down while Jax and Nick went over to speak with their parents. The two of them smiled at each other as Sir Phillip led Lady Clara out onto the dance floor. Jax danced with his aunt, Lady Caroline, since his Uncle Matthew still walked with a limp from his accident. Doctor Ramsey had said that Lord Matthew would probably always have to walk with a cane from now on. The

Chapter Nineteen

With the help of the Duke's men, they were able to move Nancie, Lady Emily, and Rachel safely to Hartford Place that night. Jax thought that it was best to move all three of the women, since the Blume'N Brew had been attacked by Roger Holden's men. With Holden and Prescott trying to kill him and Lady Emily, Jax was sure that those around them were not safe either.

The year-round staff at Hartford Place was minimal, only four servants lived here. The housekeeper, Nolia Cornwell, and the butler, Abe Hadley, went straight to work preparing rooms for everyone. The cook, Alma Jennings was thrilled to be preparing large meals again. The stable hand, Davie Mullins, took excellent care of their horses.

Things were different at Hartford Place than they were at the pub. Lady Emily only left her room during mealtimes. This had Alex seriously frustrated. Jax finally convinced his cousin to settle down. Emily needed time to come to terms with the fact that Roger Holden was planning on murdering her. After much protest, Alex finally gave in. He hoped that Jax was right. Alex busied himself with making sure that the house was well guarded and that Emily and Jax were safe from Roger.

On the second evening, Jax and Nancie enjoyed some time sitting out on the private terrace behind the house. Hartford Place was not as grand and elegant as most of the noble's homes were in London. This house was cozy and comfortable. It was the perfect place to relax. Still, it was well protected by a rock wall. This gave Jax a great deal of comfort. He and Nancie could enjoy an evening in the small private garden without worry of being attacked again.

"Maxx and Emily's father did a great job keeping his family protected here." Jax led Nancie from the terrace out to the garden.

"He wanted to make sure that Lady Spencer and Emily were safe when they came to London." Nancie could not tell Jax that this house was also a safe place for Maxx if it was ever needed.

"I noticed that you and Lord Mason are still not on friendly terms." Jax brought the matter up as they sat down on the garden bench.

The matter had been troubling Jax. If Lord Mason was still causing Nancie grief over what had happened between her and his daughter, Abby, Jax wanted to put an end to it. It had been two years now and Abby and his cousin Gavin were doing fine at Ellis Manor.

"That is a matter that will probably never settle. I think we tolerate each other to help Maxx when it is necessary." Nancie looked away. She did not wish to discuss this.

"Surely Lord Mason and Abby do not still hold you any ill will for it." Jax was determined to find a solution.

"They both are Mason's at heart. They make bad decisions without a second thought of what those decisions do to other people." Nancie looked down and nervously straightened her skirt.

"Is Lord Mason and Abby still causing you grief?" Jax could hear a bit of worry in Nancie's voice. He wondered why she was troubled so deeply over this.

"No. Lord Mason spoke his peace that day." Nancie was sure that Lord Mason was just being a protective father. That was something she missed having. "And Abby and I have not spoken since that day."

"There is something more here that you are not telling me." Jax was sure of it. He had seen the look on Nancie's face as she glared at Lord Mason in the pub that night.

"Thank you for a lovely evening." Nancie quickly stood up. "I shall retire for the night."

"I will let the matter rest." Jax stood and placed his hands on her shoulders. "Just please do not go. It has taken us a long time to get to where we are. I do not wish to lose that."

"And just where do you believe we are?" Nancie looked Jax in the eye. She did not mean to be so offended. "What do you honestly believe will come of this?"

"You know that I care for you." Jax narrowed his eyes. He did not know how this conversation had turned into him having to defend what was between them.

"Your family will never accept me," Nancie whispered.

Nancie's plea was clearly visible in her eyes. She wished that it were possible for Jax's family to truly accept her, but she felt in her heart that it was not. She knew firsthand just how a family could shun one of their family members for making a choice that did not line up with the rules of society.

"You should give my family a chance to show you that they are not like everyone else in London." Jax cupped her face in his large hands. "And I am not bound by titles and birth rank."

"You are still part of that world," Nancie whispered.

"Then I will gladly leave that world just to be part of yours." Jax rested his forehead against hers.

"I cannot let you do that." Nancie closed her eyes. Oh, how she wished it were truly possible to be with Jax.

"You, my dear, cannot stop me," Jax declared.

Jax's lips lingered above hers for a moment. Gently his lips touched hers. Nancie's hands slid up his chest and around his neck. She pulled Jax toward her. It was an open invitation for more and Jax deepened their kiss.

When their lips parted, Jax once again rested his forehead against hers. Nancie released a small gasp when she realized that her feet were no longer on the ground. She looked down, but she could not see her feet for her skirt. Jax grinned as he slowly set her back on her feet.

Nancie smiled and quickly gave Jax another kiss before he released his hold on her. She wondered how this Shaw could cause her to lose herself to where she was not aware of her own surroundings. Jax Shaw had found a way into her heart. It was something that she had sworn, years ago, to never let happen.

They sat back down on the garden bench. Jax wrapped his arms around her and pulled Nancie to him. Nancie leaned back against Jax's chest. She enjoyed the feel of his muscular arms around her. It was comforting and peaceful here. Here in Jax Shaw's arms, she felt safe. It was a feeling she had not felt in a long time.

"In about three weeks, on August seventeenth, there will be a grand party at Ellis Manor." Jax spoke softly, next to her ear. "It is my Aunt Caroline's birthday and my cousin's anniversary."

"I know." Nancie put her arms over Jax's and nestled closer to him. "Maxx goes every year."

"I wish for you to join me there this year." Jax made his request.

"I am not sure." Nancie thought on the matter for a moment.

Could she really attend a family celebration with Jax? Since it was Gavin and Abby's anniversary, as well as Lady Caroline's birthday, she would have to finally speak to Abby. She was not sure if she was ready for a family gathering with Jax.

If she went and problems arose, she was sure that Jax would stand up and defend her. That would be something that would cause problems between Jax and his family. She did not wish to cause division of any kind for the Shaw's. If something did go wrong at the party, it would also be enough for her to prove to Jax that a relationship between them would not work out. She sighed. What was she to do here?

"My mother was kind to you at Ms. Rhodes' party. Plus, you already know that Nick's wife, Elizabeth, thinks highly of you." Jax wanted to encourage her to decide to go on her own. He did not want to demand anything of Nancie. "And you would get to meet my niece." Everyone at Kinsley Estate had already fallen in love with Nick and Elizabeth's little girl.

Nancie had helped Jax's brother, Nick, and the Duke's sister, Elizabeth, when they showed up at the Blume'N Brew last year. Elizabeth's insistence on her and Rachel attending the party at Greyham Court was a dream come true for Nancie. She had always wanted to go to one of those society parties. That world was one that she had been left out of and she had wanted to part of it for so many years.

After Ms. Rhodes' End of the Summer Party a few nights ago, Nancie no longer wished to join that world. She much rather loved the parties that Lady Spencer would hold at Hartford Manor. Those parties were more like huge family gatherings rather than the stuffy society parties in London. No one was looked down upon because of their birth status at Hartford.

"I would love to go with you," Nancie replied softly.

"Plus, Maxx will also be there to watch over you. Maybe Lady Emily will attend as well." Jax froze. "Wait, did you just accept my invitation?"

Jax had been wanting to ask Nancie all day to be part of his family's celebration. He was shocked that she had so easily agreed to go. He figured that he would have to beg and plead with her for days. All day he had been working out all the arguments, in his mind, that could take place. He was confident that he could put all her arguments to rest on the matter. Now, he had accomplished this and won his fight without a fight. Jax was amazed.

"Yes, I will attend Lady Caroline's birthday, and you cousin's anniversary, celebration with you." Nancie turned around in Jax's arms and tenderly kissed him.

She figured, if she was going to give in, then she should do it whole heartily. Jax was not about to complain. There was no way that he would let an opportunity to kiss her go by either. He held Nancie tighter and kissed her deeply, until they both were out of breath.

Chapter Twenty

The next day, Jax was struggling to stay calm. He did not like hiding behind a wall like this. Jax knew that he was here to help protect Nancie, Lady Emily, and Rachel. Being here also ensured his own safety, which he was sure that gave his mother's mind great peace. The problem for him was, he felt like a coward. He had served in the military, he was a knight, and he was not afraid of Roger Holden's threats.

"Perhaps you could take some men and go order a new replacement window for the pub." Nancie suggested during their lunch.

"It has been quiet. There has not been any sign of Roger Holden the last couple of days," Rachel added.

"I cannot leave you." Jax wanted to go, but he did not want to risk Nancie's safety.

"We are fine here," Nancie assured him. "Very few people know where this house is, or that Maxx owns it."

"You have nothing to worry about. Paul is not about to let us outside the security wall." Emily pushed the food around on her plate with her fork. She did not like being shut in either.

"I know you hate this." Alex reached over and squeezed Emily's hand. "It will all be over soon."

"I hope that you are right." Emily stood up from the table. "Will you all please excuse me?" She quietly went to her room without eating.

"Do not fret, Lord Alex." Rachel grabbed Emily's plate. "I will see to it that she eats something." Rachel hurried away and carried the plate to Emily's room.

"Hopefully, Maxx will return soon." Nancie propped up on her elbows.

"If Maxx takes the time that the Duke gave to allow him to rest, he has about another week." Paul had finished eating and stood up to go. "I will make a round to make sure that the grounds are safe. If you do go, take your cousin and a few men with you. I promise to keep the ladies safe here while you are gone."

"If you do go, use my carriage and bring Doug here. We can help to take care of him. I am sure he would get better care here with us, rather than at the pub." Nancie hoped that Jax would take her up on this. He was really getting irritable being confined inside like this.

"What do you think?" Jax turned to Alex.

"I do not like it, but Doug would probably recover faster here." Doug had become a good friend to their family over the years. Alex would like to help the man if they could.

Jax took Nancie's hands in his. Even she could see that Jax was already thrilled to be doing something besides sitting around. She knew they were fine here at Hartford Place. It was Jax's safety that had her truly worried. In a fair fight, she had no doubts that Jax would best any man. However, Roger Holden and Edmond Prescott did not fight fairly.

"Do you honestly believe that you will be safe if we leave?" Jax would not go if she were not sure.

"I have no doubts on the matter. I do not trust Roger Holden so, talk to Paul before you go." Nancie smiled. She was glad that she could give Jax encouragement. "You be sure to take Alex, Brady, and Eli with you so that I know you will return safely."

"We will be safe. I promise." Jax gave her a quick kiss before hurrying out to find Paul.

Alex stood and paused at the door. He looked down the hallway that Emily had taken when she left the dining room. She had used the servant's stairs to go to her room on the second floor. He did not wish to leave her. Since getting to Hartford Place, Emily had become another person. She was quiet and distant from everyone. This troubled Alex greatly. Paul would protect her with his own life, Alex was sure of it. Right now, his restless cousin needed him.

"Do not worry." Nancie put her hand on Alex's arm. "She will be safe here."

With a nod, Alex turned to follow Jax out the kitchen door. They would find Paul and discuss a plan before leaving. Jax was proud of

his work at the pub. It was only natural that he would like to see it fixed again and before Maxx returned to London if that were possible.

Paul sent Brady and Eli with them. He also sent a couple more of Maxx's sailors as well, just to be on the safe side where Holden was concerned. They stopped at the Blume'N Brew to get a list of the materials that would be needed to replace the window and some of the floorboards that had burned in the pub. They made the arrangements with Harper about moving Doug to Hartford Place when they returned from the mill.

The entire afternoon, Jax and Alex looked over their shoulders. There were no signs of Holden or Prescott on the streets of London. The only problem with that was, they had no idea who all the men on Holden's payroll were. Ned Wilson had been tricked into helping attack the pub a few nights ago and he lost his life. Hopefully, decent men would walk away from Roger after hearing about Ned. Sadly, Prescott knew how to pull in shady men to help him.

With everything for the pub ordered, and Doug safely in Nancie's carriage, they headed for Hartford Place. Doug was thrilled to be getting out of the pub. Harper was doing his best to tend to Doug but even Doug knew that the ladies would do a better job of it.

"It is not like Holden to give up." Jax looked around the street as he rode next to Alex.

"Oh, Holden has not given up. You can be sure of that." Alex too looked over his shoulder. "That snake is hiding somewhere."

Jax was glad that the streets to Hartford Place were not like the busy streets that were up in the heart of the city. At least out here, on the edge of London, they could spot movement easily. Alex had a keen sense and he noticed almost everything that moved around them.

The sun had set by the time Hartford Place came into view. Thankfully, they had made it back before darkness had fallen. The gates opened before they got near them. Jax and Alex looked at each other questionably. Had Paul been watching for them to return and had the gates opened early for them?

Earl of Claybourne was not happy with the doctor's recommendation.

"Who is the lady with Lord Mason?" Maxx flopped down in the chair next to Nancie.

Nancie looked across the room and saw Lord Mason with a lady clinging to his arm. Until now, she had not even noticed that the Earl of Huntington was here.

"I have never seen her before." Nancie thought the young girl by the mysterious woman's side did look familiar.

"That is Ms. Mary Branton." Elizabeth told them. "Her late husband was a lawyer, I think."

Nancie watched as Lord Mason walked around the room with Mary Branton on his arm. The young girl followed closely behind them, and she only spoke when she was introduced to the other guests. Seeing Lord Mason happy greatly troubled Nancie. She looked at Maxx and gave a quick shake of her head. She could not watch Abby's father's happiness any longer. Nancie turned away, refusing to look in that direction again.

"Is there something wrong with Ms. Branton?" Elizabeth was now curious.

"I do not know the woman," Maxx replied. "I have met the daughter though."

Jax and Nick returned to their table. Jax was carrying two apple tartlets. He set one on the table in front of Nancie. He smiled at her and turned to go.

"Leaving so soon?" Nancie playfully asked.

"This one is for my mother." Jax held the second tartlet up.

"Oh, let me." Nancie jumped up and took the dessert plate from Jax.

Nancie grabbed a glass of wine from the tray as a waiter passed by her. She hurried over and handed the tartlet and wine to Lady Clara. As she was talking with Jax's parents, Lord Mason and his guests stopped by to say hello. Lord Mason proudly introduced Ms. Branton and her daughter Felicia to them.

The way Ms. Branton was eyeing Nancie made her feel uncomfortable. Nancie thought that it was best for her to leave so she said goodbye to Lady Clara.

"I am shocked that woman is even here." Ms. Branton turned her nose up as she spoke loudly.

Nancie froze when she heard Mary Branton's statement. She quickly turned around to find the woman on Lord Mason's arm glowering at her.

"Ms. Branton, Nancie is my son's guest." Lady Clara informed the woman.

"Then your son should be disowned." Mary Branton made a sound of disgust and looked away from Nancie.

Nancie looked from Lady Clara to Sir Phillip. Was this what everyone thought of her when she was not around? She closed her eyes and shook her head. Of course, this is exactly what high society people thought of women like her. She was wrong to have believed that she could be part of this world.

This was what she had been afraid of all along. She knew what being disowned would do to someone. It was a world that was cold and dark. It would be lonely nights of tears and deep sadness from the loss of a family. It was something that she would not let happen to Jax. She cared too much for him to allow this darkness to fall upon him.

"Excuse me." Nancie curtsied to Lady Clara. "I will take my leave of your family now."

With that, Nancie slightly lifted her skirts and rushed from the ballroom. Mary Branton smiled at her accomplishment.

Chapter Twenty-Four

No one in the Shaw family knew what to say to Maxx. Alex poured a glass of brandy and handed it to his friend. He figured that Maxx needed a stiff drink after Mary Branton's statement. The woman had stunned everyone in the room.

"Maxx, are you sure that there is no chance of this girl being your sister?" Gavin asked.

"I am positive." Maxx handed Alex back the empty brandy glass.

"Benjamin, did you know any of this?" Lord Matthew wondered if Mary Branton had shared her family history with him.

"Mary said nothing to me on the matter." Lord Mason was as stunned as everyone else was.

Mary Branton was introduced to Lord Mason, by the Duke's mother, at Ms. Rhodes' End of the Summer Party three weeks ago. Benjamin Mason was intrigued by the attention Mary Branton had shown to him. He had not noticed anything in her behavior that would imply of her attitude here tonight. Not once, in the past three weeks, had they talked about the late Daniel Spencer. Lord Mason had assumed, as everyone else had, that Mary's late husband was her daughter's father.

"Maxx, what will you do?" Nancie was worried for Maxx.

"I will deal with Mary Branton's accusations on another day." Maxx took Nancie's hands in his. "Right now, we are here to talk about you."

Nancie was not comfortable talking about her life. She rarely ever spoke to Maxx or Rachel about what her true feelings were on matters. She was always the strong one that helped to care for everyone around her. What people thought of her did not usually bother her, not until now anyway.

"What Mary Branton, and people like her, think does not matter." Jax was ready to resolve this issue, once and for all.

"Jackson is right, my dear." Lady Clara smiled at Nancie.

115

"Our family looks beyond titles and social statuses," Lady Caroline assured Nancie.

"We look at the heart." Dani walked over and put her arm around her mother. Lady Caroline smiled tenderly at her daughter.

"It is true that our family could face some ridicule because you own a pub, but I think we Shaw's are strong enough to face that." Lord Matthew put his arm around his wife.

"Jax loves you and so do we." Abby knew what it felt like to feel as though you were not good enough to belong among a grand family. She used to think that she was not worthy to be Gavin's wife.

"You belong here." Jax's eyes pleaded with her to believe in his family.

"I…" Nancie looked around the room. She did not know what to say.

"You do belong in this world and it is true not because of Jax." Maxx looked Nancie in the eye. "You were born into this life." Maxx motioned around the room.

"Maxx, no." Nancie shook her head. "You cannot."

"What are you talking about?" Jax demanded. Caleb and Nick had to once again, hold their little brother in his place.

"Nancie's mother was the daughter of an Earl." Maxx's reply had everyone curious.

"Maxx, please just leave it be." Nancie's plea was a whisper.

"Why would you want this kept quiet?" Jax did not understand her reasoning on the matter. "This proves Mary Branton, and others like her, wrong."

"Because it hurts!" Nancie snapped at Jax.

Jax hated seeing Nancie upset but he was glad to see that her fiery spirit had returned. She was not the quiet and calm type. Nancie had always spoken her mind. If she got angry enough, perhaps then they would finally get to the heart of the matter. Once her true fears were released, Jax would be able to help her silence them forever.

"Maxwell, what do you know?" Lady Caroline thought they all needed answers.

"Nancie's mother's name was Ella." Maxx turned to face Lord Mason.

The realization of what Maxx was saying hit Lord Mason hard. He blinked several times as he looked between Maxx and Nancie. His mind struggled to understand how it could possibly be true.

"That simply cannot be." Lord Mason put his arm around Abby's shoulders as she hurried to his side. "It just cannot be true."

"Father, are you alright?" Abby had seen her father's expression cloud over with memories like this when he had told everyone about his long-lost daughter Emerald, which she hoped to find one day.

"Benjamin, you told us that your sister had died." Lord Matthew understood what Maxx had said. He remembered Ella Mason well.

"I guess that was one way of not having to deal with it," Nancie mumbled.

"Is this really true?" Abby looked between her father and Maxx. Her eyes finally rested on Nancie. "Is Nancie truly my cousin?"

"It cannot be true!" Lord Mason snapped out of his stunned state and stepped forward. He took Abby by the arm and turned her to face him. "My sister died in 1756, two years before you were even born."

Nancie and Abby were the same age. Lord Mason could not believe this to be true. He was away in Scotland, with his mother's family, for six months that year. He returned to England when the message arrived that his sister Ella had died from a fever. He had always assumed this was the same fever that Abby's mother had also died from.

"Maxx, please let this go," Nancie pleaded. "I have done without them my entire life. I do not have to have them in my life now."

"No!" Jax no longer cared for the warnings from Maxx and his brothers. He pushed Caleb and Nick aside. He quickly closed the distance between him and Nancie. He gently placed his hands on her upper arms, leaving her no choice but to look at him. "I care not of your birth status. However, this is about your mother and she is extremely important to you. I want to hear your story from you, not from anyone else in this room."

Nancie hated that Maxx had put her in this position. This was a family secret that she would have carried to her grave. She had promised her mother, before she died, that she would keep this secret. She felt like she was betraying her mother.

117

Since this matter was now out in the open, Nancie had no choice but to tell Jax her family story. Her mother's life was a story of sadness, sorrow, and loss. It broke her heart to have to put all that pain into words now. How could she possibly explain her mother's pain to anyone?

In 1756, two years before Nancie was born, her mother's father and grandfather, the former Earls of Huntington were working to secure a marriage contract for Nancie's mother with a nobleman's son in France. Ella Mason did not wish to leave England and marry Lord Alarie, the Duke of Marseille's son.

Ella Mason stood before her father and grandfather and declared her love for Danny Blume, the son of a lowly pub owner in St. Hartford, the main village on Maxx's family's lands. The pleas and cries from Ella and her mother went unheard that day. Ella Mason was immediately disowned and banished from her family that very hour.

Ella found herself locked outside the fortress walls of Huntington Estate with only a satchel, that her mother had quickly prepared for her, and the clothes that she wore that day. Ella's mother was not allowed to ever speak her daughter's name again or she would be banished as well. Ella's father's words were harsh, and his actions were cruel. If her mother did not comply with Ella's banishment, she would never see her son again.

Since Huntington Estate was closer to London than it was to Hartford Manor, Ella walked to London alone. The journey took her three days on foot. Once she reached London, Ella found the Brewer Pub, which is now the Blume'N Brew. Ella knew that Carl Brewer was friends with Danny Blume's father. Mr. Brewer gave Ella a room and sent a messenger straight away to Hartford Manor. Four days later, Elijah Spencer, Maxx's grandfather, and the Earl of Hartford at the time, showed up at the pub. He, Maxx's father, and Danny Blume carried Ella to Hartford. Danny and Ella were married a week later.

"So, you see, I cannot allow you to be disowned." A tear escaped from Nancie's eye. "I have seen what that does to a person's soul.

My mother spent years broken and grieving for a family that she could no longer be part of."

Jax's heart was pierced many times over as Nancie told her mother's story. He pulled her into his arms and held her tightly to his chest. He wanted to absorb all the hurtful feelings she had within her. He was at a loss for words. What could anyone say after hearing Ella Mason's sad story? All that he could do was hold Nancie as she silently cried. She was a strong little woman, and she would try to hide her tears.

Jax shielded Nancie from the view of the others in the room. He allowed her time to find her strength again. He would not release her from his arms until she had done so. He looked over his shoulder, into the eyes of his family members. Something dark filled him when his eyes met with Lord Mason's.

"Can you prove any of this?" Lord Mason asked Maxx.

"You will never believe anything that we say." Nancie's strength had returned. She pushed away from Jax and faced Lord Mason, her uncle. "I would expect nothing less from you anyway. My mother always said that Mason men always made horrible decisions." From how she saw things, the women did not do much better either.

"Nancie, regardless of who your parents are, our family would never disown my son for loving you." Lady Clara stepped in front of Nancie, blocking her view of Lord Mason.

"But Mary Branton…" Nancie did not get to finish her protest.

"Mary Branton, nor anyone else, tells our family what to do. There is no way that a Shaw would disown one of our own." Sir Phillip stood by his wife's side.

"We can prove who Nancie's mother is." Maxx informed Lord Mason as he turned to face him. "You should take a close look at the brooch that Nancie is wearing."

Nancie's hand automatically covered her mother's brooch that she was wearing under her shawl. Jax tenderly moved her hand aside and pushed back the thin shawl, to reveal the brooch.

Lord Mason stepped closer and stared at the silver butterfly brooch with amethyst stones that had once belonged to his grandmother. The brooch was the only thing of value that Ella's mother had been able to hide in the satchel she had packed for her daughter the day she was disowned.

"My father said that my sister was buried with this family heirloom." Lord Mason was in awe.

"In a way, I guess she was," Nancie whispered.

"I hope that someday you are able to forgive my family for what they have done to you. If I had known that my sister was alive, I would have come for Ella. You should have grown up at Huntington Estate." Lord Mason took Nancie's hands in his.

"My mother thought that you knew of her banishment." Nancie looked up into the eyes of her uncle.

"I assure you; it would have not been allowed, if I had known." Lord Mason placed his hand against Nancie's cheek. "I have a niece."

"And a nephew," Maxx added. Lord Mason quickly looked at Maxx. "Nancie has a brother that is a year older than herself. Frank is in the colonies, fighting with the King's army."

Abby rushed over and pushed Jax, her father, and Maxx aside. Filled with excitement, Abby wrapped her arms around Nancie. This was a joyous occasion for their entire family.

"You are truly a part of our family." Abby whispered in Nancie's ear.

Nancie hugged Abby tightly. She too hoped for something more for their family. She was beyond happy that she would no longer have to feel as if she were alone in this world. Perhaps Jax was right all along, maybe she really did belong here.

Chapter Twenty-Five

The next morning after breakfast, Maxx, and everyone with him from the Blume'N Brew, left for Hartford Manor. Maxx wanted to warn his mother of Mary Branton's claims. Jax considered himself part of the crew at the pub, so naturally he went with them. Of course, everyone knew it was because he was not going to leave Nancie's side.

Maxx greatly protested the need of the Shaw family sending Alex and Caleb along with them. However, it was extremely hard for Maxx to say no when Lady Caroline and Lady Clara insisted their sons travel to Hartford. Since Roger Holden and Edmond Prescott were trying to kill Jax, the family felt better if Alex and Caleb journeyed with them. In the end, Maxx reluctantly gave in.

When they arrived at Hartford Manor, Lady Spencer was waiting for them on the front steps. She ran to Maxx and tightly hugged him the moment he dismounted his horse. Lady Spencer was overjoyed to see everyone. Nancie hugged Maxx's mother and introduced her to Jax. Once all the greetings were made, Lady Spencer took Maxx and Paul's arms and led everyone inside the manor.

"I will be thrilled when Rosa finally comes home to Hartford." Lady Spencer smiled up at Paul. "I have no doubts that you will be as well."

"Aye, I will." Paul's smile broadened into a wide grin. "This will be the best Christmas that Hartford has seen in a while."

Rosa had agreed to stay with Abby at Ellis Manor until Lord Alastair was a year old. After many years of service, Rosa would be returning to Hartford in December to take over as head housekeeper at the manor.

"Will we be seeing Lady Emily?" Alex asked Lady Spencer as they entered the sitting room.

"Emily will probably join us for dinner," Lady Spencer replied.

"Is she alright?" Alex followed Lady Spencer over to the refreshment cart in the room.

"Emily is fine." Lady Spencer glanced over at Maxx then back to Alex. "She has been rather quiet lately though. Roger Holden's threat to kill her has us all deeply concerned."

Lady Spencer hurried away to make sure that dinner would be ready in time. She sent maids to quickly prepare rooms for everyone so they could rest before dinner was served.

"Lady Spencer!" Nancie ran down the hallway to catch up with Maxx's mother. "What can I do to help?"

"Would you mind going with some of the guards down to St. Hartford? One of the merchant's supply wagon broke and the delivery, that was due today, could not be sent. You were always a great help with the village merchants." Lady Spencer was relieved to have Nancie's help.

"I will get Jax and we will make sure the supplies are delivered to the manor." Nancie turned to head back to the sitting room for Jax.

Lady Spencer caught Nancie by the hand. "I saw the looks exchanged between you and Jax Shaw. I am so happy for you, my dear. You deserve to be happy."

Nancie hugged Lady Spencer. Maxx's mother had always treated her as part of the Spencer family. She quickly returned to the sitting room for Jax. If they leave now, they would be back in time for dinner.

Jax and Nancie road on the back of the wagon from Hartford Manor to the village. Nancie talked the entire way to St. Hartford. She told Jax about her life here, before her mother died. It was wonderful to see Nancie happy and smiling.

Jax had never been to St. Hartford. His first glimpse of the village was impressive. He did not realize that Maxx had such a large village on his property. He had heard many stories about Hartford and knew, without a doubt, that this place was much different from the other properties in England.

Today, as Jax witnessed the interactions of the villagers, he could almost swear that there was something extraordinary and almost magical about this place. The joy on Nancie's face when she talked about growing up here told Jax that this place was home to her. Home was always a special place indeed.

When Jax and Nancie entered Welborn's, they were greeted by Abner and Laura Welborn, the shop owners. Their shop was the main grocer in St. Hartford. Jax was surprised by how large the shop was and by all the supplies they carried here. Shops this size and grand were expected to be found in London, not in some country village.

"It is so good to see you." Laura Welborn was excited to see Nancie. She hugged Nancie before pulling her over to the counter. "You must visit us more often."

"Your brother needs to get himself back to England and take over that pub so you can return home to Hartford." Mr. Welborn grinned and hugged Nancie as well.

"That would be nice." Nancie politely smiled at the elderly couple. She really had not given much thought to returning to Hartford.

Jax leaned against the counter and listened as Nancie talked with the Welborn's, while the wagon was being loaded by the guards from Hartford Manor. There was something wonderfully different here in Hartford. Miss Nancie from the Blume'N Brew did not exist here. Here, she was Nancie Blume, a daughter of Hartford. Jax suddenly realized a factor that made this place so special. Here, the people were not fighting for statuses and higher places in society. At Hartford, everyone was simply family.

Once the supplies for the manor were loaded onto the wagon, Nancie said her goodbyes to the shop owners. Jax offered her his arm and they started out of the shop. Just before they exited the shop door, a little woman entered the shop. She looked sad and tired. Nancie froze when she saw the little woman.

"Hello, Nancie." The woman's voice was soft and low. "It is good to see you again, dear."

"Hello, Ms. Harbin." Nancie's face clouded over with the same sadness Ms. Harbin had. "How are you?"

"The same." Ms. Harbin looked up at Jax.

"Good day, Ms. Harbin. I am Jax Shaw. It is a pleasure to meet you." Jax offered the little woman his hand, but she did not take it.

"He is a fine young man." Ms. Harbin said to Nancie.

"Gertie, it is good to see you." Ms. Welborn hurried over and put her arm around Ms. Harbin. "Come in and let me help you."

Nancie sighed deeply and quickly left the shop. Jax felt the distance Nancie put between them almost immediately. He tried to talk with her on the ride back to Hartford Manor, but Nancie never replied. Whatever was between her and Ms. Harbin was painful.

When they arrived at the manor, Nancie excused herself and retired to the rooms her family used at the manor. Jax, needing answers, went in search of Maxx. He had to know what had changed the woman he loved so drastically today.

Jax was unable to find Maxx or Lady Spencer. One of the servants led him to Maxx's study. He found Caleb and Alex playing cards with Doug and Harper in the study.

"Come on in brother and join us." Caleb motioned toward the empty chair at the table.

"I cannot." Jax put his hands on the back of the empty chair. "Have any of you seen Maxx?"

"We have not seen him in quite a while." Harper kept his eyes on his cards.

"Hello, gentlemen." Lady Emily Spencer entered the study.

"Lady Emily." Jax hurried over to Maxx's sister. "Do you know where Maxx is? I really need to speak to him."

"Maxx and Paul went to a couple of our tenant's farms. There have been a few more break ins this past week." Emily told Jax.

"Maxx should have said something. We could have gone with them to help out." Jax looked over at his brother and cousin at the card table. "They could do something useful rather than playing cards."

"You were helping Nancie and we all thank you greatly for that, by the way." Emily stepped closer to the card table. Jax followed her. "With Holden trying to kill you too, Maxx thought it was best for you all to stay close to the manor."

"How kind of Little Man," Alex said sarcastically.

Alex looked up from the cards in his hands. He eyed Emily over and slyly smiled at her. She had left London without saying goodbye.

Now, with her standing here before him, Alex was not sure of what to say to her. She was lovely. She was always lovely to him.

"Perhaps you can help me then." Jax turned to face Emily. "Who is Gertie Harbin and what does she have to do with Nancie?"

"Harbin?" Caleb looked up at his brother.

"Yes, Gertie Harbin. We ran into the little woman in the village. Nancie has not been the same since." Jax watched his brother's face cloud over, just as Nancie's had. Caleb slowly laid his cards down on the table.

"Oh my," Emily whispered.

"Lady Emily, you are going to have to tell me what is going on, for that name is now affecting my brother as well." Jax demanded an answer.

"Easy, cousin." Alex eyed Jax over his hand of cards. He would make sure that Jax kept his temper in check.

"Gertie Harbin is John Harbin's mother." Emily dropped her head. This was really something that Nancie herself should be telling Jax.

Caleb pushed away from the card table and hurried from the study. Jax and Alex looked at each other, they did not understand. Somehow, John Harbin was connected to both Nancie and Caleb.

"That name is familiar, but I cannot remember who he is." Alex was puzzled. Jax nodded, he felt the same as his cousin on this.

"John Harbin was killed, along with several other young men, during a military training exercise." Emily sighed deeply. She remembered the accident well.

Jax leaned his head back as the realization of who John Harbin was came to him. He also remembered that horrifying accident. Something went wrong with one of the cannons during the training exercise that day. It was believed, but never confirmed, that something with the manufacturing of the cannon had caused it to explode that day. For some reason, a small barrel of powder was found placed by the cannon, during the investigation. A spark had ignited the barrel of powder causing a greater explosion to happen.

John Harbin and Caleb had become good friends while in military service. John was one of the six men that were around the cannon during the exercise. None of them had survived. John was killed instantly.

Caleb had taken John's death hard. He was supposed to have been with John and the others for that exercise. The Shaw's had been called to the Captain's tent just before the accident happened. Both of their father's had come to the encampment to let them know that their grandmother had taken gravely ill.

Jax understood his brother's sadness over John Harbin's death. He did not understand why it affected Nancie so strongly. He did not know a lot about Nancie's past, and he hated asking others about her, but he needed answers so he could help Nancie.

"Was John and Nancie related?" Jax asked.

Emily, Doug, and Harper paused and looked at each other. There was no easy way to tell Jax wanted he wanted to know. The only thing to do, was to tell him the truth.

"John was Nancie's fiancé," Emily replied.

Chapter Twenty-Six

That evening, since Nancie had not come out of her room, Emily went and led her out to the garden. After seeing Gertie Harbin, Nancie was beginning to shut herself off from everyone, like she had done with John died seven years ago. Since Jax had his hands full trying to keep Caleb from becoming depressed again over John's death, Emily volunteered to help with Nancie.

"Why are we out here?" Nancie was dragging along behind Emily.

"I thought that you would enjoy a nice walk through the gardens." Emily pulled Nancie along, by the hand, like a little child.

"I have seen the gardens here at Hartford many times." Nancie did not wish to walk through the gardens today. It was easier just being sad in her room, but Emily would not take no for an answer.

"But you have not seen it like this." Emily smiled as she pulled Nancie over to a private area in the gardens.

This secluded area was a special place in the garden that Lady Spencer had created not long after she and the former Earl of Hartford were married. This special place was hidden from view of the garden paths and from the windows in the manor. The shrubbery and flowers created a small maze at the entrance.

The private garden area had a small fountain and a table for two, where many romantic dinners had taken place. The small pavilion was decorated as wonderfully as the bedchambers in the manor were. Lord and Lady Spencer had spent many summer nights here in this private oasis. Lady Spencer had said many times that those evenings were like falling in love all over again, every time.

Nancie knew that the gardens behind Hartford Manor were special. She had visited these gardens many times over the years, but she had never seen this private area before. As Emily led her around the last part of the maze entrance, Nancie was in awe of the beauty of this place. Before her was a beautiful, special, and very romantic outdoor room.

Torches and lanterns were lit all around the area. In the center was a table, already set with dinner for two. There, standing by one of the chairs, was Jax. Emily had helped to set this evening up for them. After an emotional day, she thought that Jax and Nancie could enjoy having their dinner away from everyone else.

"Enjoy your meal." Emily whispered, before she hurried away, leaving Nancie and Jax alone.

"You look lovely this evening." Jax walked over and took Nancie by the hand.

"I should have known that Emily was up to something." Nancie rolled her eyes as she sat down. "She is sneaky."

"I believe this entire family is sneaky." Jax took his seat across the table from her. "I got my eye on the mother too." Nancie smiled and nodded her head, she had to agree.

"The grandmother is even worse," Nancie whispered loudly.

"I have not met her yet." Jax was sure that Maxx's entire family was a lively bunch.

"This was a lovely idea." Nancie was still sad, but she did appreciate the trouble Jax had gone through for this private dinner. "Thank you."

"Well, I did have a lot of help." Jax reached across the table and took her by the hand. "I did not wish for you to remain sad."

"My sadness cannot be helped." Nancie looked down at her plate. After seven years, John's death was still hard for her to deal with.

"Emily told me about John." Jax thought that it was best to not have any secrets between them. "John and Caleb were good friends."

Through their meal, they talked about John Harbin. Jax told her the stories of Caleb and John's hunting and military adventures. Nancie shared how she and John had met. She did not tell Jax everything about her relationship with John Harbin. She did not want Jax to feel like he would always be in John's shadow.

Nancie was seventeen when John Harbin died. After that day she spent her time next to her father at the Blume'N Brew, learning how he ran the pub. At the time, she did not realize that her father was keeping his medical condition from her. A little over a year after John's death, her father died from a weak heart. She blamed herself a little for her father passing so soon. If she had known of his illness, she would have taken over the running of the pub much sooner.

"After my father died, that is when I became Miss Nancie." It felt good for her to finally tell someone her personal story. "My brother was away with the military and I had just lost two important people in my life, so I became devoted to protecting Maxx. I could not save John or my father, but I could help Maxx."

"So that is why Maxx had you to use the wigs and makeup. You were only eighteen and he was trying to make you look older because you were running the pub." Jax leaned back in his chair and laughed.

It was a crazy idea and one that should have never happened. Still, Maxx and Nancie had pulled off the ruse of Miss Nancie perfectly. Jax was sure that he was going to have to keep his eye on Nancie as well. She was also sneaky. That probably came from spending so much time around Maxwell Spencer.

"Maxx's father had helped greatly in all that planning. Then sadly, a year later, Lord Spencer was thrown while training that horse. His injuries were too great, he could not heal from them." Nancie sighed. This was too much death to be talking about at one time.

"It really scared my family when my Uncle Matthew had that accident last year while training a horse." Jax had learned how to train horses from his uncle.

"I feel as if everyone that is close to me dies or leaves," Nancie whispered.

Nancie closed her eyes and let the memories of those that she had lost run through her mind. She missed her parents dearly and she wished that her brother would come home.

"I know it has not been easy for you." Jax's heart broke from seeing the sadness that was on Nancie's face.

"You would probably be much safer away from me." Nancie's voice was low.

"I see what you are trying to do here, but trust me when I say this, I, my lady, am not going anywhere." Jax reached across the small table and touched her face, causing Nancie to look up at him.

Jax could no longer emotionally handle talking about all the lost lives and the near losses. He quickly stood up and pulled Nancie to her feet. Putting his hand around her waist, Jax pulled her close to him.

"There is no music playing." Nancie pointed out the obvious when they slowly started to dance.

"I can hear it." Jax spoke softly next to her ear. "Close your eyes and perhaps you will hear it as well."

Nancie closed her eyes and laid her head against Jax's chest. They had danced together many times. Jax was right. With his arms wrapped gently around her, she too could hear the music. She would have never imagined that Jax Shaw would be a helpless romantic.

Over the years, many rumors came to the Blume'N Brew about Sir Jackson Shaw. He was the free-spirited Shaw, without a care in the world. The many tales of Jax's courtships with the society ladies would circulate after every party. Rachel had kept up with all the gossip from the society parties in London. She and Rachel would laugh for days over some of the outrageous rumors that followed each party.

Every time that Jax stopped by the pub, he had a lively spirit and the other patrons enjoyed having him around. He drank, laughed a lot, and played cards for hours. A few times he even sat with Will at the piano and led the songs. There was nothing that she had ever heard about Jax Shaw that would indicate that he was serious in any way. Well, except for the things Maxx had told her about how Jax stood up and led things in Nettlesville when they had to bring his cousin Nate back to London to see Doctor Ramsey.

Jax Shaw had hidden his talents of being a true leader for most of his life. He was kind and romantic, characteristics he surely got from his mother. Somehow, this Shaw was hers. Did she genuinely want this? Would he stay? Would death come for him, like it had for her other family members? She was not sure what the future would bring, but for now, she would face it with Jax by her side.

Chapter Twenty-Seven

The next morning, Alex and Caleb, along with Harper and Doug, led their traveling party back toward London. With Roger Holden plotting to kill Jax, they had him to ride in the carriage with Nancie. This was the first time Jax was not bothered with riding in a carriage. He spent most of his time sitting next Nancie with his arm around her. He passed the time by telling her many of the Shaw family stories.

Maxx had warned his mother about Mary Branton's claims. The guards at Hartford Manor were instructed to deny Ms. Branton entry to the manor. The guards and lookouts throughout Hartford were prepared to send Lady Spencer word if Ms. Branton showed up in the village.

Maxx and Paul had stayed behind. They were still investigating the recent break ins on the Hartford properties. They would meet up with everyone at the Blume'N Brew later. Alex was in a better mood, for this time, he got to say goodbye to Lady Emily.

When they reached the Blume'N Brew, Rachel and Jerry were happy to see them. Maxx had left a few men at the pub to help them keep it open while they were gone. Rachel had been thoroughly going over the plans that Nancie and Jax had left behind for the pub to start serving meals. Nancie and Rachel were sitting at the private table in the pub, going over last-minute details. Rachel was eager to try this idea, so she had everything already prepared and ready to go.

"You have done a fine job with this." Nancie was pleased with the effort that Rachel had given to this addition to the pub. Rachel's enthusiasm had Nancie excited about it as well. "We will start serving meals tomorrow for a couple of hours, around dinner time, and see how things go."

"I think that we should give this a few months before you make the final decision on whether to continue with it or not." Rachel poured them a cup of tea. She figured things might start out slowly. She did not want Nancie to give up on the idea too soon.

It was still early in the afternoon and the Blume'N Brew had not officially opened yet. Nancie and Rachel were startled when the front doors opened and a well-dressed man, they had never seen before, entered the pub. The man removed his hat and looked around the pub. He was clearly lost. He politely smiled when he saw Nancie and Rachel sitting at the table in the back corner.

"Excuse me ladies." The stranger started to approach their table.

"May I help you, Sir?" Jerry walked in from the back room.

"Oh, yes, Sir." The stranger quickly turned to the bartender. "I am looking for Sir Jackson Shaw. I was told that I could possibly find him here."

"Jax is out back with his brother and cousin. I will send for him." Jerry opened the door to the back room and yelled for Will to go get Jax.

Jerry was not aware that the front doors were left unlocked. It was a mistake that would not be made again. He was not going to leave Nancie and Rachel alone with the stranger. He hurried behind the bar where he could grab his rifle if it were necessary. After Prescott busted up the pub once, Jerry did not trust strangers. Soon, Will returned with Jax, Caleb, and Alex.

"Mr. Webb, it is good to see you." Jax hurried over and shook the man's hand.

"I am here on behalf of Lady Daphne Hale." Mr. Webb politely nodded his head once at Jax. "Lady Daphne requests to see you. She will not enter an establishment such as this. Lady Daphne is waiting for you at Alston's Restaurant."

"Tell Lady Daphne that I am on my way." Jax was thrilled.

Mr. Webb shook Jax's hand again and hurried on his way. Apparently, Mr. Webb was not comfortable being inside a pub either. Nancie assumed this man considered himself a status above pub owners, even though he was a servant.

"I guess we are going to Alston's," Caleb mumbled. He and Alex hurried to the stables to get their horses.

Jax rushed over and gave Nancie a quick kiss on the cheek. Nancie was confused by his odd behavior. Who was this Lady Daphne Hale anyway? Why did she have Jax acting all giddy?

"We will return before the pub opens," Jax assured Nancie before hurrying outside.

Jerry locked the doors to the pub so that no one else would enter without them knowing it. Nancie was still stunned. She looked to Rachel for possible answers.

"Do you know who this Lady Daphne Hale is?" Nancie asked.

"I have not heard her name in months." Rachel thought for a moment. "The last I heard of her was that her father was trying to arrange a marriage for her with a Lord's son from Scotland. I am not sure if the arrangement was ever agreed upon."

"And she just happens to summon Jax?" Nancie was furious.

"Wait." Rachel pointed at Nancie. "It might not be what you are thinking."

"Then Jax should have explained why he was so happy to be seeing this Lady Daphne Hale before he rushed out of here!" Nancie shouted.

Nancie angrily stormed over to the bar and sat down on one of the barstools. She began to help Jerry to dry the glasses he had just finished washing. The longer Nancie sat here on this barstool, staring at the door, the madder she got. Her mind was reeling with horrible assumptions of what was going on between Jax and Lady Daphne Hale. The woman's name greatly annoyed her. She knew this was wrong and childish, but she could not help herself. Was she about to lose Jax to Daphne Hale?

By the time Jax returned to the pub, over an hour later, Nancie was fuming mad. The moment Jax walked through the door, a glass slammed into the door frame and shattered to pieces. Jax, on instinct, ducked as the next glass hit the wall behind him. His eyes widened when he looked over at the bar and saw Nancie with another glass in her hand.

"Do not throw that!" Jax ordered.

His words were ignored. The glass barely missed his head. With every step that he took around the room, Nancie threw another glass.

Caleb and Alex remained just outside the doorway. They peeped through the door as Jax dodged the glasses Nancie threw at him.

"Nancie, give him time to explain!" Jerry shouted.

The bartender ducked behind the bar when Nancie turned and glared at him. Jax was grateful for the distraction. He quickly closed the distance between him and Nancie. He wrapped his arms around her from behind. He hated confining her like this but at least now she could not throw another glass at him.

"Let me go!" Nancie demanded.

"I will gladly let you go when you calm down and explain to me what is going on." Jax refused to release his hold on her.

"Who is Daphne Hale?" Nancie shouted.

"That is what this is about?" Jax was stunned. He released his hold on her enough to turn Nancie around to face him. "You are worried about Daphne Hale?"

Nancie did not reply. She stood still as a statue in Jax's arms and glared at him. Caleb and Alex snickered from the doorway. Both disappeared out to the stables when Jax sharply narrowed his eyes at them.

"I think you should quickly explain." Jerry peeped over the bar at Jax.

"Daphne Hale's family owns a piano like the one that was destroyed here. I sent a letter, asking if they would sell it." Jax calmly looked Nancie in the eye. "Daphne convinced her mother to sell it to us. I just bought you another piano. It will be delivered tomorrow."

"Oh." Nancie spoke softly. She was embarrassed and looked away.

"I think it is rather adorable that you are jealous." Jax grinned at her.

"I'm not jealous!" Nancie shoved Jax's hands away.

"Good. Then you two will not mind cleaning this mess up." Maxx was leaning against the door frame with his arms folded across his chest. "And you both owe me a case of glasses."

Jerry bravely left the safety of the bar area. He handed Nancie and Jax both a broom. With Maxx here, Jerry was sure that Nancie would calm down rather quickly.

Chapter Twenty-Eight

With the new piano, the atmosphere at the Blume'N Brew was lively again. Will Carter was pleased to be playing again. The only concern that was weighing on everyone's mind was Roger Holden and Edmond Prescott. The two half-brothers, and their men, had been quiet for the past few weeks.

Nancie and Rachel had been serving meals at the pub for the past few weeks. So far, Jax's idea had been turning them a nice profit. Rachel enjoyed preparing the meals so much that Nancie was seriously considering keeping this new addition to the pub.

Today, since things had been going so well, Jax convinced Nancie to have lunch with him at Alston's Restaurant. Of course, Caleb and Alex tagged along for safety reasons, but they gave the couple enough space to where they did not feel crowded.

Lunch went well, and on the way back to the pub, Jax and Nancie decided to walk through the park. It was now the middle of September and soon cooler weather would be setting in. Nancie was glad that they had a chance to have this outing today. Staying mostly around the pub was wearing heavily on Jax's nerves. He really was not one to be shut in for long periods of time.

Caleb and Alex walked several yards behind Jax and Nancie. They were discussing their family hunting trips for the fall season. They were the best trackers in their family. These hunting trips were always a favorite event for them both.

Jax and Nancie walked around a bend in the park path. The trees and shrubbery concealed their view of Caleb and Alex. Jax took full advantage of this brief private moment. He lowered his head and gave Nancie a tender kiss. Even a quick kiss between them held a touch of passion to it.

Before they were aware of their surroundings again, Jax and Nancie were attacked by a group of men. One man grabbed Nancie around her waist from behind with one hand. His other hand covered her mouth, preventing Nancie from screaming. Two more men grabbed Jax's arms and held him while another man repeatedly punched him in the stomach and face.

Nancie's eyes widened in horror at each punch that Jax took. She could not stand watching Jax being hit any longer. She had to do something. She began to wildly struggle against her attacker as the man was pulling her further away from Jax.

She used the heel of her boot and brought it down hard on the man's foot. It was a tactic that Maxx had taught her. After several hits from her foot, the man screamed out in pain. Finally, Nancie wiggled away enough to remove the man's hand from her mouth.

Caleb and Alex heard Nancie scream and ran to catch up with them. When the man holding Nancie saw Caleb and Alex, he flung Nancie into the small pond and ran from the park. Even though the water was not deep, Alex hurried into the pond and pulled Nancie out.

Caleb grabbed one of the men that was holding Jax by the arm and threw him to the ground. Jax now had a better chance with only having to fight two men. The man on the ground kicked Caleb hard in his leg, giving himself time to get to his feet. Caleb smiled when he recognized the man.

"So, one of the snakes has finally came out of his hole." Caleb grinned at Edmond Prescott. He was glad to finally have a chance to get his hands ahold of Edmond.

"You are not the Shaw I wanted today, but you will do!" Edmond shouted at Caleb as he pulled out a knife. "It does not matter to me which Shaw dies today!"

Edmond screamed as he rushed toward Caleb. Caleb stepped to the side and grabbed Edmond. Once again, Edmond was roughly thrown to the ground. Caleb bent over and picked up the knife that Edmond had dropped. Edmond, seeing another chance, rushed toward Caleb again. Edmond screamed when Caleb plunged the knife into his leg.

Maxx and Paul came running from the far side of the park path to help. Jax had held his own fighting against the two men. Seeing that they were now outnumbered, Randal Gates grabbed Edmond and

they hurried from the park. Nancie rushed over and put her arm around Jax's waist for support. He was tired from fighting two men at the same time. Jax pulled her into his arms and held her tightly.

"Are you alright?" Jax asked.

"I am fine, just a tad bit wet." Nancie tried to make light of the situation.

"Then let us get you back to the pub so you can get out of these wet clothes." Jax was thankful that she was alright. He placed his hand on Alex's shoulder. "Thank you, cousin."

"Where is Maxx?" Alex did not see their friend.

"Maxx and Paul are chasing after them." Caleb motioned toward the direction Maxx went.

"You have to hand it to the little guy. He sure is persistent." Jax had to admit, Maxx did not give up easily.

"Are you injured?" Alex asked Caleb.

"My pride perhaps." Caleb dusted of the dirt off. "I should have killed Prescott."

"I am sure we will get another chance." Jax knew that Prescott would not give up. "Right now, we need to get back to the pub."

"What about Maxx?" Alex looked in the direction Maxx and Paul went, but he still did not see them.

"I am sure that our little friend can handle himself." Caleb patted Alex on the back. "Besides, you and Nancie do need to get out of those wet clothes."

They all agreed that it really was best for them to get back to the pub. With Prescott now making another attempt on Jax's life, he was not safe out in the open like this. With Nancie also being attacked, Jax and Maxx were going to lose their tempers.

By the time they arrived at the pub, Maxx and Paul had caught up with them. They had chased Prescott and his men out of the park but lost them in the crowded streets of London. Rachel helped Nancie upstairs to get out of her wet clothes, giving the men a chance to talk alone. Alex hurried to his room to change as well.

"I am not going to let her be put in harm's way again if I can help it." Maxx wanted this feud with Holden and Prescott to end.

"How are we going to keep Nancie safe?" Caleb wondered.

"They are only attacking Nancie and the pub because Jax is here." Paul poured everyone a drink before joining them at the table.

"Then Jax should not be here." Jerry brought over another bottle of rum for Maxx.

"I agree, it is time for Jax to leave," Maxx stated firmly.

"I am not leaving!" Jax shouted.

"As much as I hate to admit it, brother, they do have a point." Caleb was sure that Jax would not agree.

"How can you agree with this?" Jax snapped at his older brother.

"He can agree because they are right." Alex sat down next to Jax.

"I am not leaving!" Jax pointed across the table at Maxx.

Alex grabbed his cousin's hand and pushed it down to the table. There was no doubt in his mind, or anyone else's, that Jax would refuse to leave Nancie. When Shaw men find their one true love, nothing will stop him from having her and protecting her forever. Their mothers had told them this since when they were children.

"Your presence here endangers her." Alex looked up toward the second floor.

Jax leaned back in his chair. He looked up toward the second floor too. Nancie was up there in her room. Rachel had prepared a warm bath for her. Jax wanted to do what was best for Nancie. How could he leave her though? He had waited so long to get her to believe in their relationship. It could not end like this.

"I want her safe but there has to be another way" Jax's voice was low, he almost sounded defeated.

"There may be another way," Maxx said calmly, as he poured himself another drink.

"I do not like that look, Little Man." Alex took the bottle of rum from Maxx.

Alex had seen the expression on Maxx's face many times. Usually, some ludicrous plan was about to follow. Alex was not sure how Maxx even survived half of the outlandish schemes he came up with.

"If there is another way, one where I do not have to leave Nancie, then I want to know what it is." Jax was eager to try anything.

"In the morning, we leave for Nettlesville to deliver the ship that Lord Mason is sending to the island." Maxx looked Jax in the eye. "You and Nancie, for your safety, will join us."

Alex and Caleb shook their heads. Nancie had a fiery spirit. She would not do well on a ship for a few weeks. They were not sure that this would end well. Jax, however, thought that this was a perfect solution. He grinned at Maxx and nodded his head.

"Nettlesville it is." Jax raised his class to Maxx. This was a splendid idea. Nothing could go wrong with this plan. Well, he hoped not anyway.

Chapter Twenty-Nine

Everyone met Lord Mason at the docks the next morning. Jax's cousin Nate had suggested that Nettlesville needed a small ship of their own, to help the island continue to prosper. Lord Mason was sending a small ship that the residents could use as a fishing boat and to visit other nearby ports for trading.

Nancie was not happy with leaving the Blume'N Brew. Even though she trusted Jerry, Rachel, and Will to run the pub without any problem, she hated leaving it. A member of her family had been at the pub since her father took it over. She felt like she was abandoning her duty.

"You take good care of my niece." Lord Mason looked at Nancie as he handed Maxx the folder of documents that he was sending to Nettlesville.

"Do not fret, she will be protected at all times." Maxx took the folder and walked away, giving Nancie and her uncle a moment of privacy.

"I do not like this." Lord Mason shook his head and took Nancie's hands in his. "I think it would be better if I took you with me to Huntington, rather than sending you off on a ship full of men."

"Maxx thinks that this is for the best." Nancie's voice was full of sadness.

She did not wish to go on this voyage to Nettlesville, nor did she want to go to Huntington Estate. Someday, she would go to the home her mother grew up in, but for now, she was not ready. For years she had pictured her mother being tossed outside the gates of Huntington with nothing but a quickly packed satchel and the clothes she had on. Her mother had only told that story a few times. Even after many years, the thought of it made her mother cry.

"I know that Maxwell will keep you safe. Plus, you have all these Shaw men with you. I do know them to be honorable men." Lord

Mason put his arm around Nancie. "I know that they will protect you, even though they may be the very reason you are being targeted."

"Uncle, be nice." Nancie looked up at Lord Mason from the corner of her eye.

"It is hard to believe that both my daughter, and my niece, have fallen in love with Shaw men." Lord Mason winked at Nancie. He could not help but to tease her. He was hoping to see her smile before she left.

"Yes, I do believe that the women in your family have fallen for Shaw men." Nancie was able to smile at this thought.

She and Lord Mason stood to the side and watched as Jax, Caleb, and Alex helped to load their things onto The Em. Maxx was busy going over the schedule and giving orders to the crew members of both ships.

The ship that Lord Mason was sending to Nettlesville was much smaller than Maxx's ship. Lord Mason had not named the ship. He was giving that honor to the residents of Nettlesville. The ship could be crewed well enough with only ten men if need be. Lord Mason had hired a Captain for the ship, and he let Maxx assign five crewmen for one years' time. He wanted to give the men of Nettlesville a chance to be part of the ship's crew.

Maxx found a Captain that he trusted for Lord Mason after many months of searching. His friend, Captain Victor Dupont, had a younger brother named Francis that would be taking the position. Francis Dupont would meet them in Nettlesville. Victor was not comfortable sailing to London Harbor just yet, not with all the fighting going on between the English and French in the colonies.

"We cannot sail a ship without a name!" Ollie shouted.

"That is a bad omen indeed, Captain," Brady told Maxx.

"Right you are." Maxx agreed with his sailors. "Go grab a bottle of wine off The Em and let us temporarily name this ship."

"This should be interesting." Jax lightly laughed as he joined Nancie and Lord Mason.

"Sailors do have strange customs." Nancie had laughed many times over the tales Maxx had shared with her about sea superstitions.

Brady soon returned from The Em with a bottle of wine. Maxx took the bottle and put his arm around Ron, one of his most trusted sailors, shoulders.

"Alright, Captain Ron." Maxx motioned toward Lord Mason's ship. "For your ship's one and only voyage, what would you like to name her?"

Ron threw his hands up high as the other sailors cheered at his temporary promotion. Ron was a lively little fellow that was well loved by everyone. He had the ability of finding humor in almost every situation.

"Ron?" Maxx patted Ron on the back to get his attention. "I need a name."

"Girlbee!" Ron shouted as he held his hands high again. The crew of both ships erupted into joyful shouts again.

Maxx dropped his hand to his side. He looked at Ron blankly. He slowly looked up at Paul, who was standing by his side. It was not often that Maxx was stunned like this.

"Captain Ron, what is a Girlbee?" Paul was as stunned as Maxx was over the ship's name.

"The woman of my dreams!" Ron shouted. Again, he held his hands high and the sailors shouted even louder.

"Oh, dear Lord help us," Paul mumbled and walked away shaking his head.

"Alright, Captain Ron. As you wish." Maxx took the bottle of wine and walked to the edge of the dock. "For its one and only voyage to Nettlesville, under this name, we here by dub this ship as The Girlbee!" Maxx threw the bottle and it shattered against the ship.

Captain Ron and the sailors of both ships cheered loudly. Maxx had to grab Ron by his shoulders to get his attention. Ron was excited to be Captain for this trip. Maxx placed a Captain's hat on Ron's head. Ron grinned proudly as he touched the hat.

"Captain Ron, take your men and board your ship." Maxx motioned toward the small ship. "The Girlbee awaits her Captain and crew."

"My good men!" Ron shouted with his hands held high. "We shall conquer the seas and rest in Spain!" Again, the sailors shouted.

"Captain Ron." Maxx had to step in front of Ron to get his attention this time. "You will follow The Em to Nettlesville. This ship best not end up in Spain."

"Right, Captain." Ron turned back to his crew. "My good men, we shall guard The Em and rest in Nettlesville!"

"Board your ship, Captain Ron." Maxx laughed as he put his hand on Ron's shoulder. "We set sail soon."

"Aye, Aye, Captain." Ron happily led the crew of The Girlbee on board.

"Brady, you take Doug and Harper with you and navigate that ship," Maxx ordered. The three men hurried on board The Girlbee behind Captain Ron.

"Do not let them lose my ship," Lord Mason warned.

"Do not worry, they will be within sight of The Em at all times," Maxx assured Lord Mason. He turned to Nancie. "Once you have said your goodbyes, we will set sail."

"Little Man, you take some crazy chances." Alex laughed as he followed Maxx on board The Em.

"I really should take you to Huntington with me." After witnessing the naming of the ship, Lord Mason had serious doubts about Nancie leaving with these men.

"I am sure that Maxx will not allow that." Nancie hugged her uncle goodbye. She was grateful for his concern for her. She hated that her mother had missed this from her brother for so many years.

"Do not worry, Lord Mason." Jax shook Nancie's uncle's hand. "I will protect her with my life."

Chapter Thirty

The trip to Nettlesville went slower than they all had hoped. Even with the shorter route, that the Duke had shown to Maxx, this trip was still taking them at least ten days. The Em had to always stay within sight of The Girlbee. There were many dangers at sea for a small ship and Maxx was not taking any chances. Even with a strong wind in her sails, The Girlbee could not keep up with The Em.

Nancie did not like being on the ship. The sea was not comforting and pleasing to her as it was to the others on board. She could not understand how Maxx stayed out at sea for months at a time. To her, this was lonely and depressing. She was not seasick, she just did not like being on a ship.

In the evenings, she went up on deck and sat on a barrel near the ship's railing. Jax had set this spot up for the two of them near the stern of the ship. Here, at this spot, they were out of the way of the sailors and their duties.

When Nancie went up on deck this evening, she noticed that Paul was at the helm. Maxx was sitting near Paul on his seat by the railing. Jax had told her that this was Maxx's favorite spot on the ship. Maxx would sit there for hours, just resting and watching the sea.

Jax was talking to Caleb and Alex. It appeared that the three of them were teasing Maxx. This was something that the Shaw's did quite often. Maxx was leaning back against the ship's railing. His eyes were closed, but it was unclear to her if Maxx was resting or not. The little Captain was obviously ignoring the playful banter of the three Shaw men.

Nancie smiled and went to her quiet spot on the other side of the ship. Ollie was at his post a few feet away. He was keeping a vigil over The Girlbee. Nancie did admire the dedication that Maxx's sailors had. She knew they were loyal and trustworthy but until she

145

had seen them pulling together onboard The Em, she had not realized just how close of a group these men truly were.

"Ollie, why don't you give me your spyglass for a while? You can go below and have your dinner." Nancie held her hand out. "I will watch The Girlbee until you return."

"Thank you kindly, ma'am, but I am sure Eli will replace me soon enough." Ollie was not one to leave his post.

"It is quite alright. I am sure that Maxx will not mind." Nancie once again offered to take the spyglass.

"It is fine, Ollie." Jax sat down one of the barrels next to Nancie. "We do not mind watching The Girlbee for a while. You go on and get your dinner."

"If the Captain gets angry, I am sending Maxx to you two," Ollie teased. He was grateful to be getting his dinner early tonight. He handed Nancie the spyglass and hurried below.

Nancie sat down beside Jax and looked through the spyglass. The Girlbee was following The Em exactly like she was supposed to be. She could not help but to wonder why Maxx and the crew of The Em were so worried about Lord Mason's ship.

Ron was a good sailor. He had been with Maxx for many years. Maxx's father had hired Ron on as one of ship's first crewmen when Maxx had taken over The Em. Besides, Brady, Doug, and Harper were on board The Girlbee, so there was no way the ship would get lost. Then again, Ron was as free spirited as Maxx was, so she guessed there really was a chance that Captain Ron would sail to Spain on a whim. Maxx had done this many times. The thought made her laugh.

"I am glad that you are finally enjoying yourself." Jax had not heard Nancie laugh since they had left London.

"I was thinking of Captain Ron and Spain." Nancie had to admit that it felt good to laugh again.

"Maxx would go berserk if that happened." Jax did not like seeing Maxx angry. He was a little fellow, but when Maxx was angry, no one could handle him, except for Paul.

"You, Caleb, and Alex should not tease Maxx as much as you do." Nancie had wanted to say something earlier about this.

"Hey." Jax playfully narrowed his eyes at her. "You know, Maxx starts half of that. We only play along, most of the time anyway."

"You are probably right about that." Nancie knew Maxx well and had to agree with Jax. She lightly laughed and then looked through the spyglass again.

"You really do make a cute sailor." Jax winked when Nancie looked at him from the corner of her eye.

"I am just happy to have something to do." Nancie found sailing to be extremely boring.

"You have been helping Cook prepare the meals." Jax had seen her slip to the galley on several occasions.

"I like cooking and so does Rachel. I think I am going to keep serving meals at the Blume'N Brew. Thank you for suggesting it." Nancie hoped that Jax would stay on and help at the pub some more, but she was sure that his family members were ready to return home.

"You miss the pub." Jax was sure that she did.

"I have been at the Blume'N Brew for over half of my life." Nancie's voice was sad. "My mother died when I was twelve. My father was so overcome with grief that he just could not remain at the pub in St. Hartford anymore."

"Is that when your family moved to London?" Jax asked. Nancie's reply was the nod of her head.

Jax was beginning to understand why Nancie's father had brought his young daughter to live above a pub. He had been wondering why a father would do such a thing, but after hearing parts of Nancie's story, it was becoming clearer to him. Danny Blume could not stay in Hartford because of the grief he had over losing his wife. He had brought his young children with him because he could not stand to be parted from them.

"It is alright to learn new things." Jax wanted her to know that she was not betraying her parent's memories by doing something different.

"Change is hard for me," Nancie whispered.

"Your parents will always be with you, no matter where you go or what you do. I know that they would be proud of you no matter what you did." Jax took her hand in his.

"I could never leave the pub." Nancie looked out at the sea. She did not wish to discuss this matter.

"The building next door to the Blume'N Brew is for sale. It would be the perfect place to start a small restaurant and soup kitchen." Jax eyed her closely as he brought the matter up.

He had been wanting to talk with Nancie about this for weeks. He had acquired about the vacant building, for he truly wished to start a small soup kitchen like they had in Nettlesville. Jax knew that he had to approach this subject cautiously. Nancie was a loyal person, and she did not accept change easily.

"You wish for me to leave the pub because it would be a scandal for your family." Nancie sighed and dropped her head.

"You really would not be leaving. You would only be moving next door." Jax tried to explain the benefits of the restaurant. "There are rooms above it that could be turned into living quarters, just like you have at the pub. It would be perfect for us, and for Rachel."

"Us?" Would *'us'* truly ever work?" Nancie was hysterical. "You are asking me to leave my home, just to save your family of a scandal."

"That is not what I am doing." Frustrated, Jax got up and walked over to the ship's railing. "I only want to offer you something more." He turned to face her again. "You deserve more than a life in a pub."

"So, now I am not good enough for you?" Nancie was angry. "Well, my father thought that it was a good enough life for me. I do not see why I need to change it."

"You are twisting what I am saying." Jax struggled to remain calm.

His mother had always told Jax, and his brothers, that you must always speak calmly to a woman, especially if that woman holds your heart. He loved Nancie, but she did not seem to understand what calm was. How could he convince her that he was only trying to offer her another choice? It did not mean that what she knew was wrong.

"I will not leave my post." Nancie stated firmly. She held the spyglass up to her eye. She was done with this conversation.

"Your post?" Jax could not remain calm now. "You mean your promises to Maxx? Well, all of this seems to be Maxwell Spencer's fault, and he needs to fix it!"

Jax started to storm off and find Maxx. The dear little Captain needed to release Nancie of whatever promise she was locked into. Maxx should know better than to keep someone bound by an oath or a promise. He himself was locked into a ridiculous deal with the Duke of Greyham just to see that Alex was set free from prison, a place that Jax's cousin should not have been in to start with.

Before Jax could walk away, Nancie stood up and grabbed his arm. The look of fear on her face caused Jax to halt in his tracks. He wondered what could have her so distressed. Nancie slowly handed him the spyglass.

"Look." Nancie motioned toward The Girlbee.

With a sinking feeling in his heart, Jax looked through the spyglass. The sun had already set, but darkness had not fully overtaken them yet. He could see The Girlbee and she was sailing along behind The Em just as she should be. Everything appeared fine to him.

As Jax looked further in the distance, he froze. That letter R on the sails, and cut into the black flag, only meant trouble. The Raven and Captain Sayer were following The Girlbee. The pirate had gotten his nickname, Sayer the Slayer, for good reason. Sayer and his crew of misfits were known for burning and sinking ships at night. Jax's cousin Gavin had barely escaped with his life a couple years ago from a battle with The Raven.

"We need to find Maxx, now." Jax grabbed Nancie's hand and hurried toward the helm of the ship.

Chapter Thirty-One

Maxx rushed to the stern of the ship. He quietly watched The Girlbee and The Raven though the spyglass for several minutes. The entire crew of The Em stood at alert and waited for their Captain's orders.

"Drop anchor!" Maxx turned and shouted to the crew. Immediately, the sailors rushed to their posts to follow the order.

"What are we doing?" Jax was confused. He was concerned for Nancie's safety. Maxx was known for doing idiotic things at times.

"The Girlbee cannot defend herself against The Raven." Maxx tried to quickly explain his plan. "We are going to put The Em between her and The Raven."

"Do you really believe that The Raven is going to attack The Girlbee?" Jax put his arm around Nancie as he asked Maxx this question.

"More than likely, Sayer is just curious of a new ship in these waters, but we are not going to take any chances." Maxx turned and pointed at Nancie. "You, my friend, get below deck, now."

"I can stay and help." Nancie protested going to her quarters. She did not like being ordered around.

"That is really not a good idea." Jax was not going to let this happen.

"I cannot allow you to remain on deck." Maxx agreed with Jax and shook his head. "It would better if you went below."

"You have never ordered me about like this." Nancie narrowed her eyes at Maxx.

"Jax, get her to her quarters, now." Maxx did not have time to argue with Nancie.

"You cannot do this to me!" Nancie stomped her foot.

"On this ship, yea ma'am, I can." Maxx hated being so stern with her. "You have never sailed. You would only be in the way up here if a battle does happen."

"Because I am a woman and women do not belong on ships?" Nancie challenged Maxx. "Isn't that almost hilarious?"

"I know that you are hurt right now and that you do not understand, but do *not* do this." Maxx was not laughing.

"Jax, get her to her cabin, *now!*" Alex stepped in to help Maxx.

"Maxx, I…" Nancie did not get to finish apologizing. Before another word could be spoken, Jax took her by the waist and ushered her down the stairs.

Nancie did not struggle, or protest being sent below deck anymore. She felt terrible about what she had just done to Maxx. Jax's oldest brother, Nick, had done the same thing to Maxx last year and she was furious with him for it. Now, she had challenged Maxx as well. How could she ever make up for it?

"I know that you hate this, but it really is for the best right now." Jax told her when they reached her cabin, across from the Captain's quarters.

"I need to apologize to Maxx." Nancie was devastated.

"You will get your chance to apologize later. Besides, you did not really say anything too badly to him." Jax opened the door to her quarters.

The moment Jax opened Nancie's door, Maxx's little dog, Lucy, came running. Without waiting to be invited in, Lucy ran into Nancie's cabin. Jax rolled his eyes and shook his head. He never understood why Maxx had a dog on a ship to begin with.

"You have to tell Maxx that I am truly sorry." Nancie's plea was urgent as she grabbed Jax's arm.

"I will not pretend to understand the relationship between you and Maxx, but something sure needs to change here." Jax was now determined to find out just what Maxx had over Nancie.

"Just promise me that you will tell Maxx that I am sorry." Nancie bent down and picked up the little dog at her feet.

"I will." Jax gave Nancie a quick kiss on her cheek. He petted Lucy on the head before hurrying back on deck.

Jax went over and stood next to Maxx as they waited for The Girlbee to pass by. Maxx was unusually quiet. Jax was not sure if it was from the threat of Captain Sayer or if it was because of what had happened with Nancie. Hopefully neither issue would truly become a real problem. Perhaps Maxx was right, Sayer could just be curious of the new ship, and surely the matter with Nancie would be resolved easily.

Jax figured that the relationship between Nancie and Maxx was more serious than he had first thought. He looked down at Maxx from the corner of his eye. Whatever was between them, it had created a strong bond. When the threat with the pirate was over, Jax was going to have a long talk with Maxx.

"She did not mean it." Jax eyed Maxx closely.

"I am sure that she did not." Maxx never took his eyes off The Girlbee.

As Lord Mason's ship passed by The Em, Captain Ron stood on deck and waved at Maxx. Harper gave a small salute to assure Maxx that they were aware of the situation. Brady had spotted The Raven before anyone else had.

"The Em to the rescue!" Captain Ron shouted as The Girlbee sailed by.

There were no shouts of joy from the sailors of either ship this time. Waves of gratitude came from the crew of The Girlbee. Maxx admired Ron's ability to stay cheerful in a stressful situation. A captain's attitude always affected his crew. Maxx waved to Ron before motioning for the crew of The Em to pull anchor.

"Can The Em really protect both ships if Sayer attacks?" Jax was not aware that The Em was prepared for a battle.

"We can hold our own. The crew is already on standby to pull the cannons if we need them." Maxx went over and joined Paul at the helm.

"There are cannons on this ship?" Alex followed Maxx.

"The cannons are hidden on the second and third levels." Caleb answered his cousin's question.

"How do you know that?" Jax was curious for he and Alex knew nothing about cannons being on The Em.

"I helped Maxx and Paul to load them last year." Caleb took the spyglass from Maxx. "I will go and keep an eye on The Raven."

Jax was not aware that his brother knew anything about sailing. Caleb was not one to sit around Kinsley Estate for long periods of time. At times, Caleb would disappear for weeks. After Caleb's military service, he sometimes needed time alone to think things through. Those times usually had their mother overly worried. His older brother must have helped Maxx on some of his wayward trips to London.

"You and I need to have a long conversation." Jax pointed at Maxx. He wanted answers and he would not give up until he got them.

"After we dock in Nettlesville tomorrow, you and I, may or may not, have a long talk." Maxx stood boldly in front of Jax. "Tonight, I will stay right here on deck and watch that pirate ship. You will go below and keep our little blonde friend happy."

Maxx turned away from Jax and started giving more orders to the crew. The tone in Maxx's voice was enough for Jax to know that he should not push the little Captain further right now.

He narrowed his eyes at Maxx as horrible thoughts went through his mind. Was the tension between Nancie and Maxx so strong right now because something more than friendship had once been between them? This was not a pleasing thought for Jax. He could never imagine a romantic Maxwell Spencer.

"Do not test Maxx right now," Alex warned Jax. "There is a lot weighing on Maxx's mind."

"I understand why you are so loyal to Maxx. I really do. He did our family a great service by getting you out of prison, and I thank him greatly for that." Jax put his hand on Alex's shoulder. "There are just some things our little Captain needs to fix with Nancie. She is devasted right now."

"Maxx will settle things with Nancie. That is something you can be sure of." Alex knew their friendship meant a lot to Maxx.

"I hope you are right, cousin." Jax decided to let the matter drop, for now.

Alex did not push any further either. He went to stand watch with Caleb at the stern of the ship. Jax stood there for a moment and watched Maxx and Paul at the helm. Maxwell Spencer had secrets,

153

way too many secrets. Jax trusted Maxx for he had proven his loyalty to his family many times over the years. However, Jax just did not like secrets, they usually hurt more than they helped.

For now, Jax would let the little Captain keep his secrets. Once they were settled in Nettlesville, he would talk with Maxx. Jax had to have answers. He could not stand here and continue picturing Nancie and Maxx in an intimate relationship. He shook his head to clear the horrid thought from his mind.

Somehow, he would have to find a way to free Nancie from her promises to Maxx without losing their family friend in the process. It was going to be a delicate matter, but it was one that had to be dealt with, and soon. He liked Maxx, as did most of his family. Things were still questionable between Maxx and his Uncle Matthew, but that matter was beginning to settle.

Jax hurried down the stairs. Hopefully, Nancie would be calmer by now. He doubted that anyone on The Em would get much sleep tonight with The Raven behind them. Well, Lucy might be the only one that would get any sleep tonight.

Chapter Thirty-Two

The crew of The Em was exhausted when they reached Bryson's Landing in Nettlesville. The sailors had kept a constant watch on The Raven throughout the night. The pirate ship kept a safe distance and followed them to Nettlesville.

The Girlbee was now safely docked at the third dock at Bryson's Landing. This new dock had been built separate from the other two docks. This dock would permanently harbor the ship Lord Mason had sent to the island. Jax was glad to see that Lord Mason had listened to his cousin Nate and honored the request for a ship to be stationed here in Nettlesville. This would help the residents of the island greatly.

Maxx and his crew remained on board The Em and kept watch as The Raven docked at dock two. Jax took Nancie to the town inn. Ms. Dudley squealed with excitement when Jax walked through the door. Jax hurried over and wrapped his arms around the little woman.

"Jackson!" Miss Margaret rushed in through the door that connected her restaurant to the inn.

Jax had an arm around each of them as both ladies hugged him at the same time. Nancie could already tell that Jax was well loved by the residents here in Nettlesville.

A little girl hurried in from the restaurant behind Miss Margaret. She waited patiently while Jax hugged the two ladies. She rocked from side to side, causing her long straight brown hair to sway. When Jax noticed her, he stepped away from Ms. Dudley and Miss Margaret with a huge grin on his face.

"Hello, Jackson." The little girl held the skirt of her dress out as she properly curtsied before Jax.

"Why, Miss Macie Simmons, just look at you." Jax bowed before Macie.

Jax took Macie's hand and twirled her around a few times. The little girl giggled with delight. She wrapped her arms around Jax and hugged him tightly.

"I am glad you came back." Macie smiled up at Jax.

"We will not be staying long, but it is so good to see you." Jax spoke so tenderly to the little girl. "You have grown since I saw you last."

"I did!" Macie giggled as she bounced up and down. "And I am eleven now."

"You sure are growing up to be a fine young lady." Jax complimented Macie, causing her to blush. The encounter between Jax and Macie made Nancie smile.

Macie bounced around and giggled some more. She really was not one that could contain her excitement. Nancie was in awe of how gentle and loving Jax was with Macie. She was sure that he would be a wonderful father someday. That thought shocked Nancie to the core. How could she stand here and imagine Jax Shaw as a father?

Nancie had stunned herself so much that she had to cover her mouth with her hand to try and conceal a gasp. Macie had heard her anyway. The little girl turned and stared at Nancie. Miss Margaret and Ms. Dudley had not even noticed Nancie until now.

"Who is she?" Macie shyly stepped closer to Jax.

Jax walked over and took Nancie by the hand. He pulled her away from the door. He was happy to introduce her to the ladies of Nettlesville. Nancie was not sure why, but she felt a bit nervous.

"Ladies, I would like you to meet Nancie." Jax put his arm around her. "Nancie, this is Ms. Dudley, Miss Margaret, and the ever-adorable, Miss Macie Simmons."

"It is an honor to meet you." Nancie smiled at the three ladies. Ms. Dudley was exactly how Nancie had imagined her to be. Miss Margaret, however, was a lot younger than Nance had expected.

"Are you Maxx's Miss Nancie?" Miss Margaret asked.

Maxx's Miss Nancie? Jax did not like the sound of that. He was really going to have to find out more about Nancie's relationship with Maxwell Spencer.

"I run the Blume'N Brew pub in London, if that is what you are asking." Nancie noticed the horrified expressions on the two lady's faces at her reply.

"That is not very lady like." Macie took a step back.

"Macie, that is not a nice thing to say." Ms. Dudley slightly scolded the little girl.

"But it is true." Macie was defensive. "Mother says that a lady has no business in a pub."

"Macie, dear." Miss Margaret took the little girl by the hand and started leading her back toward the restaurant. "Speaking of your mother, she is expecting you for lunch. Why don't you run along on home?"

"Yes, Miss Margaret." Macie gave Jax another quick hug before hurrying home. Macie's words had hurt, but Nancie greatly admired the little girls' manners, up until that point anyway.

"Will you forgive the child, Miss Nancie?" Ms. Dudley politely smiled. "I am sure she was not aware that she was being rude."

"It is alright, I assure you." Nancie looked away, but she kept her head held high.

She could tell that these two women were not comfortable with her job. She knew that others looked down on women being in pubs. Those women were always considered something that they were not. Jax's mother was right, her job was considered scandalous.

"Ladies, Nancie runs the Blume'N Brew because it once belonged to her father and she cannot bear to part with it." Jax put his arm around her again. "Nancie is also Lady Nancie, Lord Mason's niece."

"You are our Lordship's niece and you run a pub?" Ms. Dudley looked from Nancie to Miss Margaret. Both ladies were confused. This was something they had never heard of before.

"It is true that my father once owned the pub. I took over after he died to help look after Maxx," Nancie replied.

"Oh, you are such a dear to help Maxx. He is so kind to us here." Miss Margaret kindly smiled at Nancie.

"We completely understand you helping Maxx." Joy now covered Ms. Dudley's face as well.

Jax and Nancie looked at each other. A moment ago, her owning a pub was scandalous. Yet, at the mention of Maxwell Spencer's name, all was greatly forgiven. This made Jax even more curious about Maxx's secrets. In time, and that time would be soon, he would find out just what those secrets were.

"Ms. Dudley, could we get four rooms for a few days? My brother and cousin are also with us." Jax followed the innkeeper over to the counter.

"I do not want a repeat of what happened the last time you and your brother were here." Ms. Dudley pointed at Jax as she playfully scolded him. "No more barroom brawls, young man."

"It is so nice to meet you, Lady Nancie." Miss Margaret curtsied before her. "I will go and have food trays prepared for you all. They will be sent to your rooms shortly." The little woman turned on her heels and hurried back to her restaurant.

Nancie was uncomfortable with being called Lady Nancie and being curtsied to. Was this what her life would have looked like if she had grown up at Huntington Estate? If so, this was something that she was glad she had missed.

"You should not have told them that Lord Mason was my uncle." Nancie waited patiently as Jax opened the door to her room.

"I could not watch them belittle you." Jax only wanted to protect her.

"It is still not a world that I am ready for." Nancie was not sure she would ever be comfortable among the nobles. Sure, her cousin Abby had adjusted to that world rather well, but she was afraid it was not for her.

"You should have never been cast outside the world of your birth status." Jax placed a soft kiss on her forehead.

He wanted her to be a greater part of his world in every way. For now, Jax would have to let Nancie find her own way through the changes that were coming to her life. As Lord Mason's niece, and the woman that held his heart, change was coming for Nancie's life whether she was ready for them to happen or not. Hopefully, those changes would bring them closer together rather than pushing them apart.

Chapter Thirty-Three

Jax stood outside the inn and watched as Captain Sayer, and his crew of pirates, entered Pete's Pub across the street. Sayer paused just outside the door and nodded at Jax before he entered the pub. Jax had done the same in return before going back into the inn behind Caleb and Alex.

"Where's Maxx?" Jax did not see any of Maxx's crew outside.

"Maxx is exhausted. He and the rest of the crew are resting on the ship." Alex yawned. He had remained on deck all night with Maxx and Paul.

"Maxx and Paul will join us for dinner at Miss Margaret's." Caleb rubbed his eyes. He too had remained on deck all night.

"Was there any trouble with Sayer at the docks?" Jax asked.

"None." Alex shook his head.

"You two go on up to your rooms. You will find a lunch tray waiting for you." Jax could tell they both needed to get some rest. "I will keep an eye on Sayer and see you at dinner."

Caleb and Alex could not protest that offer. Both were practically asleep on their feet. They would be grateful for a few hours of rest. After his brother and cousin went to their rooms, Jax decided to take a walk around the village. At least here he did not need guards following him around. Roger and Edmond were not allowed in Nettlesville anymore.

Jax met up with Marty Dudley, Ms. Dudley's son, and walked around the village. Marty had been appointed the Overseer of the community by Lord Mason. He had done a fine job following up on the plans for the island that Nate had left behind. Hopefully, someday, Nate would be able to return to Nettlesville and see how the community was prospering.

Even though Marty was the Overseer, he was also the village carpenter and he needed to get back to work on an order. Jax left Marty at his shop and walked out to Trevor Bryson's little fishing dock at the river. As he passed Trevor Bryson's house an eerie feeling came over him. It was good to see that the house and property was being well kept. Lord Mason made sure of this just in case his daughter, Abby, ever wanted to visit the house she grew up in.

Jax remembered the day they had found Trevor Bryson's body in house and Nate's wife, Olivia, was curled up, on the floor, in one of the bedchambers. Olivia did not see who threw the dagger that killed Abby's grandfather. She only knew that one of her half-brothers, Roger Holden or Edmond Prescott, were responsible for the old man's death. One day, Holden and Prescott would be held accountable for their crimes. Until that day, Jax would help to ensure that the members of his family were safe.

On the way back to the village, Jax ran into Hannah Simmons. He walked with her as she told him about some of the village gossip. To be such a small village, Hannah had some interesting tales that made Jax laugh out loud.

"I heard that my sister offended Lady Nancie earlier today." Hannah felt bad for what her little sister had said.

"So, you have also heard that Nancie is Lord Mason's niece?" When Hannah had referred to Nancie as Lady Nancie, Jax knew that word had already reached her family's home.

"Yes. Mother had visited Arthur Murray's shop earlier." Hannah looked at Jax and smiled. "You are in love with her, are you not?"

"Yes, I am." Jax's grin widened. It felt good to openly admit his feelings for Nancie.

"Have you told her?" Hannah had the uncanny ability to read people well.

"Sadly, no, I have not." Jax hated to admit this.

"Until you do, things will never move forward in your relationship." Hannah stopped outside of Miss Margaret's restaurant.

"Now, would you be talking from experience there, Miss Hannah?" Jax teased her.

"Well…" Hannah blushed as she looked down the street.

Jax's mouth dropped open when he saw Marty Dudley, standing at the door of his carpenter's shop, waving at Hannah. This was a match he would have never expected.

"That is a fine match, Miss Hannah." Jax truly meant it. "I am happy for you both."

After Hannah went into the restaurant, Jax looked up at the second floor of the inn. Nancie was standing in the window of her room. Jax smiled and waved at her. Nancie did not do the same. Instead, she frowned and turned away. They needed to talk, and soon. Jax did not like the distance that seemed to be growing between them.

"Hello, Jax." Polly Wilson, one of Miss Margaret's cooks, was pushing a food cart out of the side entrance of the restaurant.

"Here, let me help you with that." Jax hurried over and took the cart away from Polly. "I am guessing that we are taking this over to Pete's Pub."

"Yes." Polly was grateful for the help. There was extra food on the cart, and it made it difficult for her to push it by herself without spilling any of it. "Even though Miss Margaret has told the pirates that they could eat at the restaurant, they still prefer to have their meals in the pub."

"Miss Margaret does not serve ale and rum." Jax laughed at the shocked look on the young girl's face.

This was one of the reasons that he suggested serving meals at the Blume'N Brew to Nancie. Sailors, and just about every pub patron that he knew, loved food and drinks. Having both in one place was bound to attract more business for her. However, he truly hoped that she would consider the restaurant next door to the pub. She and Rachel could send food carts over the pub like Miss Margaret does here in Nettlesville.

Polly held the door to the pub open while Jax pushed in the food cart. The pirates sat together in the front right corner of the room, like they always did when Jax stayed in Nettlesville. Today, Captain Sayer must have brought his entire crew along with him. The pirates filled almost the full right side of the pub. The only table left empty along that wall was Maxx's favorite table in the very back corner.

"Awe, look." Cooper, Captain Sayer's first mate, raised his mug of ale to Jax. "The noble knight has been reduced to waiter."

The other pirates laughed and cheered as Jax helped Polly to set the platters of food on the tables. Captain Sayer sat calmly with his chair leaning against the wall. Jax had never seen the pirate Captain lose his temper. Well, there was that one incident where Sayer had threatened to kill Maxx when the pirates first showed up in Nettlesville, but that was quickly forgotten. Jax had never understood how Maxx and Sayer had agreed on their odd truce that day. Of course, he never really understood anything Maxx did.

"It is kind of you to return to Nettlesville." Sayer spoke calmly to Jax.

"I see that you still enjoy visiting Nettlesville." Jax set Captain Sayer's food tray on the table in front of him.

"I like the people here." Sayer continued to watch Jax closely. "I hear that the little pub owner from the Blume'N Brew is with you and that she is actually Lord Mason's niece."

"You do not need to trouble yourself over Lady Nancie." Jax snapped at the pirate.

"Lady Nancie?" Captain Sayer remained calm, even though his crew was now on edge with Jax's outburst. "You and I both know, that will be a hard one to pass over with the ladies in London's society set."

"I do not care what a bunch of silly gossiping women have to say." Jax struggled to control his anger.

"Ah, so the rumors are true." Captain Sayer leaned back in his chair and grinned at Jax. "Sir Jackson Shaw has fallen for the little pub owner."

"I can understand why." Cooper grinned slyly at Jax. "Without all that makeup, wig, and outlandish dresses, that little blonde pub owner makes a fine catch indeed."

"Fishing for blonde pub owners now, are ya?" Abe, one of the other pirates, slapped Cooper on the back. Abe's jest riled the pirate crew into shouts, cheers, and laughter.

"You will stay away from her!" Jax roared as he stepped closer to Cooper.

"Easy." Captain Sayer stood up and stepped in front of Jax. "No one here will ever harm your woman."

"You make sure that every member of your crew knows that." Jax angrily poked Sayer in the chest with his finger.

Jax's action caused every pirate in the pub to stand to their feet. Jax did not care. This crew did not frighten him like they did so many others. He continued to boldly stand there looking down into Captain Sayer's eyes. Sayer was taller than Maxx, but he was still short to Jax.

"Do not make me kill you." Sayer was calm and stern as he delivered his threat to Jax. "The last thing I ever want to do is help out Holden and Prescott."

"Jax." Pete took Jax by the arm and gently pulled him away from the pirates. "You go on and take Polly back to the restaurant. Tell Miss Margaret that I will have Sal to return the food cart back to the restaurant later."

Pete did not want to see a brawl here today. This one would not end like the one between Jax and his brother Caleb. This fight would surely end in Jax's death. One man could not take on an entire crew of pirates.

"Jax, please." Polly's plea snapped Jax out of his rage.

"I am not your enemy," Sayer said as he sat back down.

Polly was waiting by the door. The young girl was trembling with fear when Jax reached her. Jax took her by the arm and quickly led her out of the pub. He was going to have to suggest to Miss Margaret to not have Polly wait for the food cart ever again. Pete could always arrange for the cart to be returned to the restaurant.

"Go on." Jax motioned toward the restaurant. Polly heeded Jax's advice and quickly ran across the street.

Jax needed a few moments to calm down. He did not think it would be best for him to return to the inn in his current state of mind. He did not wish to run into Nancie when he was upset like this.

Jax decided to walk back out to Trevor Bryson's dock. He sat down on the edge and stared at the water. It was peaceful for him out here. He had spent many evenings sitting here, just thinking. Right now, he had a lot to think about.

No matter what, what was best for Nancie would always be his main concern. He loved her. There was no denying that fact. He knew that his family would never disown him for loving her. Still, he understood their concern. Scandals in London often ruined families.

There had to be a way for him and Nancie to be together without it destroying everything the Shaw family had built. Once everyone in London found out that she was Lord Mason's niece it should help a bit. Then again, Sayer was right, the women in London's society set were a cruel and vicious lot.

Jax sighed deeply and ran his fingers through his hair. He shook his head. How was he sitting here listening to the words of a pirate? Somehow, this pirate was well informed on matters in London. It had not escaped Jax that Captain Sayer was aware that Roger Holden and Edmond Prescott were trying to kill him.

Chapter Thirty-Four

That evening, Maxx and Paul joined the Shaw's and Nancie at Miss Margaret's restaurant for dinner. Even with a few hours of rest, Caleb, Alex, and Maxx were still tired. Paul had to rub his eyes several times to stay awake.

"We need more butter rolls." Jax said as he took the last one off the platter.

"I can see why you like them so much." Nancie had to agree with Jax, Miss Margaret really did make the best butter rolls she had ever tasted.

"I will get them." Maxx stood up and stretched before hurrying off to the kitchen.

"Do you not wish to follow him?" Alex teased Paul often because he was so protective over Maxx.

"It is just the kitchen." Paul narrowed his eyes at Alex. "I am sure the Captain will be fine."

"Of course, the Captain will be fine." Alex put his arm around Paul's shoulders. "You have guards at the back door, right?"

"You need more sleep." Paul, annoyed, shoved Alex's arm away.

"You two, play nice." Nancie pointed between Alex and Paul.

"Has Maxx said when we will be heading back to London?" Jax asked.

"The Captain wanted to leave in the morning, but I refused to let that happen." Paul rubbed the back of his neck with his hand. The entire crew of The Em was too tired to set sail again so soon.

"Wait." Alex turned his head sharply toward Paul. "*You* ordered our little Captain? How is that possible?"

"Maxx listens to me." Paul reached for his cup of coffee. "I step in when I need to."

"*You step in*?" Alex was beyond stunned. "Have you not been paying attention to half the things that Maxx does?"

"Alex, I am sure that Paul is aware of everything that Maxx does." Jax could already see the argument that was about to happen.

"Apparently not!" "Alex snapped at his cousin. He quickly turned back to Paul. "Half the things that Maxx does is ridiculous, not to mention dangerous. Did you forget to *'step in'* on those occasions?"

"I weigh in on almost everything Maxx does!" Paul shouted at Alex. "I never said that Maxx always listens to me. On those occasions, I do what is necessary to keep Maxx safe."

"Why are you two shouting?" Maxx came back with a platter of fresh baked butter rolls. "I could hear you all the way in the kitchen."

"We all are just tired." Paul refused to carry on with this conversation with Alex any longer.

"He is right." Alex did not want to argue with Paul either. Truth be told, Paul really did keep Maxx safe. "We are just tired."

"We were wondering, when will we be going back to London?" Nancie thought that it was best to change the subject.

"More than likely, in a couple of days." Maxx sat down between Nancie and Alex. "It might be longer though. It will depend on just how long Sayer stays here."

"We cannot leave until Sayer does?" Nancie did not like the sound of this. She had been away from the Blume'N Brew long enough.

"Sayer has done nothing to harm the people here. I doubt he ever will." Caleb was really shocked that Sayer liked Nettlesville so much.

"Do not fret." Jax covered Nancie's hand with his. "Sayer rarely stayed longer than a day or two when I was here. I am surprised that he has stayed this long. He usually makes his trades and leaves."

Captain Sayer and his crew had returned to The Raven for a few hours, but they did not leave the island. Jax had watched from the window of his room at the inn as Sayer visited a few of the shops in the village. Sayer continued to trade with the shop owners here. Jax did not understand why the pirate was helping the island prosper.

"Lady Nancie, would you care for some more tea?" Miss Margaret brought over a fresh pot of tea.

"Yes, thank you." Nancie politely smiled at Miss Margaret. She still was not used to being treated as a noble Lady. "This is excellent tea, Miss Margaret." Nancie complimented the restaurant owner after sipping the tea.

"Maxwell made it." Miss Margaret smiled sweetly at Maxx before walking over to another table.

Everyone at their table turned to stare at Maxx. Nancie knew that Maxx made great tea, but it had been a while since he had done so.

"Should we be worried?" Alex could not keep a straight face. "I mean, if you wish to give up rum and open a tea parlor, Little Man, go on ahead. We all will surely help you with that adventure."

Jax and Caleb could not contain their laughter any longer. Caleb laughed so hard he almost fell out of his chair. Nancie swatted Jax on the arm for laughing at Maxx. Surprisingly, Paul even laughed.

"My mother taught me how to make tea, I have you all to know." Maxx, being defensive, shoved Alex so hard that he did fall out of his chair.

Alex was stunned, but he was in such a hysterical state that he could not bring himself to be angry with Maxx. Instead, Alex looked up at Maxx, from the floor, and laughed even harder. Frustrated, Maxx grabbed a butter roll of the platter and stormed out of the restaurant.

"Do you all really have to tease Maxx so?" Nancie looked at Jax for help. "Maxx did not start that one."

Jax straightened up and wiped the grin off his face. She was right, Maxx did not do anything to prompt this. He wanted to keep peace with her. This was the most Nancie had talked to him since he announced that she was Lord Mason's niece. That was something he should have asked her permission of first.

"Cousin, you should ease up on Maxx," Jax scolded Alex.

"Thank you!" Paul snapped at Alex as he stood up.

"You are more than welcome, mate." Alex finally managed to get up off the floor. "All though, I am not sure as to why."

"You do realize that I now have to go across the street and make sure that the Captain does not get into a fight with a bunch of pirates, do you not?" Paul threw his napkin on the table and stormed out the door after Maxx.

"Oh, Jax!" Nancie quickly grabbed Jax's arm. For a moment everyone had forgotten about the pirates. "Please do not let Maxx get into a fight with those pirates. Sayer will surely kill Maxx if he has too much to drink."

Jax narrowed his eyes at Alex. He would love to thrash his cousin right now. Since they were not leaving Nettlesville in the morning, Jax was hoping to spend this evening with Nancie. He would love to walk with her around the village and introduce her to everyone. Now, thanks to his wonderful cousin, he had to go across the street to Pete's Pub and babysit Lord Maxwell Spencer. Trouble usually did follow the little Earl of Hartford.

"Do not fret. We will keep Maxx safe." Jax gave Nancie a quick kiss on her cheek. He waved his finger between Alex and Caleb. "You two can help me."

"You do realize that Maxx can take care of himself." Caleb did not doubt Maxx's abilities.

"In a normal fight, yes." Jax would agree with his brother. "But we are dealing with pirates, and pirates do not fight fair."

"Maxx is not loony enough to pick a fight with a bunch of pirates." Alex thought for a moment. "Aye, you are right. We should go watch out for Little Man."

Jax paused at the door and looked back at Nancie. She could see his reluctance to leave her. Nettlesville was a strange place for her. She was sure that Jax did not wish to leave her by herself. Maxx was tired and not thinking straight. After a few mugs of rum, Maxx would be a handful for Paul.

"You go on. I will be fine here." Nancie smiled. "Miss Margaret and Ms. Dudley will keep me company."

"Are you sure?" Jax wanted to stay with her, but Paul may need their help tonight.

"I am sure." Nancie walked over and stood on her tiptoes and placed a tender kiss on Jax's cheek. "I will see you after Maxx is safely back on The Em for the night."

Jax placed his hand against her cheek. Her green eyes held happiness tonight rather than the sadness that was there since they had left London. Her smiled moved him and he could not help but to lean down and press his lips to hers. Slowly, he raised his head. He grinned when the gentle gasped escaped her lips.

"Wait up for me." Jax whispered next to her ear.

With a new kind of hope in his heart, Jax hurried across the street to Pete's Pub. Somehow, they had to get Maxwell Spencer to his ship for the night, and they needed to do it quickly.

Chapter Thirty-Five

When Jax entered Pete's Pub, Captain Sayer was sitting at the table next to Maxx's. This was a little too close for comfort for Jax. Sayer was sitting against the wall calmly surveying the room, as he had always done when Jax stayed in Nettlesville last year.

Maxx was at the bar getting a bottle of rum from Pete. The room was filled with local villagers, pirates, and the crew of The Em. Captain Ron was lively tonight. He sat in the middle of the room still cheering the sailors on with his temporary promotion.

"Captain Ron." Maxx walked over and put his hand on Ron's shoulder. "This all ends at midnight. Tomorrow, I fully expect my crewman Ron to be back on The Em, like always."

"Aye, Aye, Captain." Ron turned and shouted to the crew. "One final volley for Captain Ron and the crew of The Girlbee!"

The sailors, once again at Ron's prompting, erupted into shouts, cheers, and laughter. Ron really was good for the moral of the crew. The pirates looked at each other and snickered as the sailors got another round of drinks.

"And they call us loony." Cooper leaned over and whispered to Captain Sayer.

Captain Sayer lightly laughed and waved the matter away with his hand. His eyes followed Maxwell Spencer as the little Captain walked around the room. He had to give Spencer credit, he checked on his entire crew before returning to his table in the corner.

"That is a fine ship that Lord Mason sent to the island." Captain Sayer looked over at Maxx.

"These people need that ship!" Jax snapped at the pirate Captain.

"We would never do anything to harm the good people here." Cooper understood what Jax was implying.

"I promised your little Captain here, on the day we first met, that I would help to protect this island, and we will continue to do so." Sayer assured Jax that his crew could be trusted.

"The day we first met, that was an interesting day indeed. I remember it well." Maxx stared Sayer in the eye for a moment before turning back to his mug of rum.

"Slow down there, Little Man." Alex tried to take the second bottle of rum from Maxx. "You should really go on back to The Em and get some more sleep."

"Thank you, Mother, but I am fine." Maxx patted Alex on the arm.

Maxx did manage to win the battle for the bottle of rum. It was true, he was tired. Plus, these Shaw men were irritating him greatly this evening. Maxx yawned and rubbed his eyes. Perhaps Alex was right, he should go get some sleep.

"Perhaps you should consider retiring." Captain Sayer looked over at Maxx again. "It seems that sea life has finally gotten to you." Cooper and the rest of the pirates laughed.

"Retire!" Maxx shouted as he bolted upright in his chair, alarming everyone at the table. "That is exactly what I should do." Maxx slapped his hand against the table and nodded his head at Sayer.

"What are you doing?" Paul was now greatly concerned about Maxx's mental state.

"I am thinking about retiring," Maxx replied with a huge smile on his face. "I should settle down and open that tea parlor."

"You have had enough rum." Alex successfully grabbed the bottle of rum this time.

"I have not had near enough rum," Maxx informed Alex.

"Settle down? Do you mean, get married?" Caleb was shocked. He never imagined Maxx married before.

"Just who would you marry anyway?" Jax could never picture a romantic Maxwell Spencer. Thankfully, Maxx and Rachel did not openly show affection at the Blume'N Brew.

Jax could not help but to laugh at the thought of Maxx getting married. He knew that he was supposed to be keeping Maxx calm tonight, but right now, Maxx was out of his head. Paul needed to get him to the ship and soon.

"Your cousin," Maxx declared as he pointed his finger at Jax.

"What!" Everyone around Maxx shouted the word at the same time, even Captain Sayer.

"Little Man, you are not marrying my sister!" Alex grabbed Maxx and turned him until their eyes met.

"Why not? It would solve so many problems." Maxx patted Alex on the arm. "Dani would make a fine wife, and she could help out at the tea parlor."

"You are not marrying Dani." Jax liked Maxx well enough but he was not the man to be marrying his little cousin.

"You already refused to marry Dani," Caleb reminded Maxx.

"I have changed my mind." Maxx turned up his mug of rum and finished it off.

"You cannot seriously let him marry your sister." Captain Sayer leaned over and spoke to Alex.

"Maxx is not marrying my sister," Alex assured Sayer. "My mother has already said no."

"Your father would greatly approve. It would put an end to this silent feud he and I have." Maxx got up from the table and got another bottle of rum from Pete.

"For the last time, you are not marrying my sister!" Alex shouted at Maxx.

"I will duel you for her!" Maxx shouted as he unsheathed his sword.

"That is not happening." Paul stepped in between Maxx and Alex.

"Oh, it certainly is." Maxx started for the door. "In the street Shaw! I have a wife to win!"

The entire crew of The Em hurried outside behind their Captain. Even the pirates followed along to see if this duel would take place. Paul tried to settle the crew down, but no one listened to him.

"Maxx is tired and drunk." Jax pulled Alex to the side. "You cannot duel with him."

"It is better for me to duel with Maxx, rather than one of these pirates." Alex whispered and pushed Jax aside.

"This cannot be happening," Captain Sayer mumbled as he followed everyone outside.

"Captain, we should stay out of this." Cooper warned Sayer.

"And let Spencer…" Sayer could not even say the words.

"This is not your battle today. Lord Alexander has this under control." Cooper tried to hold Sayer back but failed to do so.

The street outside the pub was soon crowded with onlookers. The duel between Maxx and Alex quickly caught the attention of every shop owner in the village. Everyone gasped in horror as Captain Sayer unsheathed his sword and stepped into the street next to Alex.

"Stay out of this!" Alex shouted at Sayer.

"I am helping you to defend your sister's honor," Sayer explained.

"If I win, I will marry your sister and open that tea parlor!" Maxx shouted and pointed his sword at Alex. He paid Sayer no mind.

Soon, Polly Wilson came running into the restaurant. She screamed and cried as she tried to find Miss Margaret. The hysterical girl alarmed everyone in the restaurant.

"What is the matter?" Nancie jumped up and grabbed the young girl by her shoulders.

"It is horrible, My Lady, just horrible." Polly cried and ran to the back of the restaurant.

Nancie and Miss Margaret hurried outside. The crowd circled the street, preventing a clear view of what was happening. Ms. Dudley was in tears and clutching the post at the edge of the walkway. Shouts and the clashing of swords soon filled Nancie's ears.

"Maxx," Nancie whispered. She just knew that, somehow, Maxx had managed to pick a fight with a pirate.

Nancie stepped down off the wooden walkway that was connected to the inn and the restaurant. She had to see what was happening. Somehow, she had to help Maxx.

"Lady Nancie, please wait here," Miss Margaret cried.

Nancie ignored the woman and pushed through the crowd of men. She finally managed to make her way to the front of the crowd. Jax grabbed her and held her back. He stood in front of her, blocking her view of the duel.

"What is happening?" Nancie cried. "You were supposed to keep Maxx safe. Now, a pirate is going to kill our friend."

"Maxx is dueling with Alex," Jax told her.

"What?" Nancie was confused. "Why would he do that?"

"Maxx wants to marry Dani." Jax stepped aside to let her see the duel.

Maxx and Alex stumbled around in the street, shouting at each other. Neither of them could hold their swords well and stand up straight at the same time. At times, both fell to the ground. Captain Sayer was circling around them, waiting for a chance to enter the battle.

"They both are clearly drunk." Nancie grabbed Jax's arm. "You have to stop this before one of them gets hurt."

"How?" Caleb could see no easy way to break up this duel. "In their state, they will more than likely kill anyone who interferes, without even realizing what they are doing."

"Look over there." Jax put his arm around her and pulled her close to his side, as he pointed across the street. "See, Paul is trying to get close to Maxx. When he grabs Maxx, I will run in and grab Alex."

"They could seriously hurt each other before then." Nancie was now furious. She huffed and stormed back into the restaurant.

Nancie knew there was not a moment to spare. This duel had to end now. Since no one else would step in, she would just have to take matters into her own hands.

"Lady Nancie, what are you doing?" Miss Margaret called out from behind her. She and Ms. Dudley followed Nancie into the kitchen.

"Come, ladies." Nancie motioned for the two women to continue following her. "We are going to stop this outlandish duel."

Chapter Thirty-Six

Miss Margaret and Ms. Dudley followed closely behind Nancie, out into the street. Each of them carried a pail of cool water. Nancie had instructed the two ladies to quickly hand her the pails as she needed them, then to hurry back to the safety of the restaurant. She would take full responsibility for her actions this evening.

Nancie made sure to avoid the area where Jax and Caleb were standing. She knew, without a doubt, that Jax would stop her when he realized what she was about to do.

The sight before her would have been hilarious if it were not for the fact that Maxx and Alex were clearly drunk and tired. Plus, there was a pirate just waiting for an opportunity to join in the fight.

Neither Maxx nor Alex could manage to wield a sword properly. Maxx, even in his drunken state, still managed to knock Alex's feet out from under him several times. Nancie could not believe that this outrageous duel was over Maxx wanting to marry Dani. Maxx would probably regret this tomorrow.

"You are not marrying my sister!" Alex shouted as he stood to his feet again.

"I am an Earl!" Maxx yelled. "Your sister would be set for life!"

Captain Sayer continued to circle close, but he did not interfere, yet anyway. Now, was Nancie's perfect opportunity. The three unsuspecting duelers were close. She made her move and pushed through the final group of men between her and the battle. The element of surprise was going to be her only advantage here. She just hoped that Miss Margaret and Ms. Dudley had stayed on her heels as she had instructed them to do.

Once she was in the open, Nancie took the pail in her hands and threw the water in Maxx's face just as he turned in her direction. Alex, shocked by the action, quickly turned to see what was happening.

Nancie dropped the pail in her hand and took the one Miss Margaret was handing to her. She quickly threw the water in Alex's face as well. Without missing a step, Nancie grabbed the third pail and threw the water on Captain Sayer.

Thankfully, with the three drunken duelers unable to continue the duel, their protectors stepped in. Paul grabbed Maxx and started pulling the little Captain toward the docks. Jax and Caleb grabbed Alex and pulled him into the inn. Cooper took Captain Sayer back into Pete's Pub. Once Paul had Maxx on The Em, Cooper would take Sayer to The Raven.

"Gentlemen, that is it for today." Nancie quickly clapped her hands and held them out to the crowd. "Show's over."

Once inside the inn, Jax handed Alex off to Caleb. He could not believe this ridiculous duel had even taken place just now. He was even more shocked at how Nancie had put an end to it. He should have known that she would not walk away quietly.

"Take him to his room and see that he does not come out anymore tonight." Jax was furious.

"I will lock him in if I have to." Caleb took Alex by the arm and pulled his drunk cousin up the stairs.

"What were you thinking?" Caleb pushed Alex into his room.

Alex sighed deeply and pulled off his wet shirt. Once he had changed clothes, Alex laid down on the bed and smiled as he looked up at the ceiling.

"Dear cousin, at least have Miss Margaret to send me up a food tray," Alex requested.

"Wait." Caleb walked over to the side of the bed. "You are not drunk, are you?"

"Not at all." Alex stretched his legs out and put his hands behind his head.

"Why would you do that?" Caleb had been completely fooled by his cousin's little ruse.

"Like I told your brother, it was better for Maxx to duel with me, rather than one of those pirates." Alex explained his actions.

"Right." Caleb understood what Alex had just done for Maxx. "If I have to, I will bring the food tray to you myself."

Alex's ruse was just as ridiculous as Maxx wanting to duel over marrying Dani. Still, Alex had kept one, tired and drunk, little Maxwell Spencer safe tonight. For that, Caleb would make sure that Alex got everything he needed tonight.

With his cousin now dealt with, Jax hurried back out to the street. Nancie was there, dismissing the crowd. He noticed that Miss Margaret and Ms. Dudley were standing outside the restaurant door, clinging to each other. No doubt they were scared out of their minds, but still, they managed to bravely help Nancie tonight. Jax's heart almost fell from his chest when he saw Nancie and these two ladies step out of the crowd with the pails of water.

Nancie was one to think fast on her feet. Jax was proud of that fact about her. She also was not afraid to act when others would not. This fact scared him beyond belief. He was going to have a hard time protecting his feisty little blonde pub owner.

Jax went over and took Nancie by the hand. She looked up at him and sweetly smiled. For added measure, she even batted her eyes at him.

"Oh no, My Lady." Jax waved his finger back and forth in front of her face. "That little trick does not work with me."

"Well, somebody had to do something." Nancie was now serious again.

"You are right, but what you did was dangerous. Promise me that you will never do anything like that again." Jax bent down and gathered up the three pails.

"I cannot promise that." Nancie shook her head. It was a promise that she would never be able to keep.

"Trust me, I already know." Jax motioned toward the restaurant. He and Nancie started walking in that direction. "You cannot blame me for trying though."

"Would the two of you like to finish your dinner?" Miss Margaret asked as she took the empty pails from Jax.

"Miss Margaret, we would love to, but it has been a trying evening for us all." Jax kindly declined her offer.

As they entered the restaurant, Caleb came from the kitchen with a food tray. Jax was surprised, for Caleb did not usually take a second meal so soon.

"Did watching the duel give you an appetite?" Jax teased his brother.

"This is for Alex." Caleb ignored his little brother's jest.

"He should go to bed without his dinner." Nancie was extremely upset with Alex. "He should have known better than to have a drunken duel with Maxx."

"Alex is not drunk." Caleb did not like the tone in Nancie's voice.

"Are you sure?" Jax narrowed his eyes and thought for a moment.

"It was all an act," Caleb replied before going back to the inn.

"Why would Alex pretend to be drunk?" Nancie did not understand.

"Aw." Jax sighed and leaned his head back. "Of course, Alex said before the duel, that it was better for him to duel with Maxx rather than one of those pirates."

"So, Alex was protecting Maxx all along?" Nancie would never understand how the minds of men worked.

"It appears so." Jax was rather pleased with his cousin.

"Miss Margaret, I think that we will take that dinner after all." Nancie smiled at the little woman. "Would you mind sending us up a tray up to my room?"

"Not at all, Lady Nancie." Miss Margaret was thrilled with the idea. She quickly disappeared into the kitchen.

"You wish for us to dine, in your room?" Jax was a bit stunned at this change in events.

"Now that Maxx is safely back on The Em and we do not have to worry about taking care of your drunken cousin, yes. I do believe that I would love to dine with you in my room." Nancie was sure that this was cause a scandal back in London. However, they were not in London right now, were they?

"My Lady, you greatly surprise me." Jax brought her hand up to his lips.

"I will go and change out of these wet clothes. I suggest that you, my dear sir, go and do the same." Nancie gently squeezed Jax's hand before hurrying to her room.

Jax quickly went to his room. Grabbing Alex had gotten him wet as well. He was excited that Nancie wanted to dine with him, alone in her room. Could the walls that she had built around herself finally be falling? Could this be a major turning point in their relationship? Jax was eager to find out.

After changing, Jax ran into Miss Margaret outside of Nancie's door. He took the food tray from her and placed a light kiss on her cheek, to say thank you. Miss Margaret had always been his favorite person in Nettlesville.

Their meal was a wonderful time between them, where they talked and laughed the entire time. After the meal was over, Nancie had Jax to light the fire in the fireplace while she spread out a blanket on the floor.

"I rather like this side of you." Jax sat down beside her and wrapped his arms around her. "I could really get use to this."

"If only we could stay like this." Nancie snuggled close to his side.

"We will have many decisions to make soon." Jax would love nothing more than to clear all the obstacles out of their way.

Nancie turned in Jax's arms to face him. The warmth of the fire was soothing to her. It was the end of September and there was a chill in the air, coming off the sea. She did not wish to discuss troubling issues tonight. Tonight, she only wanted peace and Jax's arms around her.

"Not tonight." Nancie spoke softly as she placed a finger to Jax's lips. "Tonight, I only want this."

Nancie pressed her lips to his. Her boldness sent Jax's emotions out of control. He wrapped his arms around her and pulled her even closer to him. Slowly, he lowered her down to the blanket. When their kiss ended, Nancie nuzzled close to Jax's side. There were no more words passed between them this night. As they lay on the floor, with only the sounds of the fire and their beating hearts, all else was forgotten. Sleep soon found them both.

Chapter Thirty-Seven

The next morning, Jax and Nancie found Maxx at Miss Margaret's restaurant. Maxx's eyes were closed, and his head was leaned back. A cool cloth was across Maxx's forehead to try and ease the ache in his head. Paul poured the little Captain another cup of coffee.

"Good morning." Jax grinned at Maxx. Paul quickly shook his head.

"Here is your morning remedy." Miss Margaret set a glass in front of Maxx. "Mandy Bryson's recipe sure works wonders."

Maxx sat up straight and rubbed his eyes. When he opened his eyes, Alex was sitting across the table from him. For a moment, Jax feared that these two would start fighting again. Thankfully, neither of the two spoke.

Maxx was not used to being on the losing end of things. Of course, the duel had not come to an actual end, but still, the little Earl had not officially won the battle.

"Are we all good here?" Jax looked between Alex and Maxx.

"That will be up to Little Man there." Alex did not wish to continue arguing with Maxx.

"We are fine," Maxx mumbled.

Maxx picked up the glass in front of him. He did not like the looks of this 'morning remedy' that Miss Margaret had given him. He eyed the glass closely for several minutes.

"You two should know better than to argue with each other." Nancie looked at Maxx out of the corner of her eye, as she poured herself a cup of coffee.

Maxx ignored her and finally decided to just turn the glass up and drink the contents. Everyone was startled when Maxx spit some of the liquid out. Nancie quickly grabbed a napkin in fear that Maxx was about to lose his stomach.

"That is horrible." Maxx snatched the napkin out of Nancie's hand and wiped his mouth.

"When you act less than a gentleman, horrible things will happen." Miss Margaret took the glass from Maxx and poured him another cup of coffee.

Maxx nodded his head at Miss Margaret but made no reply. There was really nothing that he could say. He was embarrassed over his own actions yesterday. The others grinned at Miss Margaret's remark but decided it was best to not say anything. That was, until Caleb joined them.

"Is this feud really over, or are you still insisting on marrying Dani?" Caleb got straight to the point, as he sat down next to Alex.

"I have no desire to marry your cousin or any other woman." Maxx stood up. "We sail in the morning." With that, Maxx left the restaurant with Paul right behind him.

"You should probably just avoid Maxx today." Jax looked over at his cousin. Alex nodded his head in agreement.

They all decided that it was best to just give Maxx some time to clear his head and nurse his wounded pride. They spent the rest of their morning meal discussing what they would do on their last day in Nettlesville. They all were looking forward to going back to London.

Jax was thrilled that he was going to be able to show Nancie around the village and introduce her to everyone. He really wanted to show her the soup kitchen behind the restaurant and inn.

Nancie enjoyed walking around Nettlesville on Jax's arm. However, she was still not comfortable being introduced as Lady Nancie, Lord Mason's niece. In fact, it irritated her greatly.

She could not help but to notice how excited Jax was when he showed her the soup kitchen that Miss Margaret had set up behind her restaurant. Ms. Dudley had pitched in and helped to expand the area behind the inn as well. The soup kitchen was mainly used during the winter months when times were harder in Nettlesville. Still, anytime someone needed a meal and could not afford it, they were served.

"We will have some serious decisions to make soon." Jax slowly brought the subject up as they walked out to Trevor Bryson's fishing dock.

"We do not have to do that today." Nancie walked over to the edge of the little dock.

"You cannot keep avoiding it. You are going to have to face things, and soon." Jax wished that she would allow for them to finally have the serious conversation that they needed to have.

"That is true." Nancie was aware that she needed to make some serious decisions soon, but she hoped to avoid that for a little longer.

"What are you so afraid of?" Jax gently took her by the arm and turned her to face him. If he knew the answer to this, perhaps he could help her.

"Making those decisions will mean that things will have to change." Nancie's eyes pleaded with him to understand how she felt.

"The only way for things to move forward is for them to change." Jax wanted her to understand his feelings as well.

"What if I am happy the way things are?" Nancie's voice rose slightly.

"Things have already happened that will force things to change whether you wish for them to or not." Jax reached for her, but Nancie stepped away.

"You want me to give up my pub and be someone that I am not." Nancie was extremely defensive now.

"I am offering you solutions and trying to help you become who you were born to be." Jax held his hands out as he pleaded with her.

"You only want to save your family from being shunned for knowing me!" Nancie shouted.

"You know that is not true." Jax pointed his finger at her. "Of course, I want what is best for my family, but I also want what is best for you as well."

"I am fine, right where I am." Nancie folded her arms across her chest.

"You know, it is not just my family's reputation that's at stake. Lord Mason will also be ridiculed." Jax informed her of another threat in society. "You are his niece, and he will be shunned as well."

"I did not wish for Lord Mason, or anyone else, to ever know that I was his niece!" Nancie huffed and turned her back to Jax. "Maxx had no right to do that to me."

"You may be right about that." Jax walked over to the other side of the dock with his back to her as well.

"It is best that we just leave things as they were." Nancie's voice was low as she turned to go back to the village.

"You cannot honestly mean that." Jax caught her by the arm. "Not after last night."

"I do." Nancie held her head high. Yes, this hurt her deeply, but it had to be what was best for them. "You go home to Kinsley Estate. Your mother will be thrilled to have you safely home. I will remain at the Blume'N Brew and continue to protect Maxx."

"Protect Maxx!" Jax shouted. "Maxwell Spencer can protect himself!"

"Yesterday sure proved differently," Nancie snapped. "That duel should have never taken place."

"I will grant you, that is true." Jax had to agree on that matter. "But it does not mean that you have to protect Maxx."

"Maxx needs me!" Nancie insisted.

"That's it!" Jax pointed his finger at her again. "Your relationship with Maxwell Spencer, whatever it maybe, needs to change!"

"I am going back to the inn," Nancie declared. She stomped off the dock. This conversation was over with, as far as she was concerned.

"You do that!" Jax was furious. He turned and headed in the opposite direction.

"Where are you going?" Nancie yelled.

"To find our dear little Captain. He has some explaining to do!" Jax shouted, without looking back.

Jax took the shorter path back to the docks from the river. He was finally going to get some answers out of Maxx. He knew that Nancie would never betray Maxx's trust and truthfully answer any of his questions. So, it was time for the little Earl to talk.

Chapter Thirty-Eight

Nancie hurried back to the inn. As she was walking past the restaurant little Macie Simmons walked out with two women. One, Nancie was certain was the little girl's mother. The other woman she had seen, from her window, talking with Jax in the street.

"Hello, Lady Nancie." Macie politely curtsied. The little girl really knew her manners.

"Hello, Miss Macie." Nancie smiled at the little girl.

"This is my mother and my sister, Hannah." Macie proudly introduced her family.

"It is nice to meet you." Nancie gave a slight nod of her head and turned to go.

"Are you alright, Lady Nancie?" Hannah asked before she could walk away.

"I will be fine." Nancie grinned and started to walk away again.

"Mother, why don't you take Macie on home?" Hannah turned and faced Nancie. "Lady Nancie and I will have a cup of tea at Miss Margaret's."

Nancie sighed and politely smiled. She did not wish to have tea with Hannah Simmons, but how could she refuse the young woman, without causing more problems? Hopefully, Hannah would be one to drink her tea fast with little conversation.

Hannah led Nancie over to one of the smaller tables along the far wall of the restaurant. Miss Margaret was thrilled to see the two of them together. She brought over a tray with fresh tea and biscuits.

"I am so glad that we have a chance to do this before you all leave in the morning." Hannah poured them both a cup of tea.

"Did Jax tell you that we were leaving tomorrow?" Nancie wondered what else Jax may have shared with this woman.

"No, I have not seen Jax." Hannah placed a biscuit on Nancie's plate. "I talked with Maxx earlier."

"Maxx was not very talkative this morning." Nancie sipped her tea. She hoped to finish this cup and go to her room.

"You looked a bit upset outside? I do hope that everything is alright." Hannah sat back and watched Nancie. "Can I help in any way?"

"I just have a lot of decisions to make." Nancie felt awkward talking with Hannah about this. "I am sure they all will work out for the best, in time."

"I am sure that you and Jax will figure things out as you go." Hannah reached for her teacup.

"What exactly has Jax said to you?" Nancie was deeply curious.

"All I know is, Jax loves you." Hannah set her teacup back on the table.

"So, Jax has not discussed our relationship with you?" Nancie asked.

She was still not sure how she felt about Hannah Simmons. Nancie was becoming frustrated with the woman's vague answers. While watching Jax talk with Hannah, she was aware of how easily the two of them could talk to each other. In fact, it was something that Nancie even envied a bit.

"No," Hannah replied. "I only spoke with Jax, for a moment, on the street the other day. That was the only time we have spoken since you all arrived."

The conversation that she had witnessed between Jax and Hannah from her window was a brief one. There had not been time for Jax to say very much to Hannah. Nancie wondered how the young woman seemed to know so much, with so little information.

"Thank you for the tea, and your kindness is greatly appreciated." Nancie quickly finished her tea and biscuit with hopes of leaving.

"I thought you looked as if you could use a friend." Hannah went to refill Nancie's teacup.

"It is quite alright, Hannah." Nancie touched Hannah's wrist to stop her. "I think that I am just going to retire to my room for a while."

185

"He does love you. Everyone can see that he does." Hannah spoke boldly. "It was hard for me to accept Marty's affections at first, but in time, I realized that I loved him as well."

Nancie was not aware that Hannah was being courted by Marty Dudley. Now it was clear to her how Hannah seemed to know so much. Hannah was witnessing a troubled relationship and was kindly offering friendship to her.

"He wants me to change my entire life." Nancie had no idea why she was telling Hannah this. "I do not know if I can do that."

"Is not love worth changing for?" Hannah asked.

Nancie was relieved to see Marty Dudley walk into the restaurant. He gave her the distraction she so greatly needed to make her excuse to leave Hannah. She wished the young couple well and quickly hurried up to her room.

Nancie sat down in the big chair, by the fireplace, in her room. Watching the flames of the fire brought back the memories of last night. She and Jax had fallen asleep, on the floor, by this fireplace. She had never spent the night wrapped in a man's arms before. Was loving Jax betraying John's memory?

Hannah's question haunted her mind long after Nancie had left the restaurant. Was what she and Jax had genuinely love? Was love worth changing your entire life for? Did she dare reach for a life with Jax, or was it best for everyone for her to send him away forever?

Nancie wiped the tears from her cheeks with her hands. How did she even fall in love with Jackson Shaw to begin with? Soon, she was going to have to decide if her love for Jax was strong enough for her to change her life. If not, she would need to set Jax free soon. She could not help but to wonder, was it already too late for her to let him go?

Chapter Thirty-Nine

Jax hurried on board The Em. He found Maxx in the Captain's quarters. Paul did not look pleased that Jax had barged in without knocking first.

"We need to talk," Jax demanded.

"Now is not a good time." Paul tried to push Jax out the door.

"Now is the perfect time." Jax was not taking no for an answer today. He stormed across the room and grabbed Maxx by his shirt.

"You need calm down." Maxx stared Jax in the eye.

"I need answers!" Jax shouted.

"You need to put me down before I let myself down." The look in Maxx's eyes left no room for defiance.

Jax now realized that he had pulled the little Captain of his feet. He did not wish to fight with Maxx. Gavin had done so, only once, and lost badly. Slowly, Jax set Maxx on his feet and gently patted his shoulders.

"You need to leave, now." Paul stepped between them.

"Paul, let him speak." Maxx motioned for Jax to join him at his desk. "What has you so out of sorts today?"

"You need to release Nancie from the oath and promises she has made to you." Jax would not leave here until Maxx had done so.

"I cannot do that." Maxx looked Jax calmly in the eye.

"Why not?" Jax leaned forward and hit the desk with his fist. "You know how horrible it is to be bound to someone. It was your own choosing, and I thank you for it, but you hate the deal you made with the Duke."

"I can assure you that my deal with the Duke of Greyham is nothing like the promises Nancie made to my father." Maxx reached for the cup of coffee Paul set on his desk. He was not going to argue about this matter.

"Just because you have worded it differently, does not mean that it is any different." Jax, frustrated, leaned back, and folded his arms across his chest. "At least one day, you will be free of the deal with the Duke. Nancie, however, will never be free."

"Why does Nancie's promise to Maxx matter so much to you?" Paul pulled another chair over to the desk and joined them. He was watching Jax closely. One fight between Maxx and a Shaw was enough.

"Nancie cannot move forward because of that promise," Jax explained. "She has to protect Maxx."

"Protect me?" Maxx was greatly confused. He looked at Paul then back to Jax. "What do you mean, she has to protect me?"

"She says that she cannot leave the Blume'N Brew because of her promise to you." Jax tapped his fingers lightly on the desk.

"Her promise to my family does not mean that she cannot leave the pub. Nancie can live her life as she chooses." This conversation was making Maxx's aching head throb even more. He reached for a bottle of rum from the small cabinet behind his desk.

"You do not need that." Paul snatched the bottle out of Maxx's hand before he could open it.

"Then her reluctance to leave, or to change her life, is because of her relationship with you." Jax narrowed his eyes at Maxx. "Exactly what has happened between the two of you? Have you dishonored her?" Jax's temper was starting to rise.

"Nancie is family to me." Maxx looked Jax in the eye again. "I assure you that no one has ever dishonored her."

"Then what is this promise? Just what has her so bound to you?" Jax wanted a real answer.

"I believe that Nancie is using her promise as a security net of some kind." Paul weighed in with his thoughts.

"I believe you may be right about that," Maxx agreed.

"What do you mean?" Jax felt like he was not getting anywhere with these two.

"Nancie has lost everyone she has ever cared about, and she does not handle change well. She is using the promises she made to Maxx's father because it is the only thing that has remained true in her life." Paul's explanation still did not answer any of Jax's questions.

"What did Nancie promise to your father?" Jax was done with talking in circles. He wanted to know what this promise was.

"I will talk with her and help her to move forward." Maxx avoided the question.

"This is not what I asked!" Jax raised his voice to Maxx.

"Her promise was never meant to hold her captive." Paul spoke sternly. He would remove Jax from the Captain's quarters if need be.

"How would you know anything about Nancie's promise to Maxx's father?" Jax stood up and faced Paul.

"Because I made the same promise," Paul replied.

Paul's words stunned Jax. He now wondered if everyone around Maxwell Spencer was bound by this ridiculous promise. Was this why so many people guarded the little Earl of Hartford as well as they did?

"I love her, and I deserve to know what she has bound herself to." Jax gave up fighting and sat back down. "How can I help her, if I do not know what she is defending?"

Jax was frustrated but arguing with Maxx was not going to get him any answers. All he could do now was to be open and honest about his feelings for Nancie. How could Maxx not allow him to help her?

"Do you truly love her above everything else in your life?" Maxx asked.

"I have already told her that I will walk away from my family if that is what it takes to be with her." Jax put his elbows on his knees and dropped his face in his hands.

"You are right. You do deserve to know." Maxx looked up at Paul.

"Be sure," Paul said.

Jax looked up. He did not understand the silent conversation between Paul and Maxx. This moment between Captain and first mate was intense. Something greater was passing between them that Jax could not comprehend.

"She deserves to finally have love in her life." Maxx nodded his head to Paul. Paul still was not sure.

"What are you two talking about?" Jax figured they would not answer him honestly.

"Nancie's promise was to keep my family's secrets." Maxx once again looked Jax in the eye.

"That's it?" Jax was more confused than before. That was a simple promise, yet Nancie clung to it with her entire life.

"Those secrets are costly." Paul began to pace around the room. "Many lives would be utterly ruined if those secrets ever came out. Maxx could even die."

"What did you do?" Jax grabbed Maxx's arm. Maxx was always getting into trouble.

"My people know the story and they hold my family's secrets as sacred. They have all sworn to keep those secrets even unto their deaths." Maxx's words did not comfort Jax at all right now.

"If anyone ever shares these secrets, the rest of us have vowed to hunt that person down and kill, not only them, but the person they shared the secret with as well." Paul stopped pacing. He did not like sharing this information.

"I am about to share with you something that no man in your family knows." Maxx paused for a moment and glanced over at Paul.

"Be sure," Paul said again.

"Before I do, are you truly sure that you wish to know?" Maxx asked Jax.

"I would do anything to help Nancie." Jax leaned forward. He needed to know what this mystery was.

"First, I will require the same promise and oath from you that everyone else has made." Maxx waited for an answer.

Jax could not believe what he was hearing. He could now finally know what had Nancie, and so many others, bound to Maxwell Spencer. That secret, if he chose to know it, would now bound him to the little Earl of Hartford as well, until the day he died. He loved Nancie and he would do what he must do to be with her. She deeply held his heart like no one else ever would.

"I swear," Jax stated boldly.

"Paul, bolt the door." Maxx nodded his head to Paul.

Chapter Forty

The next morning, The Em left Nettlesville on schedule. After lunch, Jax went up on deck. He had spent the entire morning in his quarters. The cabin began to feel smaller and smaller to him as each minute passed.

Jax leaned on the ship's railing and watched the sea for a long time. Maxwell Spencer had sure given him a lot to think about. He had many decisions that he would have to make by the time they reached London. He rubbed his forehead with his hand. The ache in his head grew worse as he thought on each possible outcome.

A sound caught Jax's attention. He looked over his shoulder to find Nancie sitting on one of the wooden barrels.

"I did not realize that you could move about so quietly." Still leaning on the railing, Jax turned slightly to face her.

"I am not that quiet." Nancie folded her hands together on her lap. "You were just deep in thought."

"There is a lot to think about and many decisions that have to be made." Jax hoped that she would not run from this subject today.

"I know." Nancie spoke softly as she looked down at her hands. Many changes were coming, and she was powerless to stop them.

"Good afternoon." Maxx sat down on the barrel next to Nancie. "Glad I found you two together."

"My, are you not in a cheerful mood today." Nancie was glad to see that Maxx was feeling better.

"We are at sea." Max jumped up and leaned over the railing beside Jax. "I love it out here."

"Well, you are strange," Jax mumbled. Maxx tilted his head slightly and glared at Jax.

"I am not the issue today, you two are." Maxx sat down next to Nancie again.

"You, somehow, are always the issue." Jax narrowed his eyes at Maxx.

"You two calm yourselves." Nancie laughed lightly. She could not tell if they were serious or just teasing each other. "We cannot have duels on ships."

"Oh, you can duel on a ship." Maxx grinned and nodded his head at her.

"You are not dueling with anyone on this ship!" Jax pointed his finger at Maxx.

"I do not recall promoting you to Captain." Maxx looked at Jax out of the corner of his eye.

"Be nice." Nancie patted Maxx on the arm.

Maxx's gaze lingered on Jax for a moment before he turned back to Nancie. Nancie could not help but to wonder what was going on between these two today.

"Your promises to my family were never meant to stop you from having a life of your own." Maxx held up his hand when Nancie started to speak. "You two have some serious decisions to make and you should make them together."

"You are right." Nancie sighed deeply and closed her eyes for a moment. "It is just hard."

"Yes, it will be hard for you to accept change, but you are not alone in any of this. You will have plenty of people to help you find your way through it all." Maxx took her hands in his.

"But you…" Nancie's heart was breaking.

"I will be beside you every step of the way," Maxx assured her. "We are family. You cannot ever lose me."

"It appears that we all are stuck with our dear little Captain, forever," Jax mumbled, earning him a stern look from Maxx.

"What is going on?" Nancie could clearly see that something was amiss between these two. "You two are acting awfully odd today."

Maxx turned his attention back to Nancie. It was time that she knew. Perhaps then she would finally be able to make her decisions.

"Jax is now bound by the same promises and oath that you, and everyone else, has made to my family," Maxx stated.

"Maxx?" Nancie was shocked. She could not believe that Maxx told his family secrets to Jax. "Why?"

"Because you deserve to be happy." Maxx placed a kiss on her forehead as he stood up. "Besides, if he does not keep his promise, we will just have to kill him." Maxx lightly laughed.

"This is not funny," Nancie snapped.

"It may not be funny, but it is true." Maxx glanced over at Jax to make sure that he understood.

Jax nodded his head to Maxx. He understood what was at stake here. Paul had spent over an hour last night explaining to him exactly what was at stake. Maxx's life could very well depend on his, and everyone else's silence.

"I do not know what to do." Nancie's eyes pleaded with Maxx for answers as she stood up and took his hand.

"I suggest, My Lady, that you follow your heart. Everything else will fall into place after that." Maxx gave her a hug before walking away.

Nancie's eyes met Jax's. Could Maxx be right? Was it possible for her to truly follow her heart? If it were true, her heart was standing in front of her.

"I cannot believe that you know." She was still stunned over this fact.

"Oh, I know." Jax took a step toward her. "For the reason that I know, I would not change a thing." He slowly took another step toward her. "But, for every other reason in this world, I wish that I did not know the Spencer family secrets."

"You made that promise and vow for me." Nancie's voice cracked a little as Jax took the final step that closed the distance between them.

"I did," Jax admitted proudly. "I do not wish to argue with you today, but we have to decide what we will do once we reach London."

"I know." Nancie looked up into Jax's eyes. She always got lost in his dark brown eyes.

"Lord Mason will want all of London to know that you are his niece. He probably has already begun telling people. I think that you should spend some time with your uncle. That is the only way for you to truly decide if you wish to step fully into that world." Jax put his hands on her waist.

"And what happens if I choose against it?" Standing this close to Jax always made it hard for her to breathe normally.

"Then we continue running the Blume'N Brew." Jax wanted her to know that no matter what she decided, he was not leaving her side.

"What about the restaurant and soup kitchen next door?" Nancie was stalling for more time.

"I would truly love that, but only if you wish for that to happen." Jax did not take his eyes away from hers.

"What about your family?" The answer to this question mattered the most to Nancie. She knew how important family was.

"I will still see my family. The time with them may be less than before, but I do not mind stepping away some to save them all from ridicule from society." Jax reached for her hand. His eyes still never left hers. "Rest assured, no matter what, the love of my family will never go away."

"Are you truly sure that this is a life that you want?" Nancie was running out of questions. A decision would have to be made soon.

"I have no life if you are not in it." Jax smiled. "I do love you, but if you do not feel the same, I will leave and never trouble your doorstep again."

A small gasp escaped Nancie's lips. Time was up. A decision had to be made. Whatever she decided, it would be something she would never be able to change once it was done. He loved her. She knew without a doubt that she loved him too.

Nancie smiled. She stood on her tiptoes and put her arms around Jax's neck. He was the only decision that she could make. Without him, she would have no life either.

"I love you as well." Nancie could deny it no longer.

Jax wrapped his arms around Nancie's waist and lifted her off her feet. He happily twirled her around. The sound of her laughter warmed his heart.

"Then there is only one thing left to do." Jax set her back on her feet.

"And what might that be?" Nancie reached up and touched Jax's cheek.

"This." Jax knelt before her. "Lady Nancie Blume, you will forever and always hold my heart. Will you do me the honor of becoming my wife?"

"Yes, Sir Jackson Shaw, I will," Nancie replied with tears of happiness in her eyes.

Nancie's arms went around his neck again as Jax stood up. Jax held her tightly in his arms as his lips claimed hers to seal their promise to each other.

"From the looks of that, we are about to have another special dinner in the Captain's quarters tonight." Maxx grumbled as he looked over at Paul.

Maxx was sitting on his perch by the railing and Paul was at the helm. They had been watching the happy couple ever since Jax had twirled Nancie around, bringing them into view.

"Indeed, it does, my Captain." Paul grinned.

"What?" Caleb turned away from the railing to look at what Maxx and Paul were staring at. Alex did the same. Caleb's mouth dropped opened when he saw his little brother down on his knee.

"Not again." Alex remembered when his brother Nate had proposed to his wife Olivia on The Em. "Little Man, you have gotten to stop allowing unmarried couples on board your ship."

Chapter Forty-One

The Em docked in London Harbor a little over a week later. Under the cover of darkness, everyone quickly made their way to the Blume'N Brew. Rachel and Jerry were happy to see them.

"Why are we being so secretive?" Nancie asked once they were inside the pub.

"Because the word at the docks tonight, was that Lord Mason has already begun telling people that you are his niece," Maxx told her.

"I know that you have not made your decision yet on whether or not you wish to step into society, so for now, to keep gossip down, we are keeping you hidden." Jax set their bags on the floor.

"I do not wish to alarm either of you, but it might be too late to stop the gossip. You two should get married sooner rather than later." Maxx lit the lanterns on a few of the tables.

"Is that truly necessary?" Nancie could not help but to be alarmed.

"It is my fault. I will take the blame, but sadly, I doubt anyone will care at this point." Maxx grabbed a bottle of rum from behind the bar. "I should have never put you on The Em with no maid to chaperone you."

"We have just stepped foot back in London and the horrors of society have already started to descend upon us." Nancie threw her hands in the air.

Jax took her hand and looked down into her fearful eyes. The things Nancie wanted to avoid were happening faster than either of them thought they would. The longer he was able to hold her gaze, the sooner Nancie calmed down. She could not believe that this simple act affected her so much.

"I have no problem with marrying you tomorrow." Jax winked at her.

"We will do what we must." Nancie gave in and agreed.

"We will send word to Kinsley Estate and Ellis Manor. Those that wish to be present at the ceremony can meet us at Camden Chapel in four days." Maxx announced their plan.

Maxx did not want Nancie to marry Jax without giving the Shaw family an opportunity to be present at the wedding. This was the only plan that Maxx could think of that would allow the members of Jax's family to be part of the marriage ceremony and for it to still take place quickly. He signaled for messengers to prepare for the journey.

"You will also need to send a messenger to Huntington Estate," Paul added. "Lord Mason will surely want to be present when his niece weds."

"I would like for my uncle to be there." Nancie was going to take Jax up on his suggestion and get to know her uncle.

"It is settled then. We will all get some rest, and we will leave first thing in the morning." Maxx settled the matter, and everyone went upstairs for the night.

Nancie was not able to sleep. She tossed and turned for hours. Finally, she gave up and went to make some coffee. She took her cup and walked down to the side entrance of the pub. Dawn was approaching. It was still early, so hardly anything outside was moving, except for the birds perhaps. Their songs filled the morning air beautifully.

Nancie stood in the doorway with her coffee. It was peaceful watching the dark sky of night start to lighten as it was getting closer to dawn. Doug walked past on his patrol rounds and nodded to her.

She noticed some late blooming flowers in the small garden across the drive. She hurried over and pick a few of them. The fresh blooms had a sweet aroma. She carried the flowers to the memorial plaque for her father, on the far front corner of the pub. She smiled, thinking of her father, as she placed the flowers in the iron vase that Maxx had built into the wall.

Next door was the building that Jax wanted to purchase and turn into a small restaurant and soup kitchen. The building was a little larger than the pub and would be perfect for Jax's plans. The second floor appeared to have plenty of space for living quarters. She could not argue that Jax was right, it would be a better environment for her and Rachel. She sighed deeply and placed her hand on her father's memorial plaque.

"I wish you were here," Nancie whispered.

Suddenly, an arm went around her waist, as a large hand covered her mouth. Nancie's eyes widened in fear. The coffee cup fell from her hand and shattered into pieces at her feet, as it hit the stone walkway.

"He's not here, but I am." Roger Holden growled in her ear.

Nancie struggled against Roger but could not free herself from his grasp. He quickly pulled her up the street and climbed into a carriage. Nancie kicked at the sides of the carriage, trying to make any noise that she possibly could, to alert someone to what was happening. Roger Holden held her tight against him as the carriage bolted forward.

Nancie continued to kick at the sides of the carriage. Roger held her down as the carriage raced through the almost empty streets of London. It was the early morning hours, so the crowds had not yet begun to fill the city streets. No one was aware of her need for help.

When they exited the city on the northern road, only then did Roger release his hold on her. As he did, Nancie balled her hand into a fist. She quickly turned and swiftly punched Roger in the mouth, busting the corner of his lower lip. With a forceful shove, Roger pushed Nancie onto the seat across the carriage.

"I demand that you release me now!" Nancie shouted.

"I will release you when I get what I want," Roger informed her. He held a handkerchief to his lip to stop the bleeding.

"And what exactly do you want?" Nancie's eyes bore holes into Roger.

"I want the Mason Jewel." Roger leaned forward and roughly grabbed her arm. "And you are going to get it for me."

"I do not have the Mason Jewel." Nancie knocked Roger's hand away.

"That may be, but it is connected to you." Roger jabbed his boney finger at her.

"I do not know how you figure that is possible, but you are sadly mistaken." Nancie folded her arms and continued to glare at Roger.

"That jewel is connected to Lord Mason's oldest daughter, so you will get it for me." Roger smiled. He was rather pleased with himself.

"I am his niece, and I cannot help you with this ludicrous mission you seem to be on." Nancie leaned back against the carriage.

Nancie could not believe that she was in this predicament. She now understood how Abby and Dani felt the night that Roger Holden had kidnapped them. She folded her arms and looked over at the carriage door. When the carriage slowed down, she would make a run for it. Roger noticed the movement of her eyes.

"If you try it, I will see to it that this carriage runs you over, and I will leave you to die alone on the side of the road." Roger's threat proved his cruelty.

"It does not matter what you do to me." Nancie did not fear Roger Holden. "You will never get what you seek."

"When Lord Mason finds out that I have his oldest daughter, he will willingly give me that jewel to get you back." Roger had his plan all figured out. "If he refuses, you will marry me, and I will kill him. In the end, no matter what, that jewel will be mine."

"You are completely bonkers." Nancie burst into laughter.

"Laugh now, but I assure you, I will have what I seek," Roger sneered.

"You will never have what you seek." Nancie lightly laughed. "If that jewel is connected to Lord Mason's daughter, you failed miserably at getting Abby to marry you."

The smile on Roger's face slowly disappeared. If his mother's contact from inside the Duke of Greyham's former household was wrong, he had just kidnapped the wrong woman. The last thing he wanted to do, was to have go after Abby Mason Shaw again to get his hands on the Mason jewel.

Pure hate burned within him. His eyes were as daggers as he looked at the blonde twit sitting across from him. He should kill her now and toss her body out of the carriage to rot in the dirt. He had never liked it when a woman challenged him and this one was as bad as Lady Emily Spencer was.

The former maid of the Dowager Duchess of Greyham had sworn that Lord Mason had another daughter from a brief former marriage.

His mother had said that Ella Mason had died at an early age without marrying. This niece had to be a charade to hide the fact that Nancie was indeed Lord Mason's other daughter. Roger would not let Nancie trick him into believing that he was wrong on this.

"We shall see." Roger refused to listen to Nancie anymore.

They rode through the night without stopping. Roger would not chance stopping at the Ridgewell Inn with Nancie. He already had a couple of mishaps at that inn. They only stopped in Delane long enough for Roger to trade out the horses for fresh ones.

Nancie was allowed a few minutes at the Delane Inn to freshen up. She was always under heavy guard and they only used the back entrances to the inn and stables. A maid was even hired to remain in the room with her. Roger was taking no chances this time. Nancie would not escape his grasp as Abby, Dani, and Elizabeth had.

A few days later, Nancie was forcefully dragged from the carriage. She was tired and her body already ached from sleeping in the carriage the past few nights. Roger's tight grip on her arm was bound to leave a bruise.

"Where are we?" Nancie demanded as Roger pulled her down a long hallway.

"Somewhere that you will never be found." Roger grinned. He was proud that his plan was working out so wonderfully.

"Jax will come for me!" Nancie shouted.

"That Shaw is the least of my worries. My men have orders to kill him the moment they see him." Roger halted outside a huge wooden door and waited for a man to unlock it.

True fear, for the first time, came over Nancie as she and Roger followed the large foul smelling man into the room. It was dark, damp, and musty here. Wherever this was, it was underground. The man placed the lantern he was carrying on a small table and left the room. Roger shoved Nancie further into the dark room.

"You cannot do this!" Nancie cried.

"Oh, my dear, it is already done." Roger smiled slyly. "If your father does not willingly hand over the Mason Jewel to me, then you and I will be wed immediately."

"You truly are a ruthless snake!" Nancie shouted with tears in her eyes. "I will never marry you!"

"Then, my dear, you will die here, alone and in the dark." Roger's evil laugh rang in Nancie's ears long after he had slammed the door and bolted it from the outside.

Chapter Forty-Two

For two nights Nancie slept the best she could on the dirt floor of the cellar she was locked up in. The only thing she had to keep her warm was the shawl she had been wearing when Roger Holden had kidnapped her.

The door to the cellar only opened three times each day. A young, frightened maid brought in her meals and tended to any personal needs that Nancie had. No other comforts were given to her.

When the door opened, Nancie could see that the long hallway was filled with armed guards. Roger Holden had apparently learned his lesson on how to keep someone held as a hostage. He made sure that there was no means of escape this time.

Nancie had been franticly searching the cellar for any means of escape. There was no window here to climb out of and she could not convince the frightened maid to help her. The girl hardly even spoke when she entered the cellar.

On the third day, Nancie had all she could handle of being confined in this dark and dreary place. The cellar was filled with shelves of wine, along with crates and sacks of food. She had to be below an inn or a restaurant, she was not sure which it was.

Her mind was not working clearly from lack of sleep and the stress of her confinement. There was only one thing that she could think to try, and it was not a good plan. Still, she had to try something before she went completely insane.

When the young maid brought the midday meal, she found Nancie's shawl lying on the ground near the door. The girl instantly searched the cellar, but Nancie was gone. The girl turned to alert the guards in the hallway and Roger Holden was summoned.

"Where is she?" Roger roared as he looked around the cellar.

"My Lord, I only found this by the door." The maid's hands shook as she held out Nancie's shawl.

"You let her out!" Roger shouted as he slapped the girl, sending her to the floor.

"I have no key, My Lord." The girl was too afraid to look up at Roger.

"Who let her out?" Roger turned his anger onto one of his guards.

"We do not know, Lord Holden, but we will find out." The guard bowed to Roger and hurried away.

"Bring her." Roger ordered Edmond to get the girl off the floor.

"We should have just killed Mason and took what we wanted." Edmond Prescott said, as he pulled the girl to her feet.

With a loud bang, the door to the cellar slammed shut behind them. Roger shouted more orders to the guards in the hallway. Each man quickly hurried to carry out their new orders.

Nancie sighed with relief, from her hiding place among the barrels, crates, and sacks of food. She had worked cautiously over the past two days to stack these things in a way that it would not look too suspicious. She did not believe that her little ruse would work as well as it had. Sadly, she could not chance leaving her hiding spot now. She would have to remain here until Jax came for her. Surely, he was already on his way.

***

Doug had found the broken coffee cup on the walk under Danny Blume's memorial plaque that morning. He looked up in time to see the carriage down the street as it bolted off toward the center of the city. He quickly ran inside the pub and woke everyone up.

Caleb and Alex immediately set out to track the mysterious carriage. Thankfully, it was still early, and the streets were not yet overrun with horses and carriages. However, it was a bit time consuming to have to stop and check with the local shop owners who may have seen the carriage. By noon, the two cousins were sure that the carriage was heading north out of the city. They sent word back to the pub and waited at a small inn, on the edge of London, for the others to arrive.

"We should check Ridgewell Inn." Jax started in the direction of the inn when they reached the turn off in the road.

"Brother, I do not believe that carriage went to Ridgewell Inn." Caleb shook his head.

"He's right." Alex confirmed Caleb's statement.

Before they decided on which way to go, Harper came riding up fast from the rear of their rescue party.

"We have a lot of riders coming behind us, hard and fast!" Harper shouted.

Maxx turned his horse. He and Paul quickly followed Harper to the rear of their party.

"Go with Maxx!" Jax shouted to Alex.

Alex nodded his head and hurried to catch up with Maxx. Within minutes, they all returned with Lord Mason and his army following them.

"You sure got here quickly." Jax was surprised, for their messenger should not have reached Huntington Estate yet.

"We were already on our way to London," Sir Charles, Lord Mason's Captain of the Guard, told Jax.

"You are not going to like this." Maxx was furious from what Lord Mason had told him.

"A letter was delivered at the gates of Huntington Estate this morning." Lord Mason's chest heaved with anger as he spoke, and his face turned red. "Holden has taken Nancie. He believes her to be my daughter Emerald."

"Is Holden still after the Mason Jewel?" Jax asked.

Lord Mason nodded his head in reply. Caleb quickly looked over at his brother. Jax was not known for staying calm. Hopefully, he and Alex could handle his little brother today. Jax merely closed his eyes and let his anger against Holden build even more.

"The message instructed Lord Mason to go to Delane," Maxx told Jax.

Without saying a word, Jax pulled on the reins and turned Blue toward Delane. At least now they had a clear destination. Not waiting for anyone to follow, Jax took off with his horse at a full run.

The rest of the rescue party caught up with Jax as they entered Delane. The letter that Lord Mason received instructed him to go to the town stables. Maxx, not trusting the little information that they had, still sent men to the inn, restaurant, and shops to search for more information. If Holden had truly stopped here, hopefully someone had seen Nancie. At the town stables, they found Dexter Greene waiting for them.

"What have you done with Nancie?" Jax jumped off his horse and ran toward Dexter.

Before Jax could get near Dexter, the man pulled out a pistol and pointed it in Jax's face. Caleb and Alex grabbed Jax and pulled him back.

"Alright, Greene. I am here." Lord Mason dismounted his horse. "Where is my niece?"

"We aren't falling for that ruse, old man." Dexter kept his gun pointed at Jax as he spoke to Lord Mason. "Did you bring it?"

"I no longer have the Mason Jewel. Sadly, it was lost over twenty years ago."

Dexter looked over his shoulder and nodded his head. At his signal, a cloaked rider, dressed in black, took off from behind the stables. Several of Lord Mason's guards immediately gave chase.

"No matter what you do, you will not reach her in time." Dexter started backing away into the stables. "By the time you reach her, your daughter will already be married to the Earl of Statham."

Jax tried to go after Dexter again as the man disappeared inside the stables. Caleb and Alex struggled to hold him back. Maxx quickly stepped in front of Jax and got his attention.

"Let him go. Nancie needs us more than your fight with Greene right now." Maxx's anger could be heard clearly in his voice.

"Then let's help chase that rider." Jax backed away and mounted his horse.

They did not find rest in Delane this night. They all were tired and weary, but Lord Mason gave the order to his army to move out. Soon they caught up with Sir Charles, who was waiting for them in a bend up the road.

"Did you catch him?" Jax was eager get answers out of the rider.

"No, but we will soon." Sir Charles was confident on the matter. "I have my men following that rider."

"Following him?" Jax roared. "We need to catch him now!"

Sir Charles grabbed Blue's bridle and held Jax in place before he could bolt after that rider. Jax did not wish to hurt Lord Mason's Captain of the Guard, but if the man did not move, he would trample him in the road.

"That rider may be Nancie's only hope. He will lead us straight to her." Lord Mason leaned over and touched Jax's arm.

"What if Holden forces her to marry him?" Jax did not like sitting here like this. They were wasting time.

"My men have been instructed to run Holden through before that can happen." Lord Mason tried to assure Jax that the situation was being handled.

Maxx dismounted and walked over to Jax's horse. Harper, Doug, and Brady rode past them at a full run. Jax looked down at Maxx for answers.

"I know that you wish to storm the castle and save Nancie, but that will not help her this time." Maxx took Blue by his bridle and motioned Sir Charles away.

"Where are your men going?" Jax's tone demanded an answer.

"They traded out their horses for the only rested ones in Delane. They are going to catch up with Lord Mason's men and take over." Maxx started leading Blue over to the side of the road. "They are leaving a clear trail for Alex and Caleb to follow. For now, the rest of us will water our horses at the pond just off the road here and let them rest for a while."

"But…" Jax hated this plan.

Logic told Jax that their horses needed to rest. Another night of riding, at the pace they had been traveling, would probably kill half their horses before morning.

"Trust me." Maxx looked Jax in the eye and spoke calmly. "I will never fail her."

"Uh!" Jax exclaimed loudly as he dismounted his horse.

Jax was disgusted and hated the fact that he knew they all were right. He would give Blue time to rest. Then, with or without the others, he was heading out.

"It's all that Caleb and I can do to hold you in your place." Alex watered his horse next to Jax's. "How did Little Man manage to do so on just his word?"

"Leave it be," Jax mumbled.

Jax handed Blue's reins to Caleb and walked away. He had to calm down before he exploded on everyone around him.

Chapter Forty-Three

When the rescue party rode into Camden, they found Doug waiting for them at the edge of the village. Roger Holden and his men had left Camden about an hour before Jax and the others arrived. When the cloaked rider from Delane informed the Earl of Statham that Lord Mason's army was on the way, and without the Mason Jewel, Roger abandoned his quest and fled north toward Scotland.

"Did he take Nancie with him?" Jax would chase Holden into Scotland if he had to.

"We do not know. No one here will really talk to us. All we know is, Nancie is missing. She has not been seen since yesterday." Doug was sure that this information would not be well received.

"What do mean she's missing?" Jax roared.

Before Doug could say more, Harper approached with the young maid that was carrying Nancie her meals. The young girl was trembling with fear and refused to look anyone in the eye.

"This is Lanie. She says that Nancie, somehow, escaped from the cellar under one of the restaurants." Harper had finally convinced the girl to talk. He looked Maxx in the eye. "I promised her protection from the Earl of Statham, in exchange for her help."

Maxx nodded his head that he understood and agreed. Maxx dismounted his horse and took the girl by the arm. When Lanie finally looked up at Maxx, the bruise Roger Holden had left on her cheek was visible to them all. Many of them remembered the mark that one of Roger's men had left on Alex's sister Dani's face a couple years ago.

"Tell me everything that you know, and I will see to it that you and your family are relocated anywhere you wish to go." Maxx promised the girl his protection.

"No one knows what happened to Miss Nancie. She was locked in the cellar under Huffman's Restaurant. I took her noon meal yesterday only to find her gone." Lanie spoke quickly to Maxx.

"Show me where he held her." Maxx spoke softly to the girl as he made his request. The girl was still trembling with fear and the last thing they needed was for her to become hysterical.

Lanie led the way to Huffman's Restaurant. The owner protested their entrance into the building. Lord Mason's men held Nigel Huffman in the kitchen while Lanie showed them the cellar.

Jax barged through the door. Since Nancie had escaped, the door was not locked anymore. His heart broke as he looked around the dark, damp, musty room. How could Holden hold anyone here?

"Who let her out?" Jax demanded of Lanie.

"We do not know." Lanie stepped behind Maxx when Jax raised his voice.

"There is no way to escape this cellar." Caleb looked between his brother and Maxx.

"Nancie!" Maxx shouted.

"What are you doing?" Jax thought Maxx had lost his mind.

"Shh." Alex motioned for Jax to be quiet. He was sure he heard a sound. "Did you hear that?"

"Nancie?" Jax looked around the room again. He had not heard anything.

To their surprise, a low groaning sound was heard. The sound came from under the supplies stacked in the corner. Quickly, everyone worked together to move the crates, barrels, and sacks of food. Jax breathed a sigh of relief when he saw her.

"She's freezing." Jax lifted Nancie off the dirt floor.

"Here." Lord Mason removed his overcoat and wrapped it around his niece.

"Is there a doctor here?" Maxx asked Lanie.

"Yes, My Lord," Lanie replied. She quickly led the way to the doctor's house.

Lanie stayed with Nancie while Doctor Ross examined her. Maxx thanked the young girl for her services. Guards carried Lanie home to pack her family's belongings. It was only her and her mother, and they had no other family to take them in. Still, Maxx was moving them from Camden, in fear that Roger Holden would keep his threat to Lanie of killing her and her mother.

"You had me scared there for a while." Jax sat down on the side of the bed after the doctor left the room.

"For a while there, it got scary." Nancie was tired but she still tried to smile at Jax.

"I cannot believe that you hid under all that stuff." Jax brought her hand up to his lips. The warmth was returning to her skin.

"Maxx told me to." Nancie's voice cracked. She looked over at the water on the stand that was by the bed.

"Maxx?" Jax did not understand how Maxx had helped her. He did, however, notice her need for the water and quickly reached for the glass.

"Maxx told me, long ago, that if I was ever held captive and could not escape, to look for a place to hide if possible." Nancie explained as she slid up against the head of the bed.

"Looks like our little Captain has good advice." Jax held the glass of water to her lips. "I cannot belief that Holden fell for it."

"Can we not say that name right now?" The look in Nancie's eyes was not that of fear. Hate for Roger Holden burned deep within her eyes.

"For now, of course." Jax could see that it was for the best right now.

"What do we do now?" Nancie motioned for Jax to take the water away.

"When you are better, we will get married." Jax took both of her hands in his.

"We will get married tomorrow." Nancie did not wish to wait any longer.

"We do not have to rush." Jax pushed a few strands of her blonde hair behind her ear.

"We will get married tomorrow." Nancie said each word slowly and firmly. She was not going to give Roger Holden another chance to try forcing her into marry him.

"I will have your uncle and Maxx to prepare everything." Jax took her into his arms before she could become hysterical. "If you are truly better tomorrow, we will wed."

After Nancie fell asleep, Jax relayed her request to Lord Mason and Maxx. They both agreed that this ceremony should happen quickly. The two of them set out to make all the arrangements.

Just after lunch the next day, everyone went to Camden Chapel. Ms. Crook greeted them upon their arrival and place a bouquet of flowers in Nancie's hands. The little woman was overjoyed that a wedding was happening today.

"It is good to see that the army outside is bringing the bride, rather than taking her away this time." Minister Wallace looked between Maxx and Lord Mason.

"No worries today, Minister Wallace," Maxx assured him.

Maxx was sure the minister would never forget the Duke of Greyham showing up here to take his siter Elizabeth before she could marry Jax's brother Nick. Today, Minister Wallace would finally be marrying another Shaw couple.

"Sir Jackson, if you would kindly follow me, we will start as soon as Lady Nancie is ready." Minister Wallace turned and walked to the front of the chapel.

Jax, Caleb, and Alex followed the minister, leaving Nancie with Maxx, Lord Mason, and Lanie. Lanie took Nancie's coat and placed it on a hook by the door. Maxx would be sending Lanie and her mother to a safe location after the ceremony. Sir Charles and Maxx's men took their seats on the pews of the chapel while Lord Mason's army stood guard outside. Sadly, the women of the Shaw family, and Rachel, could not be here with them today.

"Shall I escort you?" Lord Mason held his arm out for Nancie.

"That will be *my* job," Maxx stated firmly.

"You both may escort me." Nancie knew this would be odd, but she did not wish to see her dearest friend and her uncle argue.

Lanie straightened out Nancie's lavender colored dress that Lord Mason had purchased for her this morning at one of the local shops. Maxx plucked a couple of flowers from Nancie's bouquet and handed them to the young maid.

"When the music starts, you lead the way." Maxx motioned toward the front of the chapel. Lanie smiled and nodded her head. She was thrilled to be part of the ceremony today.

Lord Mason and Maxx proudly escorted Nancie down the aisle to Jax. Within a matter of minutes, vows were spoken and the ring, that Caleb had purchased for Jax this morning, was slipped onto Nancie's finger. Jax was amazed that his usually quiet brother had such excellent taste in jewelry. The stone in the ring matched the dress that Nancie wore today.

"Sir Jackson Shaw, you may kiss your bride." Minister Wallace was overjoyed to say those words, finally, to another Shaw couple.

Jax slide his hand around Nancie's waist and pulled her to him. Not wanting to wait another minute, Nancie stood on her tiptoes, put her arms around his neck, and kissed Jax, her husband.

Chapter Forty-Four

Once again, Roger Holden retreated to the safety of Statham Hall for months, after another failed attempt at acquiring the Mason Jewel. The Shaw family stayed on their guard for any possible attacks from the Earl of Statham's men. Roger often paid to have his dirty work done for him.

Christmas that year came with wonderful surprises for the Shaw family. Abby, Olivia, and Elizabeth were all expecting their second child. Nancie was thrilled for them, but she was deeply saddened at the same time. She and Jax could not share the same wonderful news with their family. Sadly, unknown to anyone in the family, a week before Christmas, Nancie had experienced a miscarriage. Jax assure her that one day, she would be a mother.

Maxx had managed to surprise Nancie with a Christmas gift that took her mind off her loss for a while. Her brother, Frank, had returned from military service. Frank's help at the Blume'N Brew allowed Nancie time to really think more about Jax's idea of a restaurant and soup kitchen next door to the pub. She finally agreed that it would indeed be a better environment for her and Rachel.

That spring, Lady Danielle Shaw was finally presented to the king and queen for the social season. Lord Matthew and Lady Caroline had hoped that waiting almost three years after Gavin's disappearance would have given London's society set enough time to get over the scandal of Dani being on Maxx's ship.

The night after Dani's presentation, the Duke of Greyham hosted a ball at his home in London. That morning, Nick and Elizabeth's son, Jacob Phillip Shaw, was christened, and the entire Shaw family was present for the celebration.

Nancie was still not fond of these types of parties, but she would not miss the celebration tonight. About halfway into the evening, after everyone had congratulated Nick and Elizabeth on the birth of their son, Jax stood and got everyone's attention.

"At Christmas, Nancie and I were not able to share the happy news that we wanted to with our families." Jax looked down at his wife and squeezed her hand. "However, today, after a few months of waiting just to be sure, Nancie and I want to share with you all, that we are indeed expecting our first child."

The ballroom erupted into shouts of happiness. The music soon started again, as the Shaw family descended upon the expectant couple. Lady Clara and Elizabeth were the first ones to congratulate Jax and Nancie. Lady Clara was overjoyed. Elizabeth had accepted Nancie as family long before she had married Jax.

Dani Shaw did not join in with her family's celebration. Instead, she watched, from across the room, as her family surrounded Jax and Nancie. Dani could not bring herself to be part of her family's happiness tonight. Tonight, she just stood here and watched. She was happy for her cousin, but she feared that motherhood would never be possible for her.

"Did you have many callers today?" The Duke stepped beside Dani.

"No, Your Grace." Dani was amazed at how silently the Duke always approached her. "No one called."

Dani was sure her lack of callers were because London's society had not forgotten the time she was on Maxx's ship. If she were to ever wed, her parents would most likely have to secure her a marriage in another country.

"Lady Danielle, would you like to dance?" Sam hated that she was saddened, but he was rather pleased that no gentlemen had called upon her today.

"I overheard something this morning." Dani turned to face Samuel Dawson. She had, without meaning to, heard her three brothers talking in the study of their family's newly renovated house in London.

"What did you hear, Little One?" Sam smiled when he noticed that she was wearing the necklace he had given to her at her brother's wedding.

"I heard that you have Maxx locked into an outlandish five-year deal of service, just so that my brother Alex would be freed from prison." Dani looked up at Sam. "Tell me that this is not true."

"You do not need to trouble yourself over my arrangement with Maxwell Spencer." Sam could no longer smile for he knew she was not pleased.

"So, it is true?" Dani sighed and looked away.

"Well, actually, I forgave Spencer a year and he's already worked off another year. So, he only has three more years left." Sam tried to explain, but he knew this would still not please Lady Danielle.

"Maxx is my friend." Dani looked Sam in the eye again. "I must ask you to kindly release him from this deal."

"Spencer is a weasel, and I cannot release my hold on him just yet." Sam wanted to grant her request, but this deal, as bizarre as it was, kept Maxwell Spencer in place.

"Then, no, Your Grace. I do not wish to dance with you." With tears in her eyes, Dani turned and hurried away.

Sam scanned the room for the object of his fury. Finally, his eyes rested upon Lord Maxwell Spencer. He hurried across the room to wipe the smile of the little Earl of Hartford's face.

"This is your fault!" Sam angrily pointed his finger at Maxx.

"Me? What did I do?" Maxx did not understand.

"Your Grace, perhaps you are mistaken." Alex stepped between Maxx and the Duke.

"Maxx has been right here, with us." Gavin stood beside his brother.

"One day, Spencer, I swear, I am going to kill you myself." Sam's eyes bore into Maxx.

"I know." Maxx nodded his head. "You tell me that every chance you get."

Frustrated, Sam shook his head and walked away. He would find some way to repay Spencer for messing up his time with Lady Danielle tonight.

"I should go and do something," Maxx said as they all watched the Duke walk away.

"Like what?" Gavin hated asking.

"I do not know, but if I am going to be accused of doing something, when I have clearly done nothing, then I should definitely go and do something." Maxx's reasoning made everyone's head hurt.

"Little Man, you are staying right here." Alex was not about to let Maxx leave to start some type of trouble.

"We are not letting you out of our sight," Nancie informed Maxx.

Maxx gave in and remained with the Shaw family. Tonight, was truly a happy occasion for them all and Maxx did not wish to disrupt that. After a while, Lady Caroline came over and joined them.

"Have any of you seen Dani?" Lady Caroline was worried.

"No, Mother." Gavin looked around at everyone as they all shook their heads. "We have not seen Dani in a while."

"I cannot find her." Lady Caroline was almost in tears now.

"Do not fret, Mother." Nate put his arm around his worried mother. "We will help you search for her. I am sure that she has not gone far."

"Your Grace!" Jax stopped the Duke as he walked by. "Have you seen Danielle?"

"I spoke with Lady Danielle right after you made your happy announcement." Sam angrily looked over at Maxx again. Because of Maxx, Dani had refused to dance with him tonight.

"That was over an hour ago." Alex was now deeply worried.

"Everyone, spread out and search for her." Gavin quickly ordered.

"Olivia and I will stay with Lady Caroline." Abby hurried over and took Lady Caroline by the arm. She and Olivia led their mother-in-law over to a nearby chair.

After half an hour of searching the house, Dani could not be found. The search was now being expanded to the gardens and grounds around Greyham Court.

"We have to find her." Lady Caroline cried. Abby held her tightly.

"It is getting late. I will take Nancie back to the Blume'N Brew and return to help search for Dani." Jax took their leave from Gavin.

Nancie and Jax hurried to their carriage. Normally, Nancie would protest being sent home, but tonight she would not. She would love to help everyone search for Dani. However, being in her condition, she would not put their baby at risk.

Chapter Forty-Five

Jax and Nancie's carriage hurried through the streets of London, toward the Blume'N Brew. Jax needed to get back to Greyham Court quickly so he could help his family search for his little cousin.

"Did you enjoy your evening?" Jax had to get his mind off Dani before his anger was out of control.

"It was a lovely evening." Nancie smiled across the carriage at her husband. She hated that Dani was missing but up until that point, it was a lovely party.

"Do not worry, we will find my cousin." Jax could see the worry on Nancie's face. He did not wish for her to become too distraught over the matter.

"Do you think that our rooms above the restaurant will be ready soon?" Nancie too was trying to keep their minds on happier things right now. She knew that Jax was pleased with the purchase of the building next door to the pub.

"They should be ready within a month." Jax was glad that his wife was ready to move out of the pub. He did not truly wish for their child to grow up in a pub.

As the carriage turned by the park, a thud sound was heard. Nancie and Jax were both alarmed.

"What was that?" Nancie leaned forward a bit.

Jax leaned his head out the carriage window. Something was sticking out of the carriage door. Jax retrieved the object and brought it inside the carriage. Jax became seriously alarmed when he realized he was holding a dagger.

Before Jax could shout to the driver, or cover Nancie for protection, something spooked the horses and they bolted at a full run. When the sound of shots was heard, Nancie slid to the floor of the carriage. The driver could not control the horses. As they made the next turn, the carriage overturned in the street. Several shots rang out again. Their driver, and horses, now lay dead in the street.

Jax reached for Nancie and helped her to sit up. Jax managed to push the door opened and climbed out onto the side of the overturned carriage. He reached down and took Nancie's hands. Carefully he pulled her out of the carriage. Once Jax was on the ground, he reached up and helped Nancie off the carriage.

"You're bleeding." Nancie felt the blood on Jax's arm as he set her on the ground. "Were you shot?"

"No. It was this." Jax held up the dagger.

Nancie bent over and ripped one of her petticoats. She tied the makeshift bandage around Jax's arm. This would have to do until they could reach the pub. Jax checked the driver, one of Lord Mason's men, but there was nothing he could do for the man.

"We need to get to the pub quickly." Jax took Nancie's hand. He had to get her to safety.

"Jax?" Nancie swayed and tightened her grip on Jax's hand. "Something is wrong."

"Nancie!" Jax shouted as his wife collapsed in his arms.

Jax scooped Nancie up in his arms and ran the two blocks to the pub.

"What happened?" Frank demanded as he helped Jax get Nancie upstairs.

Frank, after hearing about the accident, sent Jerry to get Doctor Ramsey. He had Rachel to stay with Nancie while he armed the stable hands. They had heard the gun shots from the pub, but they did not know that it was Jax and Nancie that were in trouble.

After Jerry returned with the doctor, Frank sent him to find Maxx at Greyham Court. Soon, several members of the Shaw family, along with Lord Mason, showed up at the Blume'N Brew.

While the doctor tended to Nancie, Frank cleaned and bandaged Jax's arm. Frustrated, Jax got up and began to pace. He could not stay still when he did not know if his wife was alright or not. Jax took the dagger and threw it into the pub wall.

"Where did you get this?" Maxx pulled the dagger from the wall and examined it closely.

"It was thrown into the side of the carriage just before the accident." Jax was more worried about Nancie than a dagger.

"Paul, look." Maxx held the dagger up. "Check the ship, now."

Paul and Brady rushed out the door and headed to the docks. In less than twenty minutes they returned with a dagger identical to the one Jax had. The design in the handles of the two daggers were the same.

"Where did you get that?" Alex asked as he looked over Maxx's shoulder at the two daggers.

"This one, Jax found tonight." Maxx held up the second dagger. "This one, you pulled out of Trevor Bryson's chest in Nettlesville."

Before anyone could speak, Doctor Ramsey came down the stairs. His heart was heavy, and his expression was grim.

"How is she?" Jax rushed over to the doctor.

"Nancie will recover, in time." The doctor looked Jax in the eye, but he did not smile.

"And our baby?" Jax's voice cracked. He already knew.

"I am sorry, Sir Jackson." Doctor Ramsey placed his hand on Jax's arm. "It was too early, and your son did not survive."

"Son..." Jax stumbled and his father, Sir Phillip, caught him. "My son is gone."

Sir Phillip held his youngest son on the floor and cried with him. Everyone in the pub's heart broke. They did not know what to say or do in this moment.

"Gather your strength, Sir Jackson." Doctor Ramsey knelt in front of Jax. Sadly, he had seen these types of occasions before and he offered what help that he could. "Your wife needs you now, more than ever. Your family will surely mourn with you in the days to come."

Jax sat up. The doctor was right. Nancie needed him and he needed her. Sir Phillip wiped the tears from his son's face. Nick and Caleb helped Jax and their father to their feet. Somehow, Jax had to find his strength for Nancie's sake.

"Holden will pay for this." Jax vowed as he looked around the room. Everyone nodded their heads in agreement.

"You go and be with her." Maxx stood in front of Jax with his hands on Jax's arms. "Your family will search for your cousin. Lord Mason and I will handle everything else."

"Maxx, I…" Jax had no words.

"You are one of mine now. When she can travel, I will be moving you to Hartford. For now, you only need to go upstairs and be with your wife." Maxx assured Jax that everything would be taken care of. Maxx was sending little Danny Johnathon Shaw to Hartford, to rest next to his grandparents Danny and Ella Blume.

Jax clung to the railing as he climbed the stairs. He would not dwell on Roger Holden just yet. Right now, his wife needed him. When he opened the door to their room, Rachel dropped her head and quickly left.

Jax climbed in bed next to his wife and took her in his arms. He was unsure of what to say to her. Perhaps words were not needed just yet. For now, they held each other and cried together.

"He's gone." Nancie cried with her head against Jax's chest. "I am so sorry."

"This is not your fault." Jax leaned back and tilted Nancie's chin up so he could look into her eyes. Seeing her bright green eyes clouded over and flooded with tears broke his heart even more. "We will see our son one day, just not in this world."

"What if I was not meant to be a mother?" Tears flowed uncontrollably down Nancie's cheek.

"You are a mother, and I am a father. I do not understand why our children could not be here with us." Jax spoke softly. Nancie laid her head against Jax's chest again. "I promise you, my dear loving wife, one day you will hold many children within your arms and watch them grow to become amazing men and women."

"I love you," Nancie whispered.

"And I love you." Jax wrapped his arms around his wife and held her tightly. He would see to it that happiness found her again soon.

While Jax comforted his wife, Sir Phillip remained at the Blume'N Brew to be his son's strength. The rest of the family, Maxx, and the Duke continued to search for Dani. Lord Mason's men surrounded the pub to keep his niece safe. It was a sad day for them all, for Roger Holden had finally managed to kill a Shaw.

My Dear Reader,

Thank you for being a part of the Shaw family journey with me. I hope that you enjoyed *Capturing A Knight's Heart*, Book Four in the *For the Love of a Shaw* series. I know that this is a sad moment for Jax and Nancie, but the family story is not over.

I know that up until this point, I have given you the first chapter of the next book at the end. However, I cannot do that for Book Five. I hope that you can forgive me for that but starting in Book Five some major reveals will take place and I wanted you to have that all at the same time, cover to cover.

There will be three more books in this series. I hope that you will join me soon in *A Duke's Treasure*, Book Five in this series. We will find out what happened to Lady Danielle Shaw.

I would love to hear from each of you. So, please send your messages. If you are enjoying this series, please encourage your family and friends to follow along with us. It would be a great gift to me if you did. Another wonderful gift would be, if you would kindly write a review for this book, and the others in the series, on Amazon and Goodreads. You can find ways to connect with me on the About the Author page.

Again, I want to thank you dearly for following along with me on the amazing journey. I cannot tell you how much it truly means to me that you are here with me. I love these characters and this story. I hope that you too, fall in love with a Shaw!

Blessings to you,
Debbie

Other Books by the Author

Christian Writings:

Stamped *subtitle*: Breaking Out of the Box
Please look for the 2nd Edition.

Her *subtitle*: Beautiful, Loved, Wanted, Matters, Priceless!
Her: Beautiful, Loved, Wanted, Matters, Priceless!
subtitle: Devotional Guided Study Journal

Fictional Writings:

Historical Romance:
For the Love of a Shaw series:

When A Knight Falls: Book One
Falling for the Enemy: Book Two
A Knight's Destiny: Book Three

Fiction: Preteen – Young Teen, (Kids of All ages!)

Forest Rovania series:
Jasper's Journey

Cookbook Journals:

My Thanksgiving Recipes
(A blank journal for your recipes)
4 Cover Designs to choose from.

My Halloween Recipes

Coming Soon!!!

For the Love of a Shaw series:

A Duke's Treasure   Book Five

Pre-teen – Young Teen

Forest Rovania series:

Kevin's Mission   Book Two

Debbie Hyde

About the Author

Debbie Hyde has a love for writing! She enjoys reading books from many different genres such as: Christian, Romance, Young Adults and many more. You will always find wonderful clean stories in her fictional writings.

When not reading or writing, she enjoys using her talents in cooking, baking, and cake decorating. She loves using her skill as a seamstress to make gowns, costumes, teddy bears, baby blankets and much more.

She is currently working on the *For the Love of a Shaw* book series in historical romance and the *Forest Rovania* book series in Preteen – Young Teen Books with her granddaughter, Nevaeh.

Debbie started Letters To You on Facebook after God put it on her heart to "Love the lost and lead them to Jesus". This wonderful community of amazing people allows her to continue her mission to Just #LoveThemAll.

Connect with Debbie at:

Email: debbiehyde5@yahoo.com

Facebook:
Letters To You – Debbie Hyde for her Christian writings
Debbie Hyde & Nevaeh Roberson for her fiction writings
Instagram: debbie_hyde_author
Debbie would love to hear from you and see your reviews!

Made in United States
Troutdale, OR
12/22/2024

27190064R10128

Debbie Wylde

"First, we have to get you to safety." Nancie put her arm around Emily.

"I have a plan." Paul nodded before walking over to Gavin and Jax. "It is not safe for Lady Emily to be here at the pub anymore. We will take her to Hartford Place for the night."

"Where exactly is Hartford Place?" Alex did not like the sound of this. Gavin shook his head at his brother. He had never heard of Hartford Place.

"Hartford Place would be perfect." Emily stepped forward and agreed with Paul's suggestion.

"My men will make sure that you get there safely." Sam slightly bowed to Emily.

"Thank you, Your Grace." Emily curtsied to the Duke. She and Nancie hurried upstairs to pack a few things.

"I still do not know where Hartford Place is." Alex narrowed his eyes at Paul and the Duke.

"You and Jax should go with them." Sir Phillip suggested. This pleased Alex greatly. Paul however, rolled his eyes. He was sure that protesting would do no good. It looked as if Alex Shaw would be following Lady Emily no matter what. Jax, however, had no intention of letting Nancie leave without him being by her side.

strangling Dexter Greene. The entire room fell into silence whey they noticed Emily standing on the bottom step of the stairs.

Nancie hurried over and hugged Emily, but Emily did not hug her back. There was the look of shock on Emily's face. She knew that Roger Holden would be furious that his plans for the evening had failed when she refused his proposal, but plotting her death was not something that she was expecting to hear. Alex also tried to hug Emily, and just like with Nancie, she was as still as a statue.

"Doctor Ramsey was able to remove the bullet. Doug will have a rough night. We will know more on his condition in the morning."

Emily spoke slowly and calmly.

"There is a way to stop it all." Dexter smiled slyly at Emily. He did not like that Ned had given away part of their plan.

The sound of the man's voice snapped Emily back to reality. She could not believe what the horrid man was implying. She and every man in the room was now infuriated.

"You mean to say, that I have to marry Roger Holden or everyone, including myself, will die?" Emily was appalled.

Jerry, being the closest to Dexter, punched the horrible man in the mouth. Jax agreed with Jerry. Dexter Greene deserved to be hurt. Nancie and Sir Phillip grabbed Jax before he could reach Dexter.

"You help take care of Lady Emily. Do not worry, we will hold him in his place." Caleb assured Nancie that Jax was taken care of. He was concerned that since she was so small, his brother could hurt her in his rage for Dexter.

When Captain Cromwell and the King's Guard arrived, Sir Phillip and Gavin filled them in on what had happened. Dexter Greene was taken into the King's custody and escorted out of the pub. He refused to answer any of Captain Cromwell's question and went with them quietly. The King's Guard also took Ned Wilson's body. They would see to it that he was returned to his family for burial.

"We have gotten to do something." Nancie whispered to Paul and Emily.

"We need Maxx," Emily replied in a whisper as well. Nancie and Paul both agreed.